Tsutomu Sato

ustration **Kana Ishida**

ustration assistants **Jimmy Stone,**

asuko Suenaga

esign **BEE-PEE**

Magic High
School

Honoka Mitsui

Class 1-A. Miyuki's classmate.
Specializes in controlling
light-wave vibration magic.
Rather subjective in her outlooks.

"But
competition
is important...
I think fussing
over winning
and losing
will help us
get better."

Angelina Kudou Shield

A USNA (United States of North
America) student who came to Magic
High as part of a foreign exchange
program, switching places with Shizuku
Kitayama. A blonde-haired, blue-eyed girl
with unequaled magical abilities

"I don't think you should care so much about winning or losing."

Miyuki Shiba

The younger sister of the Shiba siblings. Part of Class 1-A. An elite who entered Magic High School as the top student. A Course 1 student, called a "Bloom," whose specialty is cooling magic. Her lovable only flaw is a severe case of a brother complex.

Leonhard Saijou

Nicknamed "Leo." Part of Class 1-E, like Tatsuya. His father is half-Japanese and his mother a quarter. Specializes in hardening magic.

"Hey, that hurts!"

Erika Chiba

Tatsuya's classmate. Has a bright personality; a troublemaker who gets everyone involved. Her family is large and famous for *kenjutsu*—a magical technique that combines swords and magic.

"Miki, you take the one with the coat. I'll stop the one with the mask!"

She's not the only one having trouble.

Mikihiko Yoshida

Part of Class 1-E. Tatsuya's classmate. Belongs to a distinguished family of old magic. Has known Erika since they were children.

"You cannot defeat me."

Vampire

A mysterious being who stalks the night and extracts the blood of magicians.

"With my authority as Stars commander, I sentence you."

Angie Sirius

Commander of the USNA's magician force, the Stars. Rank: major. One of the Thirteen Apostles, strategic magicians.

I absolutely cannot lose!

I'll crush
you with
everything
I have!

State of the World in 2095

World War III, also called the Twenty Years' Global War Outbreak, was directly triggered by global cooling, and it fundamentally redrew the world map.

The USA annexed Canada and the countries from Mexico to Panama to form the United States of North America, or the USNA.

Russia reabsorbed Ukraine and Belarus to form the New Soviet Union.

China conquered northern Burma, northern Vietnam, northern Laos, and the Korean Peninsula to form the Great Asian Alliance, or GAA.

India and Iran absorbed several central Asian countries (Turkmenistan, Uzbekistan, Tajikistan, and Afghanistan) and South Asian countries (Pakistan, Nepal, Bhutan, Bangladesh, and Sri Lanka) to form the Indo-Persian Federation.

The other Asian and Arab countries formed regional military alliances to resist the three superpowers: the New Soviet Union, GAA, and the Indo-Persian Federation.

Australia chose national isolation.

The EU failed to unify and split into an eastern and a western section bordered by Germany and France. These east-west groupings also failed to form unions and now are actually weaker than they were before unification.

Africa saw half its nations destroyed altogether, with the surviving ones barely managing to retain urban control.

South America, excluding Brazil, fell into small, isolated states administered on a local government level.

Strategic Magicians: the Thirteen Apostles

Because modern magic was born into a highly technological world, only a few nations were able to develop magic strong enough for military purposes. As a result, only a handful were able to develop "strategic magic," which rivaled weapons of mass destruction.

However, these nations shared the magic they developed with their allies, and certain magicians from those allied nations with high aptitudes for strategic magic came to be known as strategic magicians.

As of April 2095, there are officially thirteen magicians publicly recognized as strategic magicians by their nations. They are called the Thirteen Apostles and are seen as important factors in the world's military balance. The Thirteen Apostles' nations, names, and spell names are listed below.

USNA

Angie Sirius: Heavy Metal Burst
Elliott Miller: Leviathan
Laurent Barthes: Leviathan
* The only one belonging to the Stars is Angie Sirius. Elliott Miller is stationed at Alaska Base, and Laurent Barthes outside the country at Gibraltar Base, and for the most part they don't move.

New Soviet Union

Igor Andreivich Bezobrazov: Tuman Bomba
Leonid Kondratenko: Zemlja Armija
* As Kondratenko is of advanced age, he generally stays at the Black Sea Base.

Great Asian Alliance

Yunde Liu: Pilita (Thunderclap Tower)
* Yunde Liu died in the October 31, 2095, battle against Japan.

Indo-Persian Federation

Barat Chandra Khan: Agni Downburst

Japan

Mio Itsuwa: Abyss

Brazil

Miguel Diez: Synchroliner Fusion
* This magic program was named by the USNA.

England

William MacLeod: Ozone Circle

Germany

Karla Schmidt: Ozone Circle
* Ozone Circle is based on a spell co-developed by nations in the EU before its split as a means to fix the hole in the ozone layer. The magic program was perfected by England and then publicized to the old EU through a convention.

Turkey

Ali Sahin: Bahamut
* This magic program was developed in cooperation with the USNA and Japan, then provided to Turkey by Japan.

Thailand

Somchai Bunnag: Agni Downburst
* This magic program was provided by Indo-Persia.

The Irregular at Magic High School

The Irregular at Magic High School

VISITOR ARC Ⓘ

9

Tsutomu Sato

Illustration **Kana Ishida**

YEN ON

NEW YORK

THE IRREGULAR AT MAGIC HIGH SCHOOL
TSUTOMU SATO

Translation by Andrew Prowse
Cover art by Kana Ishida

MAHOUKA KOUKOU NO RETTOUSEI Vol. 9
© TSUTOMU SATO 2013
First published in Japan in 2013 by KADOKAWA CORPORATION, Tokyo.
English translation rights arranged with KADOKAWA CORPORATION, Tokyo, through Tuttle-Mori Agency, Inc., Tokyo.

English translation © 2018 by Yen Press, LLC

Yen On
1290 Avenue of the Americas
New York, NY 10104

Visit us at yenpress.com
facebook.com/yenpress
twitter.com/yenpress
yenpress.tumblr.com
instagram.com/yenpress

First Yen On Edition: September 2018

Yen On is an imprint of Yen Press, LLC.
The Yen On name and logo are trademarks of Yen Press, LLC.

Library of Congress Cataloging-in-Publication Data
Names: Satou, Tsutomu. | Ishida, Kana, illustrator.
Title: The irregular at Magic High School / Tsutomu Satou ; Illustrations by Kana Ishida.
Other titles: Mahōka kōkō no rettosei. English
Description: First Yen On edition. | New York, NY : Yen On, 2016–
Identifiers: LCCN 2015042401 | ISBN 9780316348805 (v 1 : pbk.) | ISBN 9780316390293 (v. 2 : pbk.) |
    ISBN 9780316390309 (v. 3 : pbk.) | ISBN 9780316390316 (v. 4 : pbk.) |
    ISBN 9780316390323 (v. 5 : pbk.) | ISBN 9780316390330 (v. 6 : pbk.) |
    ISBN 9781975300074 (v. 7 : pbk.) | ISBN 9781975327125 (v. 8 : pbk.) |
    ISBN 9781975327149 (v. 9 : pbk.)
Subjects: CYAC: Brothers and sisters—Fiction. | Magic—Fiction. | High schools—Fiction. |
    Schools—Fiction. | Japan—Fiction. | Science fiction.
Classification: LCC PZ7.1.S265 Ir 2016 | DDC [Fic]—dc23
LC record available at http://lccn.loc.gov/2015042401

ISBNs: 978-1-9753-2714-9 (paperback)
        978-1-9753-2715-6 (ebook)

10 9 8 7 6 5 4 3 2 1

LSC-C

Printed in the United States of America

The Irregular at Magic High School

VISITOR ARC ①

An irregular older brother with a certain flaw.
An honor roll younger sister who is perfectly flawless.

When the two siblings enrolled in Magic High School,
a dramatic life unfolded—

Character

Tatsuya Shiba

Class 1-E. One of the Course 2 (irregular) students, who are mockingly called Weeds. Sees right to the core of everything.

Mikihiko Yoshida

Class 1-E. Tatsuya's classmate. From a famous family that uses ancient magic. Has known Erika since they were children.

Miyuki Shiba

Class 1-A. Tatsuya's younger sister; enrolled as the top student. Specializes in freezing magic. Dotes on her older brother.

Honoka Mitsui

Class 1-A. Miyuki's classmate. Specializes in light-wave vibration magic. Impulsive when emotional.

Leonhard Saijou

Class 1-E. Tatsuya's classmate. Specializes in hardening magic. Has a bright personality.

Erika Chiba

Class 1-E. Tatsuya's classmate. Specializes in *kenjutsu*. A charming troublemaker.

Shizuku Kitayama

Class 1-A. Miyuki's classmate. Specializes in vibration and acceleration magic. Doesn't show emotional ups and downs very much.

Mizuki Shibata

Class 1-E. Tatsuya's classmate. Has pushion radiation sensitivity. Serious and a bit of an airhead.

Subaru Satomi

Class 1-D. Frequently mistaken for a pretty boy. Cheerful and easy to get along with.

Shun Morisaki

Class 1-A. Miyuki's classmate. Specializes in CAD quick-draw. Takes great pride in being a Course 1 student.

Akaha Sakurakouji

Class 1-B. Friends with Subaru and Amy. Wears gothic Lolita clothes and loves theme parks.

Eimi Akechi

Class 1-B. A quarter-blood. Full name is Amelia Eimi Akechi Goldie.

Azusa Nakajou

A junior and is student council president after Mayumi stepped down. Shy and has trouble expressing herself.

Mayumi Saegusa

A senior and the former student council president. One of the strongest magicians ever to grace a magical high school.

Hanzou Gyoubu-Shoujou Hattori

A junior and the former student council vice president. Is the head of the club committee after Katsuto stepped down.

Suzune Ichihara

A senior and the former student council treasurer. Calm, collected, and book smart. Mayumi's right hand.

Koutarou Tatsumi

A senior and a former member of the disciplinary committee. Has a heroic personality.

Mari Watanabe

A senior and the former chairwoman of the disciplinary committee. Mayumi's good friend. Good all-around and likes a sporting fight.

Isao Sekimoto

A senior. Member of the disciplinary committee. Wasn't chosen for the Thesis Competition.

Midori Sawaki

A junior and a member of the disciplinary committee. Has a complex about his girlish name.

Kei Isori

A junior and the student council treasurer. Top grades in his class in magical theory. Engaged to Kanon Chiyoda.

Kanon Chiyoda

A junior and the chairwoman of the disciplinary committee after Mari stepped down. Engaged to Kei Isori.

Katsuto Juumonji

A senior and the former head of the club committee.

Masaki Ichijou

A freshman at Third High. Participates in the Nine School Competition. Direct heir to the Ichijou family, one of the Ten Master Clans.

Shinkurou Kichijouji

A freshman at Third High. Participates in the Nine School Competition. Also known as Cardinal George.

Midori Ichijou

Masaki's mother. Warm and good at cooking.

Takeaki Kirihara

A junior. Member of the *kenjutsu* club. Kanto Junior High Kenjutsu Tournament champion.

Sayaka Mibu

A junior. Member of the kendo club. Placed second in the nation at the girls' junior high kendo tournament.

Koharu Hirakawa

Senior. Engineer during the Nine School Competition. Withdrew from the Thesis Competition.

Chiaki Hirakawa

Class 1-G. Holds enmity toward Tatsuya.

Satomi Asuka

Nurse. Gentle, calm, and warm. Smile popular among male students.

Kazuo Tsuzura

Teacher. Main field is magic geometry. Manager of the Thesis Competition team.

Akane Ichijou

Eldest daughter of the Ichijou. Masaki's younger sister. Mature despite being in elementary school.

Ruri Ichijou

Second daughter of the Ichijou. Masaki's younger sister. Stable and does things her own way.

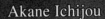

Haruka Ono

A general counselor of Class 1-E.

Harunobu Kazama

Commanding officer of the 101st Brigade of the Independent Magic Battalion. Ranked major.

Shigeru Sanada

Executive officer of the 101st Brigade of the Independent Magic Battalion. Ranked captain.

Muraji Yanagi

Executive officer of the 101st Brigade of the Independent Magic Battalion. Ranked captain.

Kousuke Yamanaka

Executive officer of the 101st Brigade of the Independent Magic Battalion. Physician ranked major. First-rate healing magician.

Kyouko Fujibayashi

Female officer serving as Kazama's aide. Ranked second lieutenant.

Retsu Kudou

Renowned as the strongest magician in the world. Given the honorary title of Sage.

Zhou

A handsome young man who brought Lu and Chen to Japan.

Yakumo Kokonoe

A user of an ancient magic called *ninjutsu*. Tatsuya's martial arts master.

Toshikazu Chiba

Erika Chiba's oldest brother. Has a career in the Ministry of Police. A playboy at first glance.

Naotsugu Chiba

Erika Chiba's second-oldest brother. Possesses full mastery of the Chiba (thousand blades) style of *kenjutsu*. Nicknamed "Kirin Child of the Chiba."

Ushiyama

Manager of Four Leaves Technology's CAD R & D Section 3. A person in whom Tatsuya places his trust.

Rin

A girl Morisaki saved. Her full name is Meiling Sun. The new leader of the Hong Kong–based international crime syndicate No-Head Dragon.

Xiangshan Chen

Leader of the Great Asian Alliance Army's Special Covert Forces. Has a heartless personality.

Ganghu Lu

The ace magician of the Great Asian Alliance Army's Special Covert Forces. Also known as the Man-Eating Tiger.

Sayuri Shiba

Tatsuya and Miyuki's stepmother. Hates them both.

Maya Yotsuba

Tatsuya and Miyuki's aunt. Miya's younger twin sister. The current head of the Yotsuba.

Hayama

An elderly butler employed by Maya.

Miya Shiba

Tatsuya and Miyuki's actual mother. Deceased. The only magician skilled in mental construction interference magic.

Honami Sakurai

Miya's Guardian. Deceased. Part of the first generation of the Sakura series, engineered magicians with magical capacity strengthened through genetic modification.

Mitsugu Kuroba

Miya Shiba and Maya Yotsuba's cousin. Father of Ayako and Fumiya.

Ayako Kuroba

Tatsuya and Miyuki's second cousin. Has a younger twin brother named Fumiya.

Fumiya Kuroba

A candidate for next head of the Yotsuba. Tatsuya and Miyuki's second cousin. Has an older twin sister named Ayako.

Angelina Kudou Shields

Commander of the USNA's magician unit, the Stars. Rank is major. Nickname is Lina. Also one of the Thirteen Apostles, strategic magicians.

Benjamin Canopus

Number two in the USNA's magician unit, the Stars. Rank is major. Takes command when Major Sirius is absent.

Silvia Mercury First

A planet-class magician in the USNA's magician unit, the Stars. Rank is warrant officer. Her nickname is Silvie, and Mercury First is her code name. During their mission in Japan, she serves as Major Sirius's aide.

Mikaela Hongou

An agent sent to Japan by the USNA (although her real job is magic scientist for the Department of Defense). Nicknamed Mia.

Alfred Fomalhaut

A first-degree starred magician in the USNA's magician unit, the Stars. Rank is first lieutenant. Nicknamed Freddy. Currently on the run.

Charles Sullivan

A satellite-class magician in the USNA's magician unit, the Stars. Called by the code name Deimos Second. Currently on the run.

Claire

Hunter Q—a female soldier in the magician unit Stardust (for those who couldn't be Stars). The code name Q refers to the seventeenth of the pursuit unit.

Rachel

Hunter R—a female soldier in the magician unit Stardust (for those who couldn't be Stars). The code name R refers to the eighteenth of the pursuit unit.

Glossary

Course 1 student emblem

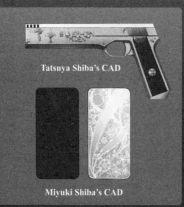

Tatsuya Shiba's CAD

Miyuki Shiba's CAD

Magic High School

Nickname for high schools affiliated with the National Magic University. There are nine schools throughout the nation. Of them, First High through Third High each adopt a system of Course 1 and Course 2 students to split up its two hundred incoming freshmen.

Blooms, Weeds

Slang terms used at First High to display the gap between Course 1 and Course 2 students. Course 1 student uniforms feature an eight-petaled emblem embroidered on the left breast, but Course 2 student uniforms do not.

CAD (Casting Assistant Device)

A device that simplifies magic casting. Magical programming is recorded within. There are many types and forms, some specialized and others multipurpose.

Four Leaves Technology (FLT)

A domestic CAD manufacturer. Originally more famous for magical-product engineering than for developing finished products, the development of the Silver model has made them much more widely known as a maker of CADs.

Taurus Silver

A genius engineer said to have advanced specialized CAD software by a decade in just a single year.

Eidos (individual information bodies)

Originally a term from Greek philosophy. In modern magic, *eidos* refers to the information bodies that accompany events. They form a so-called record out in the world, and can be considered the footprints of an object's state of being in the universe, be that active or passive. The definition of *magic* in its modern form is that of a technology that alters events by altering the information bodies composing them.

Idea (information body dimension)

Originally a term from Greek philosophy; pronounced "ee-dee-ah." In modern magic, *Idea* refers to the *platform* upon which information bodies are recorded—a spell, object, or energy's *dimension*. Magic is primarily a technology that outputs a magic program (a spell sequence) to affect the Idea (the dimension), which then rewrites the eidos (the individual bodies) recorded there.

Activation Sequence

The blueprints of magic, and the programming that constructs it. Activation sequences are stored in a compressed format in CADs. The magician sends a psionic wave into the CAD, which then expands the data and uses it to convert the activation sequence into a signal. This signal returns to the magician with the unpacked magic program.

Psions (thought particles)

Massless particles belonging to the dimension of spirit phenomena. These information particles record awareness and thought results. Eidos are considered the theoretical basis for modern magic, while activation sequences and magic programs are the technology forming its practical basis. Yet, all of these are bodies of information made up of psions.

Pushions (spirit particles)

Massless particles belonging to the dimension of spirit phenomena. Their existence has been confirmed, but their true form and function have yet to be elucidated. In general, magicians are only able to sense energized pushions. The technical term for them is *psycheons*.

Magician

An abbreviation of *magic technician*. *Magic technician* is the term for those with the skills to use magic at a practical level.

Magic program

An information body used to temporarily alter information attached to events. Constructed from psions possessed by the magician. Sometimes shortened to *magigram*.

Magic-calculation region

A mental region that constructs magic programs. The essential core of the talent of magic. Exists within the magician's unconscious regions, and though he or she can normally consciously use the magic-calculation region, they cannot perceive the processing happening within. The magic-calculation region may be called a black box, even for the magician performing the task.

Magic program output process

❶ Transmit an activation sequence to a CAD. This is called "reading in an activation sequence."

❷ Add variables to the activation sequence and send them to the magic-calculation region.

❸ Construct a magic program from the activation sequence and its variables.

❹ Send the constructed magic program along the "route"—the lowest part of the conscious mind to highest part of the unconscious mind—then send it out the "gate" between conscious and unconscious and output it onto the Idea.

❺ The magic program outputted onto the Idea interferes with the eidos at a designated coordinate and overwrites them.

With a single-type, single-process spell, this five-stage process can be completed in under half a second. This is the bar for practical-level use with magicians.

Magic evaluation standards

The speed with which one constructs psionic information bodies is one's magical throughput, or processing speed. The scale and scope of the information bodies one can construct is one's magical capacity. The strength with which one can overwrite eidos with magic programs is one's influence. These three together are referred to as a person's magical power.

Cardinal Code hypothesis

A school of thought that claims, of the four families and eight types of magic, within which exists a natural foundation of "plus" and "minus" magic programs (sixteen in all), one can construct every possible typed spell by combining these sixteen.

Typed magic

Any magic belonging to the four families and eight types.

Exotyped magic

A term for spells that control mental phenomena rather than physical ones. Encompasses many fields, from divine magic and spirit magic—which employs spiritual presences—to mind reading, astral form separation, and consciousness control.

Ten Master Clans

The most powerful magician organization in Japan. The ten families are chosen every four years from among twenty-eight: Ichijou, Ichinokura, Isshiki, Futatsugi, Nikaidou, Nihei, Mitsuya, Mikazuki, Yotsuba, Itsuwa, Gotou, Itsumi, Mutsuzuka, Rokkaku, Rokugou, Roppongi, Saegusa, Shippou, Tanabata, Nanase, Yatsushiro, Hassaku, Hachiman, Kudou, Kuki, Kuzumi, Juumonji, and Tooyama.

Numbers

Just like the Ten Master Clans contain a number from one to ten in their surname, well-known families in the Hundred Families use numbers eleven or greater, such as Chiyoda (thousand), Isori (fifty), and Chiba (thousand). The value isn't an indicator of strength, but the fact that it is present in the surname is one measure to broadly judge the capacity of a magic family by their bloodline.

Non-numbers

Also called Extra Numbers, or simply Extras. Magician families who have been stripped of their number. Once, when magicians were weapons and experimental samples, this was a stigma between the success cases, who were given numbers, and the failure cases, who didn't display good enough results.

Various Spells

• Cocytus
Outer magic that freezes the mind. A frozen mind cannot order the flesh to die, so anyone subject to this magic enters a state of mental stasis, causing their body to stop. Partial crystallization of the flesh is sometimes observed because of the interaction between mind and body.

• Rumbling
An old spell that vibrates the ground as a medium for a spirit, an independent information body.

• Program Dispersion
A spell that dismantles a magic program, the main component of a spell, into a group of psionic particles with no meaningful structure. Since magic programs affect the information bodies associated with events, it is necessary for the information structure to be exposed, leaving no way to prevent interference against the magic program itself.

• Program Demolition
A typeless spell that rams a mass of compressed psionic particles directly into an object without going through the Idea, causing it to explode and blow away the psion information bodies recorded in magic, such as activation sequences and magic programs. It may be called magic, but because it is a psionic bullet without any structure as a magic program for altering events, it isn't affected by Information Boost or Area Interference. The pressure of the bullet itself will also repel any Cast Jamming effects. Because it has zero physical effect, no obstacle can block it.

• Mine Origin
A magic that imparts strong vibrations to anything with a connotation of "ground"—such as dirt, crag, sand, or concrete—regardless of material.

• Fissure
A spell that uses spirits, independent information bodies, as a medium to push a line into the ground, creating the appearance of a fissure opening in the earth.

• Dry Blizzard
A spell that gathers carbon dioxide from the air, creates dry-ice particles, then converts the extra heat energy from the freezing process to kinetic energy to launch the dry-ice particles at a high speed.

• Slithering Thunders
In addition to condensing the water vapor from Dry Blizzard's dry-ice evaporation and creating a highly conductive mist with the evaporated carbon dioxide in it, this spell creates static electricity with vibration-type magic and emission-type magic. A combination spell, it also fires an electric attack at an enemy using the carbon gas–filled mist and water droplets as a conductor.

• Niflheim
A vibration- and deceleration-type area-of-effect spell. It chills a large volume of air then moves it to freeze a wide range. In blunt terms, it creates a super-large refrigerator. The white mist that appears upon activation is the particles of frozen ice and dry ice, but at higher levels, a mist of frozen liquid nitrogen occurs.

• Burst
A dispersion-type spell that vaporizes the liquid inside a target object. When used on a creature, the spell will vaporize bodily fluids and cause the body to rupture. When used on a machine powered by internal combustion, the spell vaporizes the fuel and makes it explode. Fuel cells see the same result, and even if no burnable fuel is on board, there is no machine that does not contain some liquid, such as battery fluid, hydraulic fluid, coolant, or lubricant; once Burst activates, virtually any machine will be destroyed.

• Disheveled Hair
An old spell that, instead of specifying a direction and changing the wind's direction to that, uses air current control to bring about the vague result of "tangling" it, causing currents along the ground that entangle an opponent's feet in the grass. Only usable on plains with grass of a certain height.

[0]

The Dallas National Particle Accelerator Institute in Dallas, Texas. It stood in the United States of North America (not the north of the United States of America, but the united states whose domain spanned the North American continent). Currently, in its linear collider with a total length of thirty kilometers, an experiment to generate and evaporate a micro black hole based on extradimensional theory was about to get underway.

Preparations had been completed two years ago, but the institute had never gotten the green light due to the unknowable risks involved. Instead, what had given this experiment the push it needed was the event that had occurred in the Far East a month prior.

On the southern tip of the Korean Peninsula, a large explosion had wiped out an armed city and its nearby fleet in an instant. It wouldn't be an overstatement to call it a major world affair rather than a simple "incident."

Not because of the destruction's scope—but because of its presumed method.

A team of scientists working at the Department of Defense had concluded after fierce debate that the explosion had been caused by the conversion of mass into energy. Three years ago, this was no more than a tentative hypothesis by a few scholars. But this time, the scientists' outlook was unanimous.

By calculating from the estimated size of the explosion, the mass converted to energy was approximately one kilogram—even if the reaction of such a huge amount of mass had never been observed before, the concept of particle-antiparticle annihilation had already been precisely measured using experimental devices, and they knew what kind of phenomena would occur.

However, data on this "Great Bomb" recorded by reconnaissance satellites hadn't displayed characteristics that matched the annihilation data measured at experimental facilities. The satellites also hadn't detected any residual matter from nuclear fission or fusion. The only thing this could mean was that someone had implemented a high-energy explosion using a method the scientists didn't know about, via either science or magic.

Their final conclusion caused anxiety to sweep through the USNA's leadership.

If the explosion had been caused by magic, the USNA wouldn't be able to emulate it, and that was that.

And that was because, despite advances in magic systematization, it was still a largely personal thing. But without understanding what the underlying mechanisms of the explosion were, their scientists couldn't even work on countermeasures. If that muzzle ever pointed at them, their only recourse would be to sit back and be devastated. It would be the very definition of a nightmare.

What was the explosion? Could they get at least a hint related to the mass-energy conversion's underlying mechanisms? Those questions were the final push needed to advance this micro black hole generation-vaporization experiment.

There was a precise hypothesis in place describing the phenomena that would occur during mass-energy conversion during black hole vaporization. Scientists had conducted experiments with micro black holes to verify that conclusion in the first place. And the data observed from the Great Bomb didn't match what had been predicted.

Hawking radiation, however, was a phenomenon the scientists

had far less observational data on than annihilation, and the USNA scientists believed they could get observational data that didn't match theoretical predictions.

Maybe they would observe characteristics matching those of the Great Bomb. The possibility wasn't zero.

At the time, the USNA's leaders were mentally cornered enough to give a dangerous experiment the green light based on something so ephemeral.

Cornered enough to ignore the unknown risks.

Retribution was about to descend upon them—no, upon the world.

Calamity quietly crept in, unbeknownst to everyone.

[1]

There was only one month remaining in AD 2095.

Looking back on the year, Tatsuya keenly felt that it had been a dizzying one. He'd fought terrorists in April, an international crime syndicate in August, and foreign invaders in October. *Turbulent* didn't begin to describe it.

But he still didn't have the luxury of leisurely thinking back on his year. Not because of the guiding motto of "There's still a month left, you never know what will happen until it's over," but because of a more pressing, realistic reason:

"...*Guh!* I just don't get it!"

"Be quiet! Stop shouting! You're so annoying!"

"L-Leo, Erika, calm down..."

It was that detestable natural enemy of almost all calling themselves students, whether in middle school, high school, or university. An unavoidable roadblock. A wall they had to overcome—exams were upon them.

The usual suspects had gathered at Shizuku's house—or mansion, rather.

Tatsuya, Miyuki, Erika, Leo, Mizuki, Mikihiko, Honoka, and

Shizuku were all there, without a single person missing, for a group study session in advance of their midterms.

Most of those in the group were high achievers, at least on written tests. The only possible exception, Leo, was still average; he didn't need to worry about failing. The practical portion was the part to really worry about, but that was outside the scope of this study session.

Despite the occasional strange cries, the room in general had the air of a peaceful teatime—that is, until the bomb Shizuku dropped.

"Huh? Shizuku, could you say that again?" asked Honoka, flustered.

"I'm actually going to be studying abroad in America," repeated Shizuku, the same exact words in the same exact tone.

"You didn't tell me!"

"Sorry. I wasn't allowed to say until yesterday."

As Honoka paled at the news and pressed her friend, Shizuku's head dipped apologetically, conveying the only emotion everyone could read on her. Now that Honoka understood that Shizuku had wanted to reveal it earlier but couldn't, she couldn't say anything more.

"You managed to get approved?" remarked Erika, but not because she doubted Shizuku's academic (or linguistic) prowess. In this age, governments restricted overseas voyages unofficially but substantially to avoid the leakage of genes—and thus of military resources—of high-level magicians.

The USNA was ostensibly an ally nation, but it was also a latent rival country in the Pacific region. Under normal conditions, studying abroad there would never be approved.

"Mm. For some reason I got permission. Dad says it's because it's an exchange program."

"Why would they be okay with it just because it's an exchange program?" wondered Mizuki.

"I dunno."

Mizuki's question was a reasonable one; the logic evaded even Tatsuya. He could try to force it into his brain regardless, but he didn't have nearly enough information to make it click. So he decided to abandon his jog in the mental hamster wheel and think about the matter at hand instead: "How long? When do you leave?"

"Right after the new year. It'll be three months."

"Only three months... Don't scare me like that!" Honoka put a hand to her chest in relief.

By Tatsuya's logic, even three months was too long (as in, he was surprised the government had approved it).

But that, too, didn't matter.

"Then we'll have to have a going-away party," he proposed to his friends.

Because that was the true matter at hand.

The midterms ended safely, bringing the date to December 24, a Saturday. It was both the last day of the second school term and Christmas Eve.

Even after weathering a third world war, the Japanese were as indifferent as ever when it came to religion. This wasn't necessarily because they lacked religious belief, but more because, in the backs of their minds, they considered even the absolute gods of the monotheistic religions single entities among many. For that reason, they celebrated the New Year and Christmas in the same general manner as before.

And that day, the streets were decorated for Christmas.

Perhaps it would be more accurate to say they were decorated for the commercialization of Christmas, but that would be pedantically cynical. It would be one thing if a person didn't have anyone to talk to while espousing that, but to assume such a perverse attitude while surrounded by cute (!) girls, to the point that it poisoned the group waters, would be ridiculously ill-advised. (Of course, in a girl's case, the phrase "surrounded by cute guys" might be more apt.)

Yes… Even if one was presented with a going-away party, its date brought purposely to December 24, and therein given a small, fresh cream cake with the words "MERRY XMAS" written in white chocolate atop it—even then, one mustn't call it *mismatched*. In the first place, going by this shop's style, it read "WEIHNACHTEN" rather than "XMAS," but that too was perhaps, well, in good sport for the cultural exchange–oriented occasion.

"Brother, does something concern you?"

He shook his head at his sister, her flowering beauty making it seem like she was dressed up despite wearing her school uniform, and muttered, "It's nothing."

Yes. It was nothing—it *had* to be nothing. He mustn't do anything that would cause their guest of honor displeasure. He was the one entertaining her today, after all.

"Does everyone have drinks? This may not quite fit the bill for a going-away party, but the owner gave us this cake, so for our toast, let's go with…merry Christmas."

"Merry Christmas!"

In response to Tatsuya calmly leading the toast, his friends responded with cheery voices, and they thrust their glasses high.

On the entrance to the café, Einebrise, was a sign saying Reserved for the Day.

Across the Pacific Ocean on the North American continent, it was still the night before Christmas Eve. The date was just about to shift to the twenty-fourth.

Compared to Japan, where the majority treated Christmas as just another event, even after weathering a war that spanned twenty long years—or perhaps *because* they had weathered it—the Americans, including those people who newly became American after the war, treated Christmas far more sincerely, piously, and fervently. In preparation for the morrow's Christmas Eve, they'd gone to sleep earlier than usual—or, at least, they should have.

Unfortunately, late on the night before Christmas Eve, there were shadowy dealings taking place on a street in Dallas, Texas, a prominent city in the central south of the USNA.

A figure, leaping from rooftop to rooftop.

Several others, encircling the suspicious person from the air. Given their usage of specialized CADs for flight magic, which had only just begun to spread, they must have been police or military magicians.

"Stop at once, Lieutenant Alfred Fomalhaut! You should realize you can't get away now!"

Directly in front of the fugitive stood a small figure wearing a mask covering her eyes.

Her high-pitched voice called for his surrender. Perhaps seeing something in her short frame, Alfred Fomalhaut stopped dead.

"...What on earth is wrong, Freddy?" she asked in a slightly immature voice with unease and distress mixed in, a definite softening of her previous overbearing tone—a shift one could call subtle. "Why would someone given a first-magnitude code name flee his unit?"

"..."

But she didn't receive an answer, only silence.

"Some are saying the serial murders happening in the city were done with your pyrokinesis. You're not doing anything like that, are you?"

"..."

"Please, answer me, Freddy!"

The answer came, but not in the form of words.

The girl leaped back instantly—leaving the stole around her shoulders behind.

The fabric spread out, hiding her behind it, and without any spark, it lit and burned up.

Pyrokinesis—the power to generate fire.

She'd been wearing the stole over her dark-mauve uniform, and all those encircling the man were wearing capes and mantles as well, all cold-weather gear that was easy to remove. However, they wore it not for its original purpose, but to protect themselves from this man's ability, which he could activate using his sight as the trigger.

As the stole's flame disappeared, the light went out all around the suspect.

It was an area-of-effect spell that reversed the direction of light within a fixed distance when centered upon a target. A spell whereby light from the outside could be shut away, trapping those within the radius in complete darkness: Mirror Cage.

The defensive spell, which was used for sealing away supernatural powers that used sight as their trigger, had been activated by a single person in the circle.

"Lieutenant Fomalhaut, with the authority of the Stars commander described in the USNA Army Criminal Law Special Provision, I sentence you to death!"

A pronouncement of death, almost a wail.

As First Lieutenant Fomalhaut waited unmoving, bound inside the dark coffin by a second spell, the masked girl—Major Angie Sirius, commander of the Stars—leveled her suppressor-equipped automatic pistol at him.

A single bullet, equipped with a strong Information Boost to disable all magical interference, shot into that bounded field of illusion and ignorance trapping Lieutenant Fomalhaut and pierced him through the heart.

Though they called it a going-away party, they knew they'd be able to see her again in the spring. And when it came to studying abroad overseas, which would never normally be approved for them, maybe it was natural their curiosity would triumph over their sadness.

"So, where are you studying in America?"

"Berkeley."

Shizuku's answer to Erika's question was a single, curt location name, but that wasn't because she was unhappy—it was just her personality.

"Not Boston?"

A sense that America's modern magic research centered around Boston was deep-rooted among Japanese magicians. Miyuki's remark arose from that assumption.

"The East Coast apparently isn't a great place to be right now."

Shizuku's answer to Miyuki's question was an unsettling one.

"Oh, yeah. The humanists, right? I see them a lot on the news lately."

Mikihiko kept in step with Shizuku's answer.

"First witch hunts, now magician hunts? They say history repeats itself, but this is ridiculous," Leo growled, his voice cold.

"It's not a perfect repeat, is it? I'm not sure what was behind the witch hunts in the seventeenth century, but the recent 'magician hunts' seem like they're rooted in neo–white supremacy." Tatsuya smoothed it over with a mollifying tone. "...But, still, maybe you're right to avoid the area."

After all, smoothing it over didn't mean Tatsuya's words were defending the practice.

"I wasn't aware of that," Miyuki interjected after her brother spoke, her gaze seeking an explanation.

Tatsuya immediately answered her: "You can spot a pretty high percentage of the same names in their active group member list. Said list isn't exactly circulating publicly, so you can't be blamed for not knowing."

"That sounds a lot more criminal to me, Tatsuya... Anyway, let's stop the depressing talk."

As Erika purposely made a joke and shook her head, Tatsuya and Miyuki gave pained grins and nodded. They were aware the topic was a bit on the shady side for the situation.

"Do you know who's coming in exchange?"

Perhaps feeling a responsibility to shift the mood, Miyuki's change of subject was a slightly abrupt one.

"In exchange?"

"It's an exchange program, right?"

Evidently, Shizuku didn't seem to grasp the question at first, but after Miyuki prodded her a second time, a look of understanding crossed Shizuku's face—albeit a hard-to-read one, as usual.

"A girl our age, apparently."

Amid a line of disappointed faces, Tatsuya smiled and asked, "Do you know anything else?"

"Nope." Shizuku nodded perfunctorily.

"...Isn't that just the way it is? You can be curious about this girl all you want, but in the end, we just don't have a man on the inside to tell us," Mizuki sighed, putting the conversation to an end.

As one would understand already from the fact that they'd had the going-away party on this day, all eight of the people gathered here had no other plans for Christmas Eve. It surprised Tatsuya that Shizuku, Erika, and Mikihiko didn't have plans at home, but the Kitayama, Chiba, and Yoshida families had thrown adult-oriented parties, leaving no room for freshmen in high school—thoughts and expectations of their parents aside.

It wasn't to say they felt none of the youthful temptation of partying all night long and deepening friendships, but unfortunately, they couldn't be out until midnight in their school uniforms.

"We can't stick around forever, or we'll cause trouble for the proprietor."

After causing the proprietor to flounder at this suspiciously sinister turn of phrase (the speaker's name omitted for privacy's sake), the eight set out for home.

Honoka boarded the same self-driving car as Shizuku, likely

because she'd be staying over. Honoka didn't seem very close to her parents—though this was the usual story for magic high school students.

Erika, Leo, Mizuki, and Mikihiko each got in their own vehicle. They couldn't help but feel at least a little hope for the possibility of unexpected happenings, but it looked like none of them were at that stage yet.

Tatsuya and Miyuki, for whom no unexpected incidents could occur anyway, boarded a two-seater ride and sat together until they returned home. On the surface, the cabinet interiors were called private spaces, but Tatsuya would never forget the old adage: The walls had ears. Whenever they spoke of entangled topics, they always obscured proper nouns. Miyuki knew to do that as well, and though she gave the impression of having something to say, it wasn't until they passed through the front door of their house and calmed down in the living room that she actually broached the subject.

"I cannot shake the feeling that Shizuku's study-abroad program is curious."

After they'd changed in their rooms and sat down next to each other on the sofa to enjoy coffee for two, Miyuki began to speak.

"Curious... I agree."

Tatsuya took the cup from his lips and wordlessly prompted her to continue. Miyuki hesitantly offered her doubts.

"First, someone with as much magical talent as Shizuku being permitted to study abroad is unnatural. Until a short while ago, I would have been convinced had she said she was studying abroad as the daughter of a wealthy businessman and not as a student of magic, but if that was the case, it's strange that we don't know anything about the one coming here to study in exchange. Come to think of it, this study-abroad talk coming up so suddenly—I cannot help but feel something else is going on. It's almost like..."

"Almost like a backroom deal made to investigate us? According to our aunt, we seem to be *under suspicion*, after all." Tatsuya gave a subtle smile and spoke with a tone implying it wasn't their problem. "Material Burst. I figured they wouldn't be able to leave that alone."

Hearing the answer come from her brother's mouth exactly as she had hesitated to suggest it, Miyuki's eyes widened, but a moment later she smiled, as though relieved.

"I see... You thought as much as well, Brother?"

"A student coming abroad to study here would be one thing, but considering it alongside our aunt's *warning*, it would probably be too naive to chalk it up to coincidence."

Tatsuya had told Miyuki of his one-on-one conversation with Maya the same day—both about what they were being suspected of, as well as who exactly was under suspicion.

"The Stars, then...?"

"Her forbidding me from contacting the major and the others is starting to hurt."

As punishment for using a strategic spell without prior permission, Maya had prohibited him from contacting the Independent Magic Battalion for a time. He had very little intention of meekly doing as he was told, but as long as the risk far outweighed the return, he wouldn't act against her directive of his own accord.

"I suppose even if we ask Aunt Maya...she wouldn't tell us."

"The study-abroad program is about to start, too. Clearly, she's given her tacit approval on this."

The Yotsuba family was currently in a position rivaling the Sae-gusa for leadership in the current Ten Master Clans. There was no way they'd be unaware of any irregular situations like a talented magic student studying abroad.

"On the flip side, though, I think it means this won't be all bad for us. Our aunt wouldn't let someone of the caliber to investigate us slip past unnoticed. There's probably some sort of trouble in America now as well. Maybe she wants us to catch them out on it."

Tatsuya's expression was closer to a resigned smile than a pained one.

"We don't know for sure yet… Perhaps it wouldn't be right to get too far ahead of ourselves."

"Yeah, you're absolutely right, Miyuki."

His lips said that, but both the praiser and the praised were sure that viewpoint suggested no more than a temporary ease of mind.

After returning to base in the Stars' fan-cluster VTOL aircraft and making her report over an encrypted channel to the Joint Chiefs of Staff, Angie Sirius, aka Major Angelina Sirius, still in uniform, flopped down onto the bed in her room.

She turned over, facedown, and buried her face in the pillow.

She couldn't get used to execution missions, no matter how many times she experienced them. She could resist the urge to vomit now, unlike after those missions early on, but that was only because her body had gotten used to her mental anguish.

And the mental anguish had only gotten worse.

He was an *American*, a *magician*, and a *member of the Stars*, the USNA Army magician unit directly under the Joint Chiefs of Staff—a comrade in three different ways, and she had executed him personally.

When they told her it was a mission granted to the unit's commander, the one with the code name Sirius, it hadn't felt real.

She'd been too excited by the fame and honor to understand what it truly meant to kill a countryman.

Angie tossed again, blocking the light with an arm. She hadn't even turned out the lights in the room yet.

Suddenly, the doorbell chimed.

A pained smile came to Major Sirius's lips. It would seem her meddlesome subordinate had come to check on her again tonight.

The Stars consisted of twelve smaller units, with the commander unifying the other unit leaders, in form at least. Her subordinates were all leaders who had to see to the needs of their own units. She didn't have any time for someone to be poking his nose into her business—

"Come in," she said curtly into the door microphone, getting out of bed and opening the door with a remote control.

"Please excuse the intrusion, Commander."

In came the person she'd expected. He was the Stars' number two, leader of the first unit and commander in the case of her absence, Benjamin Canopus.

Position within the Stars was not tied directly to military rank, making it an irregularity as a military organization. Still, they had yet to run into the theoretically possible situation where a squad leader outranked the commander. That being said, it wasn't unusual at all for them both to have the same rank.

Indeed, of the twelve unit leaders, six of them were captains and six were majors, the latter holding the same military rank as their commanders.

Even though Major Sirius was far from unhappy with this arrangement, it still made her anxious to hold the same rank as Canopus, who was far older than she.

"Refreshments, ma'am."

Benjamin Canopus, a man of about forty, had the typical appearance of a high-ranking officer, with a strong build but a slick air about him, unlike soldiers who had worked their way up through the ranks or civilian businessmen.

"Thank you, Ben."

He placed a cup of steaming honey milk on the side table. Major Sirius decided to be honestly grateful for the paternal consideration her subordinate offered. The hot milk with honey wasn't in the kind of army tumbler used during missions, but instead had been poured from a thermos into a stylish commercial mug.

She gently put it to her lips. The warmth and sweet flavors seemed to soothe her anguish.

"You're very welcome. Have you finished your preparations already, Commander?" asked Major Canopus, seeing the personal shipping containers stacked in a corner of the room.

"Yes, for the most part."

"Skillful and efficient, as always."

"I am still a girl, after all."

Major Canopus shrugged at the girl young enough to be his daughter. In fact, he did have a daughter—two years younger than she. "I would think being a girl doesn't have much to do with it... Perhaps it's your Japanese blood."

"And I would think calling all Japanese people meticulous is a thing of the past."

With her quarter-Japanese blood pointed out, this time it was Major Sirius's turn to shrug.

She wasn't especially unhappy with the comment. People who cared about race wouldn't go far—in the Stars, at least.

"Well, in any case... You'll have time to forget your mission of retribution and spread your wings for a while."

"It's a special mission, not a vacation..."

The easygoing Major Canopus's instigation met with Major Sirius's lips turning down into a pout. The expression was exactly suitable for a girl her age.

"In fact, it's miserable," she continued with a sigh. "'Dig up whether the suspects are strategic magicians,' they tell me. Maybe one of them is—but then, isn't it also likely neither of them is? Why would they assign me an undercover investigation when I've never done one before? I know there's an age requirement, but there must be plenty of others who have the specific training for this."

Major Sirius's mission was to determine the identity of the one who executed—who cast—the Great Bomb, observed in the Far East in October and believed to be a strategic-class spell. Out of the fifty-one suspects the information department had narrowed the field to, two of them were attending a school in Tokyo. So they'd assigned the undercover investigation to Major Sirius, who was in the same age range (coincidentally, the exact same age).

"There, there," said Major Canopus, putting both hands up in a pacifying gesture. "It must mean the general staff office considers them a very hard-to-manage problem. If the targets are what we predicted, they'll be magic users with the danger level of strategic nuclear weapons. Their particular magical identities were also beyond our investigation. It isn't inexplicable that HQ is prioritizing candidates on combat power rather than intelligence training."

"I understand that, but…"

"While I do feel this plan of making contact with high school suspects using another high school student is somewhat simplistic, you won't be the only one on this investigation, Commander."

Naturally, behind the scenes of Major Sirius contacting the suspects would be a large group of *experts* investigating from different angles. One planet-class magician from the Stars would also be with the major as her direct aide. There wasn't any way she wouldn't have known.

"I know that, too, but…"

Therefore, that answer could be called natural as well.

"Why not think of it this way? Your role as commander is to shake them up after making contact."

"Well… Maybe that's more realistic. I'm essentially an amateur when it comes to espionage, after all."

"Which is why I believe you should take this chance to enjoy yourself and have a good time. I think the suspects may open up to you more if you do."

Major Sirius heaved a sigh. "Yes, maybe you're right, Ben." She returned her mug to the side table, then stood up in front of Major Canopus. "Ben, I leave things in your care while I'm gone. It pains me to burden you with what should be my duty, since we haven't yet finished mopping up the rest of the fugitives…but you're the only one I can ask to stand in for me."

"Please, leave it to me, Commander. And, though it may be somewhat early—safe travels."

Major Canopus saluted with a fond smile, and Major Sirius returned the gesture with a grateful one.

[2]

Tatsuya and Miyuki greeted the new year of AD 2096 together as they always did.

Their father was spending New Year's at his lover's former primary residence, which was now her second house. Tatsuya and Miyuki would have found that more awkward in many ways, so they had no complaint about avoiding it.

Neither of them used New Year's as an excuse for a day's self-indulgence. As Tatsuya waited by the front door at around the same time they'd usually leave for school, he heard his sister call, "I must apologize for the wait," and looked up.

Clad in a long-sleeved kimono of a lustrous red fabric with a white-and-pink peony design, Miyuki gracefully descended the stairs.

On her face, so fair-skinned as to need no powder, stood a single pair of brilliantly crimson lips.

The swaying hair ornament hanging down from her tied-up hair seemed ever so slightly childlike, but it was actually a point of charm that formed an age-appropriate cuteness amid her maturity.

Her congenital beauty wasn't the only thing that drew the eye, however.

The women's clothing of yore placed pressure on the chest, and though more three-dimensional kimonos had been tailored in recent years, Miyuki wore a traditional *furisode*, which expressed the lines of her waist, so slight it might break, and of her chest, which had increased in volume; despite that, her neck was hidden modestly. It was an inexplicably elegant manner of wearing clothes.

Upon seeing his sister's glamorous figure—the prettiest in the world, he thought—Tatsuya felt brotherly pride swell.

"Mmhmm. You look very pretty."

Tatsuya placed his sister in the center of his view as she dipped her feet into her sandals, then offered this unabashed compliment.

Miyuki's cheeks immediately turned vermilion. "Brother... Please, do not tease me."

Embarrassed, though not looking away, she instead protested through upturned eyes; the gesture was powerful enough to turn to ash any nonimmunized man.

"I wasn't teasing you... Let's be off."

Tatsuya, though, handled it easily; it could be said that he hadn't been Miyuki's older brother sixteen years (fifteen years and nine months, to be precise) for nothing.

A self-driving commuter was parked in front of the gate. Though it was self-driving, it wasn't unoccupied. In the back seat sat one adult man and one adult woman.

"Happy New Year, Master."

"Happy New Year, Kokonoe-sensei. I hope you will continue to look after us again this year."

At Tatsuya's short greeting and Miyuki's polite bend at the waist, Yakumo responded with a smile, still sitting. "Well, every year you grow a good deal more attractive. Your beauty rivals that of Kichi-jouten herself. The *tenyo* on Mount Meru might hide themselves out of embarrassment."

In a way, it was exactly the kind of response expected from Yakumo.

"Sensei... Isn't there something else that needs saying?"

The interruption came from the woman sitting next to him.

Tatsuya, the words taken right out of his mouth, turned to her before Yakumo could butt in and lowered his head in a slight bow. "Happy New Year, Ms. Ono. I must ask, is it okay for you to be seen with Master?"

"Happy New Year, Shiba. Unpleasant questions right out of the gate this year, I see."

Tatsuya was actually honestly concerned, but Haruka seemed to take it as sarcasm. Mentally, he shrugged it off, though when he thought back to several of his usual habits, he was forced to realize that he couldn't necessarily blame her for the misunderstanding.

"I ran into Sensei by coincidence," she continued. "I came here today to chaperone you."

"I see. So that's your story," remarked Tatsuya. "A chaperone for high school students might feel a bit uncomfortable, but I suppose… But in that case, should you be calling him sensei?"

In the back seat, Haruka scowled.

He was right—in this day and age, as a high school student, simply paying one's first shrine visit of the New Year didn't necessitate adult supervision. If she was going to make an excuse, he'd have expected it to be that she was "going with" them, not "chaperoning" them.

And calling someone she'd run into by coincidence sensei, despite him not being in the teaching profession, carried the risk of sounding peculiar.

"Shall we think about it on the way?"

Miyuki's proposition came only after Tatsuya opened the commuter's door. Ignoring the lost-in-thought Haruka, he offered a hand to Miyuki, then closed the door and rounded the commuter to get into the opposite seat, where the driver would be. When he locked the door, the commuter pulled away toward the station.

They were paid significant attention at the station as they transferred into a private train cabinet, and they drew even more stares after getting out of the four-seater to make the five-minute walk to the meeting place.

"Wow! Miyuki, you look so pretty!"

...And when they arrived at the meeting place, those were the first words that greeted Tatsuya and Miyuki. Mizuki, wearing a long dress and a fur cape-coat, looked at Miyuki, spellbound. Her gaze was so enthusiastic Tatsuya wasn't sure she even saw him.

"Happy New Year, Tatsuya. You look nice. Which is a little surprising."

Honoka, wearing a *furisode* like Miyuki, seemed to wince at first under the pressure of her classmates' attractiveness, but she smoothly diverted those thoughts upon seeing Tatsuya, who was dressed plainly, though with a more upright air about him than usual. She quickly returned to a good New Year's smile, seeing that.

"Happy New Year," he answered. "You look nice, too, Honoka."

Honoka did indeed look good in a *furisode* kimono, so Tatsuya didn't feel like he was flattering her. She smiled happily, and he returned it, only to then consider his own clothes. "You say surprising—does this look a little weird for me?" he asked.

"Nah, not at all!" said Leo. "You look good, Tatsuya. You have a kind of commanding presence, like the leader of a crime syndicate."

"What am I, a yakuza?"

Tatsuya couldn't tell if Leo was being serious or not. After all, Leo himself was in a jacket that looked like day-to-day clothes.

Mizuki, Honoka, and Leo were the three they met up with for their New Year's shrine visit. Erika and Mikihiko were too busy helping around the house with all their followers present, so they couldn't slip out; Shizuku would be leaving for her study-abroad program very shortly and couldn't avoid things related to her father's job this time.

"You don't look particularly like a yakuza, but for sure, there aren't many high schoolers who look that good in a *haori* and *hakama*."

"It isn't so much *yakuza* as *sergeant* or *constable*."

As Haruka and Yakumo, who came a few steps later, said, Tatsuya was wearing a *haori* jacket, *hakama*, and *setta* sandals today—a pure Japanese ensemble. And as Honoka and Leo said, the outfit really suited him. In fact, the outfit felt empty without a larger waist and a truncheon attached.

"Oh, Haruka! Happy New Year."

"Happy New Year, Ms. Ono... Tatsuya, who might this be?"

After Leo's casual greeting came a more by-the-book one from Honoka, who then glanced over Yakumo. After that, she sent the questioning look to Tatsuya.

"Head priest of Kichijouji Temple, Kashou Yakumo. Maybe the rest of us would know him better as the *ninjutsu* user Yakumo Kokonoe? He's my martial arts teacher."

Hearing Tatsuya's introduction, Honoka's and Mizuki's eyes widened. He'd figured Honoka would know the name Yakumo, but Mizuki was beyond his expectations.

"I get it. That's why we were talking about going to the Hie Shrine for this."

And when Leo demonstrated an unlikely piece of knowledge, Tatsuya was outright surprised. Certainly not because he'd been looking down on Leo, but...

"What do you mean?"

...because, as one could see from Haruka being completely clueless, it wasn't a fact most normal people knew.

"Hm? *Kashou*—that means he's a Tendai Buddhist monk, right? Aren't praying to Sannou and Taimitsu rituals basically joined at the hip within the Tendai sect?" explained Leo, looking confused as to why she had asked.

However, the question marks above Haruka's head only increased with this new information.

"You're quite knowledgeable for someone so young. Your name is Leonhard Saijou, right?" Leaving behind the confusion, Yakumo addressed Leo in a jovial tone.

"Huh? You know who I am?" Leo blurted.

"Yes. I had a chance to watch recordings of the Nine School Competition," answered Yakumo. His response was also straightforward, without any twists, but when Leo heard it, he reflexively scowled. He'd probably remembered his anachronistic and out-of-place mantle getup. Apparently it was a memory he'd have liked to forget.

With preliminary introductions finished, the seven of them—the five classmates, the man with the shaven head (though he didn't wear the *kesa* robe of a Buddhist priest, but instead a normal men's kimono), and the young woman—walked in a pack toward the main shrine. Fortunately for Haruka, nobody asked her why she was going with them.

Roadside stands lined either side of the shrine approach, a sight unchanged for a century. But even this was a scene that had vanished in most places with the worsening of the global food crisis. It was likely a deeply emotional sight for those old enough to remember it, but Tatsuya and the others didn't have any such sentiment for the past.

Without any particular detours, they walked up the long staircase, passed through the shrine gates, and entered the inner yard in front of the outer shrine. There, Tatsuya suddenly felt eyes on him.

Not a rude, scrutinizing stare, but the glancing kind, of someone stealing looks at him.

"Any idea, Shiba?"

"No, ma'am."

"Heh. Maybe Tatsuya's outfit is an unusual sight for foreigners."

They quite skillfully played it casual, but there was no fooling Haruka and Yakumo's eyes. Even Tatsuya had noticed it without using Elemental Sight, so Haruka aside, it was only natural that his master would as well.

As Yakumo said, the "foreigner" had the stereotypical blonde hair and green eyes—and she was a young girl. In these times, though, that didn't necessarily mean she was a citizen of another country. Plus, her features gave off a Japanese impression, somehow.

She looked about Tatsuya's age. Considering the ethnic differences, it would be easy to mistake her for younger than she was, but Tatsuya decided that she wasn't that much younger than they were at all.

"What might you be looking at, Brother?"

He hadn't had his eyes on the girl for more than a second, but that was enough for Miyuki to notice. When she followed where his gaze was, her eyes rose in surprise.

"...Well, she *is* a pretty girl," said his sister flatly, her inner thoughts readily apparent.

To be certain, the girl was pretty enough that Miyuki calling her such wasn't sarcasm. Vividly colored hair and eyes. In a sense, her beauty was the direct opposite of Miyuki's. But that certainly hadn't been why Tatsuya was looking at her.

He glanced at Yakumo for help—and when he saw the childish smirk on the man's lips, he realized he'd have to do something about this himself.

He peered directly into his sister's eyes, and in a cool, uninterested tone of voice, he responded, "Not as pretty as you, though."

"...Please, don't think you can use that trick to fool me every time."

The words were a fierce counterattack on their own, but her giddy voice, vermilion cheeks, and wandering eyes left little need for fear.

"I'm not trying to fool you. That's what I honestly think, and I wasn't looking at her for that reason anyway."

"Brother, I swear!" Miyuki quickly went to turn her face away but then realized something that wouldn't let her turn a blind eye to what he'd said. "...Is there something suspicious about her?"

"Suspicious? Well, her clothing, for starters..." answered Tatsuya in a voice like he was about to crack a pained grin.

Miyuki stole a second glance at the blonde-haired, green-eyed girl, and was very nearly convinced of the whole matter.

A light-beige half coat and a skirt with a frilled hem. Patterned tights and long boots. Simply hearing those things wouldn't be strange. But her half coat was the same length as her skirt, which had a four-inch inseam. Apparently, it was to leave only the colorful frills decorating its hem visible. And her stretch boot soles were awfully thick, and the boots went up to her knees, combining with her tights, which had a lace pattern that revealed skin in places. And the gloves bordered with fake fur. And the animal-patterned soft hat. Based on current trends, her outfit was an incoherent medley. It was like she'd thrown together various girly fashions from before the war at random. It wasn't strange that even Tatsuya, a guy, would think it was strange.

But Miyuki knew her brother wasn't the type to seriously worry about such surface things.

"That isn't all, is it?"

This time, she directed a strong-willed gaze at the girl, unlike before.

Perhaps sensing it, though her face betrayed nothing, the girl began to walk.

Toward Tatsuya's group.

Without saying anything, she passed by them, then walked up the long staircase.

But her route made Tatsuya certain that she'd come near just to cast a glance at them.

While the mission given to Major Angelina Sirius was an undercover investigation, it also had a strong diversionary aspect to it. In accordance with that, their first contact seemed to have gone well—she'd gotten a look at her targets, and they at her. She'd been worried they wouldn't notice her, since she'd concealed her presence, but her subordinate had been right earlier—there was no need to fear. Still, being spotted so easily wasn't satisfying in and of itself, she thought as she opened the door to the apartment that would be her base of living operations for this mission.

"Welcome back."

Contrary to Major Sirius's prediction that her roommate wouldn't be back yet, a voice came from the room to welcome her.

"Silvie, you're back?"

When her older roommate came to the door to greet her, the major called her by her nickname.

This young woman's name was Silvia Mercury First. Everything past the Silvia was a code name, marking her as the highest among the Mercury-rank planet-class magicians within the Stars. Her actual military rank was warrant officer, though, and her age twenty-five. As could be understood from her being given the First code name despite her young age, she was a woman whose talents were highly rated. Silvia hadn't originally wanted to be a soldier—she'd majored in journalism. Now, though, her information analysis skills made her valuable enough to be selected as Major Sirius's aide.

"Silvie?"

Supposedly talented, Major Sirius's roommate didn't answer her words, instead staring intently at her. The major, dubious, said her name a second time, and Silvia finally spoke, her gaze steady.

"Lina… What are you wearing?"

Lina was Major Angelina Sirius's nickname when she was off the clock, and she had ordered that she be called that rather than Commander or Major during the undercover mission. Silvia had always been a free-spirited woman, so regardless of the rank and position difference between them, she quickly got used to using it—and speaking frankly.

Though she hadn't been outright rude, it wasn't something one would usually say to a superior officer. But "Lina" didn't seem to mind it whatsoever.

"Oh, this? I did some research on Japan's fashion idols from the last century so I wouldn't stand out more than I had to. It was hard work, too. How do I look?"

"…Before I answer that, I'd like to ask something."

"Yes, what is it?"

Silvia was making a face like she was nursing a headache and about to massage her temples, but Lina didn't seem to notice. "Isn't it hard to walk in those boots?" she asked.

Lina nodded, as if heartily agreeing with her. "It is! I nearly tripped a few times. I don't know how Japanese girls don't twist their ankles walking in these."

"Did you see any other girls wearing the same kind of boots?"

It should have only needed one question, but it took two. Still, Lina didn't seem very bothered. "Hmm? Now that I think of it, I didn't."

Silvia's expression changed; now it looked like she both had a headache and wanted to sigh. "Lina, I'll be frank. Those boots are way out of fashion."

"Huh?!"

Lina's eyes went wide, and the sight made Silvia's irritation explode. "Don't *huh* me! It's not just the boots! Your tights and that hat are out of fashion, too. One hundred years is too far back! And your coordination is incredibly incoherent. This isn't the fashion sense a young woman would have. I bet you stood out like a sore thumb in that."

The uncomfortable face her scolding met with told Silvia that her roommate knew what she was talking about. Truthfully, Lina had noticed eyes on her wherever she went. She'd shrugged them off, though, figuring a foreigner was a rare sight.

"I know you were supposed to draw the targets' attention...but how are you going to handle drawing the attention of people who have nothing to do with us?"

Finally unable to hold it in any longer, Silvia heaved a sigh.

"Commander."

The word was polite; the tone was cold. Lina thought she felt a cold sweat break out along her spine.

"We will cancel everything else for the day. I do not wish to be rude, but this Mercury will explain Japan's latest fashion trends in a detailed and easy-to-understand way," announced Silvia, hands on her hips.

Lina might have far eclipsed Silvia in combat power, but these were words she just couldn't fight.

After a short but eventful Winter Break, the third school quarter began.

The "eventful" things included, for one, the unexpectedly tearful parting when seeing Shizuku off at the airport (main roles: Honoka, Shizuku; supporting roles: Miyuki, Mizuki, with Tatsuya at a loss)—but Tatsuya had faith that the experience would turn into a good memory one day. He had to, or it would have been too harrowing.

The transfer student would be replacing Shizuku in Class A starting today, but it didn't have anything to do with Tatsuya. He wasn't completely unrelated as long as she was in the same class as Miyuki, but he had no desire to involve himself with her.

Speaking of classes, they were on a full-time curriculum right from the first day of the new quarter. At the end of first period, rumors about the transfer student in Class A were already making their way around, but he wasn't going to be assertive and put up an antenna for it; the gossip went in one ear and out the other.

His aloof stance, however, still placed him in the minority, and during their break after second period, he too was caught up in the vortex of rumors by a certain curious friend.

"I hear she's gorgeous," said Erika, coming up to him immediately, looking excited—or maybe feigning excitement—at which point he decided he could no longer leave things unaddressed. "Beautiful blonde hair, too. Even the upperclassmen are showing up to see her…"

"You going sightseeing, too, Erika?" he asked; for now, despite her fevered descriptions, it was all hearsay.

"No, there's way too many people for me to get in."

"Huh," interjected Leo. "I guess you *do* know how to restrain yourself—"

No sooner had he retorted with this than his hands flew over his head in defense. A moment later, there was a frog-like out-of-tune sound, and he bent forward in pain, clutching his throat—which had been left unprotected.

If he knows she'll do it, why does he bother saying that stuff?

As Tatsuya stared unsympathetically down at Leo, who was writhing after being caught in the throat by a rolled-up notebook, the perpetrator—Erika—continued to talk as though nothing had happened. "Well, I'm a girl, right? I don't care how beautiful she is—it's not worth having to jostle my way through a squeezing crowd just to see her."

Tatsuya was of the exact same opinion when it came to having no intention of actually going to see her, but as a man, in terms of opinions that linked his curiosity fully to his sexuality, he felt the need to object.

"Nobody expects transfer students at a magic high school, after all. It's only natural to be curious about one. Hasn't happened for at least ten years, right?"

"I don't know about before, but we're apparently not the only one who got an exchange student," interjected Mikihiko, just having arrived from the geometry prep room. "I hear Second, Third, and Fourth High have all accepted a short-term exchange student. A few apparently came to the university, too, under the pretense of joint research. One of our followers was talking about it."

"Oh, I heard about the university, too," said Erika. "Rumor is that when they found out how incredible flight magic is for military applications after the Yokohama incident, they were falling over themselves to come here and scope it out."

Though old magic and modern magic were different fields, the Yoshida and Chiba had many followers who used each, so the amount of information that came to them personally was on a different level than what people outside of the families could glean. Based on what Tatsuya's friends had said, the USNA had put a good deal more people into this than the families had expected. In October, the talk had been of the Stars acting by themselves; now, it looked like the situation had gotten quite a bit worse since then.

"Then you think the transfer student in Class A is a spy, too?" asked Leo, outspoken as ever, having recovered from his agonies.

"Look, you..."

Erika wasn't the only one to give a sour face—Mizuki and Mikihiko did as well.

"Leo, you're not supposed to say those things out loud..." scolded Mizuki.

"We have to support her as classmates, you know..." added Mikihiko.

Even attacked by their doubles lineup, Leo managed an argument. "You say classmates, but she's in Class A, isn't she? We'll barely see her."

"Miyuki's in Class A, stupid," said Erika, cleaving his objection in two. "The student council vice president and the first transfer student in who knows how many years. It might only be until she gets used to the school, but Miyuki will have to look out for her. If she and Miyuki are involved with each other, than we'll have to be, too."

Tatsuya, who didn't want to proactively involve himself with the new girl, sighed to himself, thinking that Erika, unfortunately, was right.

That involvement would come earlier than he thought. Actually, it was more like it was the earliest possibility out of the ones he'd predicted—a merciless actualization.

His group of friends met for lunch in the cafeteria like always. Miyuki and Honoka came, as well as one other—a blonde-haired, green-eyed girl. Seeing her wasn't exactly shocking, but it did cause Tatsuya a momentary bout of *Seriously?*

He'd heard of her hair and eye color and more than his fill of gossip about how pretty she was. Anyway, if she was just a pretty girl, Tatsuya had his resistance built up from Miyuki. No, the surprise he felt this time around wasn't because of the happenstance or her beauty; it was because the new girl was the same one they'd met—or rather, chanced to see—at Hie Shrine.

"Would you mind very much if I sat with you?"

From her mouth flowed fluent Japanese. She had something of an accent to her emphases, but one couldn't blame her. She was studying abroad in Japan, after all—though it was possible it was all pretense, meant to craft a believable infiltration.

"Sure, go ahead."

Her eyes were directed at Tatsuya. He didn't feel much need to square off against her, so he spoke candidly.

"Lina, let's get our plates first."

"Plates? …Oh, for the food. All right."

Tatsuya and the others had already gotten their meals. Prompted by Miyuki, the three of them headed for the serving counter. The buzz where they went sounded louder to him than normal. More students let them past, too, in awe.

"She really is a knockout next to the two of them, huh?"

Erika, despite also being attractive, wasn't the type to put pressure on those who saw her, and even she had to breathe a word at the sight.

"She seems to be pretty friendly with them…" said Mizuki, probably referring to how they'd just met today.

"Hey, Tatsuya…" said Leo. "I feel like I've seen her somewhere before."

"Whoa. Now *that's* an ancient pickup line." Erika immediately snapped back a retort, but she quickly realized that Leo wasn't *that* enamored by the girl, because, truthfully, she had wanted to say it, too.

"...You know, you're right." Mizuki nodded in agreement.

"Wait, you, too, Shibata? She...can't be a celebrity or a model, could she?" wondered Leo.

Of course, Tatsuya knew the truth lay elsewhere. In fact, he was surprised they didn't very clearly remember someone dressed up so *conspicuously*. As he wondered whether to clear up his friends' questions here and now, the three others came back together.

He felt many sets of eyes gather on them. Gazes pretending to be casual, but unable to hide a strong interest, from all over the room. People were always looking at Miyuki, but there were clearly more people stealing glances their way now.

"I'm sorry for the wait, Brother." Acting like it didn't bother her at all, Miyuki sat down naturally next to Tatsuya.

"I'll introduce you, Tatsuya," said Honoka, setting her tray down across from him like it was totally normal, turning to the girl who sat next to her. "Her name is Angelina Kudou Shields. As I'm sure you've heard, she's the exchange student who started in Class A today."

After hearing Honoka's introduction, Tatsuya—and the other three as well—gave troubled expressions.

"Honoka, would you introduce me to everyone else, and not just this person?"

But it was the exchange student in question who spoke for their concerns.

"Oh, ah, I-I'm sorry!"

"...Well, that's Honoka for you."

"That it is."

Erika and Mizuki both spoke truly, not trying to make fun of her. Honoka went red in the face and clammed up.

"Allow me. This is Angelina Kudou Shields. She's from America."

After Miyuki's second introduction, the transfer student gave a bow in her seat, her blonde hair fluttering. "Please, call me Lina," she said, narrowing her eyes into a beautiful smile.

Her deep-blue eyes weren't the color of water, or of ice, but the blue of the azure sky. Her wavy blonde hair, bound by ribbons to either side of her head, would probably reach to the small of her back when undone. It might have even been longer than Miyuki's. Her mature features for a freshman in high school and her coquettish hairstyle seemed somewhat unbalanced, but it served to soften the sharp impression her beauty made, giving her an air of amiability.

More eyes were on them than usual, and she was clearly the cause. After hearing her name again from Miyuki, even as they were taken by her gorgeous smile (two male students in particular), mild surprise was on their faces; Tatsuya preempted them and returned the introduction. "I am Tatsuya Shiba, from Class E. As I'm sure it's confusing to have two Shibas at the table, you may simply call me Tatsuya."

"Thanks. You can call me Lina, too. And I'd be grateful if we didn't need to speak formally with one another."

"All right, then."

"Pleased to meet you, Tatsuya."

Lina reached a hand across the table—perhaps it was customary—so Tatsuya gently took it from underneath, as though holding it up reverently.

It wasn't a handshake; the act was like that of someone asking a noblewoman for a kiss. Was it beyond her expectations?

"Tatsuya, are you by chance Miyuki's older brother?" asked Lina, confusion rising in her sky-blue eyes but her expression casual.

As he reflected on her lack of a poker face, Tatsuya nodded with a smile, careful not to chuckle. He purposely didn't point out that Miyuki had called him as much a few moments ago.

"I'm Erika Chiba. You can call me Erika, Lina." Being gregarious in times like this was doubtless one of Erika's strong points.

"I'm Mizuki Shibata. Please, call me Mizuki."

"And I'm Leonhard Saijou. Leo's just fine. I'm a little rude when I talk sometimes, but don't take it personally."

"I'm Mikihiko Yoshida. You can just call me Mikihiko, too."

Taking encouragement from Erika, Mizuki, Leo, and Mikihiko introduced themselves in turn.

"Erika, Mizuki, Leo, and Mikihiko. Nice to meet you."

Lina memorized all their names without having to ask again. It was an elementary skill, but also the first step in earning goodwill from others, and she had it down pat.

Still, when she said Mikihiko's name, it sounded like two names—Miki Hiko. His very Japanese name must have been difficult for her American tongue.

"It's hard to say, isn't it? You don't have to call him Mikihiko—you can just use Miki."

If the person himself had said it, that would have been an impressive display of consideration, but when another person said it—Erika, in particular—it seemed like more than just friendliness. At least, Mikihiko seemed to feel that way and tried to object to Erika's words (or rather, suggestion).

"Oh, is that so? I'll do that then. Is Miki all right with you?"

But right before he could, Lina asked that with a face that looked relieved—forcing him to accept the proposal.

Lina had chosen the soba noodles from the cafeteria menu, and as she wielded her chopsticks with an assured manner, she answered all the questions that occasionally came her way without so much as a sour face. It probably helped that none of the group was the type to ask anything ill-mannered. As everyone was about finished eating, Lina seemed to have opened up quite a bit. That was when Tatsuya, representing the other Class E members harboring the same question, asked it:

"By the way, Lina, would you happen to be a blood relation of His Excellency Kudou?"

Old Sage was a moniker only used by Japan's magicians. And Tatsuya personally didn't like the term. Instead, he asked the question with the term *His Excellency*, used publicly out of respect for the retired general.

"I seem to recall His Excellency's younger brother visiting America and starting a family there."

That was in an age when international marriages between magicians were encouraged. At the time, Retsu Kudou was already seen as the world's strongest—and trickiest—magician. His younger brother had moved to America and begun a family there with an American magician, which was quite a topic of conversation for at least Japan's magicians.

"Oh, I'm surprised you knew that, Tatsuya. It was quite a long time ago."

Tatsuya's speculation turned out to be right. Also, from that, he understood that Retsu Kudou's brother's bones being interred in American soil as those of an American magician was a thing of the past for her.

"My maternal grandfather was Shogun Retsu's younger brother."

She pronounced the Japanese word for *general* without the elongated *o*, which certainly wasn't Tatsuya's ears playing tricks on him—it was the medieval title itself from which the modern had come. Retsu Kudou had long held a leadership position among Japan's magicians, and even now, ones from the West still called him shogun. She may have been a quarter Japanese, and she may have been fluent in the language, but she was still an American magician through and through.

"I think the connection was how the topic of a foreign exchange program was brought to me."

"Oh, then you didn't request for it yourself, Lina?" piped in Erika casually.

The slight disturbance Lina showed at that was also likely not Tatsuya just seeing things.

[3]

Those who crawl through the dark of night aren't limited to the nefarious. That city life remains unthreatened by its outlaws—or at least remains undestroyed—is thanks to the chaos-battling disciples of law and order who frantically run through that same darkness.

Of course, not all of these "disciples of law and order" are diligent. In fact, one young man who was (or ought to have been) a defender of law and order was just busy complaining to his male partner.

"One thing after another to bother us..."

"..."

"And here I thought the disasters ended with the New Year."

"..."

"What's going on anyway? Illegal immigrants and foreign invaders made more sense than this."

"...It's our job to figure that out, remember? These incidents are keeping food on our tables, so quit your whining!"

His superior continued on after that, muttering his regrets about the incidents occurring at all. But just as the coworker sucked in his breath, ready to give an actual admonition—or rather, a scolding—to his superior...

"Yes? This is Inagaki."

...he instead answered a call that came over the receiver in his ear, making sure to mask the tension in his voice.

"...Roger. We'll head there right away."

After switching off the transmitter, he fired a harsh glance at his superior, who must have been able to guess what had happened and yet was still idling.

"Chief, it's the fifth one. Cause of death is the same as past victims—death by emaciation. No external wounds, also the same as always."

After hearing Lieutenant Inagaki's report, Chief Toshikazu Chiba spread his arms and looked up, as though entreating the heavens. "And all the blood is gone, too, right? ...The fifth freak death this month. It's getting real hard to keep the media off this."

Without speaking of the victim or the perpetrator, Chief Toshikazu Chiba breathed a troubled sigh. And though his expression said he found it all a huge pain, in his eyes there glinted the sharp light of a hunter.

Angelina Sirius's debut at First High was sensational.

Her looks, for one, became such an entity that by the end of her first day, not a student in school didn't know about them.

Until now, the seat of most beautiful girl had belonged to Miyuki. This had been a unanimous viewpoint, including from upperclassmen and female students.

But with Lina in the picture now, their "queen" had become a binary star. Their frequent opportunities to do things together only added to the impression.

Golden hair that glittered in the sunlight. Eyes that shone bluer than sapphires.

Black hair that was deeper than the night sky. Clear eyes that were darker than a black pearl.

Both equally beautiful, yet possessing contrasting types of beauty: When the two young women stood together, it seemed only to heighten their individual radiances.

Their looks alone were enough to be the subject of conversation, but...

"Here I come, Miyuki."

"I'm ready anytime. You may do the countdown."

Now, they stood facing each other, separated by three yards.

Between them, a one-inch metal ball sat atop a slender pole.

Several similar fixtures were set up in the practice room, but all their classmates stopped what they were doing to watch them.

No, not only their classmates.

The viewing seats up on a mezzanine making a circuit around the room were packed with seniors who were no longer required to attend school now that all their mandatory classes were completed.

Mayumi and Mari were among them.

"...You think her magic power really rivals Shiba's?"

"In a way, she came to Japan representing America, so I don't think it's impossible. But it's hard to believe it so suddenly—magic ability on par with Miyuki's in someone of the same age?"

"Agreed. They say a picture is worth a thousand words, and I won't believe it until I see it."

"Well, that is why we came to take a look, after all."

This practice would be a simple and highly gamelike exercise, where the two girls would use their CADs at the same time, each aiming to be the first to control the metal ball in the middle. Its simplicity would highlight pure power differential and nothing more.

The students had begun this exercise last month, and none of Miyuki's classmates could come anywhere close to beating her. There was such a difference in their magic power that even the instructors were forced to admit the exercise would be pointless for both her and her opponents.

After hearing about it, student council members old and new (plus the disciplinary committee chairwoman) took turns challenging her; that none of them could hold a candle to her was now a badly kept secret at First High.

Crushed without difficulty, their pride as upperclassmen in pieces (though Miyuki was very humble about her victories), Mayumi and Mari joining the others in spectating was only natural.

"Three, two, one…" counted down Lina in English.

The CAD they would use was a panel interface, fixed in place. When Lina said "one," they both held a hand over the panel.

"Go!"

The last signal was given by both voices.

Miyuki's fingers touched the panel, and Lina's palm slammed it.

Static and dynamic—their start-up methods reflected their colors exactly.

But the contrast was merely physical.

A flash of psionic light burst over the metal target.

Because the light was invisible to the naked eye, shutting your eyelids would be ineffective. Viewers less experienced with external magical influence–restraining techniques massaged their temples and shook their heads to clear them.

The glow vanished in an instant. The metal ball rolled toward Lina.

"Agh, I lost again!"

"Hee-hee. That's two wins in a row, Lina."

Lina making a grand show of frustration, and Miyuki giving a somewhat relieved smile: As one could see from their attitudes, the unofficial match had ended in Miyuki's victory. However, from the tone in which the "two in a row" comment had been spoken, you didn't get the impression that it was an overwhelming defeat. After all…

"…They were exactly equal," breathed Mayumi.

"In fact, wasn't the transfer student slightly faster triggering the spell?"

"Yes. But Miyuki's influence was higher, so she took control before the spell was complete. You can prioritize speed, or prioritize power... This isn't so much a victory of pure force as a victory won through tactics."

From both Mayumi and Mari's point of view, their magic power—at least, their pure magic power for basic, single-type spells—was equal.

After that, within their allotted time, they did the exercise four more times, the score for which was two to two, making today's winner Miyuki by two wins.

That afternoon, it was business as usual in the school cafeteria.

Lina was sitting with them again today, though she hadn't done so every day. She'd had several invitations from here and there during the week after she transferred in, and she ate with different people each day.

Broadening her cultural exchange with others could be called the model attitude for a transfer student. This was actually the first time she was eating with Tatsuya's group again since her first day.

"You're very popular, Lina."

"Thanks. I'm glad everyone here is so kind."

Erika's compliment had nothing hidden beneath the surface, and instead of pointlessly getting embarrassed or acting modest, Lina gave an indifferent response. The attitude was both personal and a product of national character, and it came off as new and fresh for Tatsuya's group (minus Erika).

"You were more amazing than we thought, Lina. I mean, they chose you to study abroad and everything, so I figured you were the real deal, but I never thought you'd be able to compete with Miyuki on even terms."

"I'm actually surprised myself."

At Mikihiko's compliment, Lina's eyes widened in a slight overreaction as she expressed her surprise. As an aside, Mikihiko seemed to find Lina easier to talk to than Miyuki, and though he still spoke stiffly to the latter, he'd started to loosen up with the former.

"I don't mean to brag, but I was undefeated at the high school level in the States. But I just couldn't seem to win out over Miyuki. Even with Honoka, I wouldn't lose in overall ability, but I would when it comes to precise control. Japan really is the great land of magic."

"Lina, that was just a training session, not a competition. I don't think you should care so much about winning or losing."

"But competition is important. It might be practice, but they purposely put something so much like a game into the curriculum. I think fussing over winning and losing will help us get better."

At Miyuki's gentle admonishment, Lina made a frontal objection, unafraid of conflict.

That must have been her way of doing things. This part of her, too, felt somewhat fresh.

"It's important to have a sense of competition while you're in the heat of things. But there's no reason to take it out of the practice room, is there? Exercises are only exercises—they're not like practical tests, which are connected to your grades."

So Tatsuya, too, decided to offer his own unreserved opinion.

"…Yes, maybe you're right, Tatsuya. Maybe I was getting a little too into it."

"It's not a bad thing. Miyuki will have more motivation now that she has a new rival. On that point, I'm grateful to have you here, Lina."

Lina nodded without comment at first but then returned a blank stare.

"There it is—Tatsuya's sister complex returns," said Erika from next to her, giving an exaggerated sigh.

"O-oh, I see… Tatsuya and Miyuki do seem close."

To Tatsuya, beneath the innocuous comment, the temperature of Lina's gaze felt like it had rapidly decreased.

"By the way, Lina, and this isn't important or anything, but…" He got the feeling the conversation was headed in a bad direction, so he tried to change the topic.

"What is it?" She turned an icy gaze on him. Still, it didn't seem like she was truly scorning him; he could spot a bit of acting. She was probably going along with Erika's joke.

He had no guarantee that wasn't just an optimistic outlook, but Tatsuya wasn't petty enough to grimace and stop talking at something like this.

"I thought the nickname for Angelina was Angie. Did I remember wrong?"

The question shouldn't have bothered her.

At the very least, Erika, Mizuki, and Honoka, who were sitting with them, thought as much.

But for just a moment, an unmistakable consternation crossed her face.

"No, you're not. But it's not unusual to shorten it to Lina, either. In elementary school, there was a girl in the same class named Angela, and we called her Angie, so…"

"So you came to be called Lina instead of Angie?" Tatsuya nodded, appearing convinced.

…Without letting on that he'd noticed her panic.

There were no dormitories at First High.

Out of necessity for the magic high schools, of which there were only nine in the country, some students enrolled from far away.

Thinking about it that way, it wouldn't seem strange to have dormitories, but in this day and age, aside from special schools with all-dorm systems placing heavy emphasis on the dorms as a learning environment, you never saw any such facilities. In an age where HARs had become normal household items and groceries could be bought online and delivered to your doorstep, students had no trouble whatsoever living on their own, so there was no demand for dormitories.

Thus, most students who couldn't commute from home rented

a place near school. It wasn't unnatural for Lina, a transfer student, to rent an apartment. Her room was two stations from the school by train—right nearby, given transportation in the modern era. She was renting not a single-person one-room apartment for students, but one big enough for a small family, because she wasn't living on her own.

"Welcome back, Lina."

"You're home early, Silvie."

When she opened the apartment's front door, her aide for this mission, Warrant Officer Silvia, came out as though she'd been waiting for her.

"It's already night, you know."

Lina, who had taken several detours, gave a small, pained grin at the retort. While she was still in her uniform, they moved to the dining room. And there...

"I didn't know you were coming today, Mia."

...a young woman with a tense expression greeted Lina. She was standing in front of the table, probably because she'd just been talking to Silvia.

"Yes, Major. I hope I'm not intruding, ma'am."

The woman called Mia answered in a nervous voice. Lina gave a troubled smile, then sat down at the table.

"Please, sit, Mia. Silvie, would you mind making tea?"

Normally, Silvia would have thought nothing of their rank difference and responded, "You're a girl, so you should at least make your own tea." But she could also read the situation.

"Is milk tea fine? Mia, would you like some more?"

"Ah, yes, ma'am. Thank you," answered Mia in a reserved manner, although her tension had loosened quite a bit.

Her name was Mikaela Hongou, nicknamed Mia. Like Lina, she was a Japanese American, but unlike with Lina, you couldn't tell her apart from other Japanese people. At most, her skin was a little dark, but even that wasn't particularly unusual in Japan.

She was one of the spies they'd sent into Japan ahead of Lina and

Silvia. Still, spying wasn't her main profession; her main job was as a Department of Defense magic scientist who researched emission-type magic, a girl of talent who had even taken part in the black hole experiment in November in Dallas. Since the Dallas experiment hadn't yielded many results, she'd requested this mission to search for a method of nonannihilation mass-energy conversion.

As was the case with many magic scientists, she was a magician herself. Unlike the fake students who had arrived in Japan under the pretense of collaborative research starting this month, she had infiltrated the Magic University as Mia Hongou, a sales engineer from Maximillian Devices' Japan branch, at the beginning of last month. Incidentally, her room was the one next to the one Lina was renting. Neither combat nor intelligence personnel, she was strictly part of the support staff, but also one of the "main team," working on their original goal—espionage activity—behind the scenes. She was supporting the members who had, in a way, waltzed right up to the front door this month.

"Have you found something out?"

Lina asked Silvie, who had finished arranging the teacups on the table and sat down.

"I'm going back over official databases, but at this time, I haven't found any new information."

"I see. I doubted you would get results that quickly." Next, Lina looked over to Mikaela. "What about you, Mia?"

"It's the same for me, ma'am… I'm sorry."

After seeming to have relaxed a bit, Mikaela tensed up again.

With her getting so nervous, Lina felt like she was bullying the poor girl, so she backed off. But when Lina had first come to Japan at the end of the year, the Mikaela she'd met had been even shakier and tenser than now. Despite the difference between a scientist and a warrior, Lina was the Sirius, the top of the USNA's magicians—and in her middle teens. Telling Mia not to be nervous wouldn't work. Lina and Mia could have slightly friendlier conversation now that two

weeks had passed since Lina's arrival, but only when they stuck to topics regarding daily life. Lina persuaded herself that was enough, since when it came to discussing their mission, Silvia's frank attitude wasn't the best thing, either.

"What about you, Lina?" Silvia asked. "Have you gotten a little friendlier with the targets?"

Lina's face clouded over. "I think I've gotten a little closer with them, but..." She sighed, then let out a weak smile. "Still nothing vital. In fact, I think they'll realize who I am before I uncover anything."

"...Did something happen?"

"Tatsuya asked me why my nickname wasn't Angie instead of Lina. It scared me for a second!"

"Was it a coincidence?"

"I don't know. I have no clue. I'm really not cut out for this, am I...?"

Lina heaved another sigh as Silvia poured more milk tea into her cup. Silvia and Mikaela looked at her worriedly. When she noticed that, Lina energized herself. "...It's fine. They're just high school kids. There's no way they seriously think that I'm Sirius. Even if they had suspicions, I'd never let them catch on."

A valiant comment at first, but it was clearly a bluff. To begin with, Lina was the one who was supposed to be catching on to *them*. That she felt the need to declare that she wouldn't let them get the best of her was fairly telling. Silvia realized it, too, but didn't say anything, maybe deciding it was better than Lina getting depressed over it.

However, she pointedly failed to mention that her targets weren't just any high school kids.

He handed a gown to his sister as she rose from the examination bed, fitted with only a psiometer (a psionic wave measurement device) and her undergarments. Tatsuya's android-like poker face from during the examination dissolved into a slightly anxious look, but it was still enough for Miyuki's eyes to catch it.

"...Is something not to your satisfaction? Brother, please, do not hesitate to tell me. I would do anything you tell me to do."

Still, that was an overreaction—or, rather, simply an extreme reaction overall. Feeling such, Tatsuya gave a dry smile, his expression hard to read, like he was unable to decide what countenance to put forth.

"No, if something isn't to my satisfaction, it's on me this time. The upper limit on your magic program construction scope has leveled up beyond my expectations. Because of that, your CAD's processing power can't keep up with your magical power. I thought I'd given it some room to grow when I set it up, but...I didn't think far enough ahead."

"I'm sorry..." she sighed, hanging her head.

"Why are you sorry? You should be proud." Tatsuya tousled her hair, and when she looked up, he smiled gently.

Infected by the smile, or in response to it, she gave her own smile as well, which was all well and good, but...

...*You're not supposed to blush for that.*

Sensing danger in the silence—mainly from her chest peeking through the gown seam—Tatsuya continued, his words somewhat hurried, "It looks like Lina being in your class is a good incentive for you."

The instant Lina's name came out, the mist dispersed from the flushed Miyuki's eyes.

"Yes... This may be forward of me, but I've never had anyone as strong as her to go up against."

And this wasn't because he'd offended her. Miyuki wasn't an unreasonable girl—she wouldn't flare up whenever she heard another girl's name come out of Tatsuya's mouth. The sense of transparency she gave off, which made even her expression look cold, was rooted in a different cause.

Currently, her eyes were filled with a quiet fighting spirit. "By the way, Brother, your question of her at lunch—I would presume, well..."

"It was that obvious, huh?" said Tatsuya with a chuckle before erasing his smile. "Yes, I do believe Lina is Sirius," he announced plainly. "I really can't hide anything from you, can I?"

As Tatsuya brought up his hands and smiled again, Miyuki's expression dissolved into a mischievous grin, and she pointed her index finger at him like she was posing. "Well, of course. Miyuki watches you more than anyone else, Brother."

Tatsuya seemed to force himself to laugh, but was it because he thought it was a joke, or because he'd decided to make it one?

As she laughed along with her brother, she thought to herself that she wanted to know how he really felt.

The basement (or perhaps one should say "underground facility") was climate controlled, but both of them would be restless with her in just underwear and a gown. After Miyuki changed out of her dressing gown, they moved to the living room.

Covering her slender legs were neither black leggings nor tights, but long socks. Her skirt hem was gently ruffled out and very short, and between it and her socks, her fair skin came in and out of sight.

If she was wearing that while standing upright, and then sat down or bent forward, wouldn't that be fairly bad? That's what Tatsuya thought, without thinking too hard about what exactly would be "bad."

In ignorance of her brother's thoughts—though he had no way of verifying whether she really didn't know—Miyuki placed a coffee cup in front of him, and, just for today, sat down not next to him but on the sofa across from him.

Then, she did nothing so free-spirited as crossing her legs.

She put her knees properly together, leaning them at an angle.

It was a considerably sexier pose than one that would have given him a peek under her skirt.

Tatsuya, who didn't understand Miyuki's intent (though he may have understood her surface intent, he didn't know what lay behind it), decided not to make her any more flushed.

As soon as he decided not to concern himself with it, the instability vanished from his eyes.

He got a quick glimpse of a somewhat dissatisfied look from Miyuki across the table, but he simply looked at her and spoke.

"Getting back to the previous topic, I believe with high certainty that Lina is Angie Sirius."

Two months ago, while the Stars—the USNA Army's magician force—was investigating the truth behind his strategic spell Material Burst, he'd received a warning from his aunt, Maya Yotsuba. At the time, she had also spoken of the fact that he and Miyuki had been designated targets of the Stars' information war as suspects. Tatsuya had been thinking Lina transferring to First High was part of that initiative.

"What I don't understand is how they don't seem to be trying to hide Sirius's identity whatsoever. It almost seems as though they're *trying* to get us to realize."

It was only natural he wouldn't understand. Even Tatsuya couldn't have speculated the reason was that Lina's personal—or rather, mental—guard was more lax than even the USNA Army imagined.

"And..." If he'd known the truth, laughing would have been his only recourse, but he continued his deduction, expression serious.

"Why would the USNA send in Sirius, who is essentially their trump card?" Miyuki had already switched mental gears and answered her brother seriously.

"That's right," Tatsuya remarked. "Simply based on our observations this week, Lina's abilities don't seem to be geared toward espionage work. Their true intentions probably lie elsewhere, but using her as their spy, of all people?"

"Sirius is too important..."

"If we assume that Lina is Sirius...then her spy mission would be secondary. Their real mission is something else."

"But what on earth could be so important that the USNA would send Sirius outside the country?"

At this point, they were overthinking things. Though, they had no way of knowing that.

"I don't know…but I don't think we need to let it bother us at this stage."

From an omnipotent viewpoint, his deduction was off the mark; but as it came out of Tatsuya's mouth, his tension suddenly deflated—

"America's done us the honor of providing you with a rival, Miyuki."

—but that wasn't to say that his seriousness disappeared as well. In fact, his voice was earnest.

"Yes, Brother," answered Miyuki in a formal tone, to his equally earnest gaze.

"Compete with Lina with everything you have. I know what I said before, but if she's going to get caught up with wins and losses, that will work in your favor. It will help push you to greater heights."

"Yes."

"Lina stands to grow just as much from competing with you. But you don't have to worry about that. This sort of chance rarely comes."

At his firm instructions, Miyuki gave a quiet smile without a single shadow of unease. "Yes," she said. "And I have you, Brother. As long as you do me the honor of remaining at my side, I have nothing to fear—not even Sirius."

Tatsuya had meant what he'd said in the sense of a competition partner, not a true opponent.

He couldn't deny that he felt Miyuki's words were slightly off-kilter.

But at the unflinching trust she showed in him, he nodded without hesitation.

◇ ◇ ◇

After-school hours for Tatsuya came in many variations, but they had two main patterns—either he shut himself up in the school's library, or he patrolled the halls as a disciplinary committee member. Usually, in the latter case, a veritable barrage of events occurred.

Enough to make him think it was actually a conspiracy.

And on this day, he felt that way more strongly than ever before.

Disciplinary committee members were granted the special right to carry their CADs on their person at all times, but aside from when he was doing a job for the committee, Tatsuya didn't use that right.

CADs were originally tools for activating typed spells in a short time; although they could be used with other magic, such as typeless magic, outer magic, and old magic, when it came to simple things—especially in typeless magic's case, such as simply emitting psions—forgoing a CAD wouldn't restrict a person very much.

Tatsuya, who had himself revealed at the Nine School Competition—unfortunately—that he could use dismantling magic, was mainly using typeless magic outside class during the second term. That suited his purposes quite nicely, so there was no practical need for him to carry a CAD.

Still, he equipped himself with the disciplinary committee's spare CADs when patrolling, mainly as an intimidation tactic, since you couldn't make light of a CAD even if using it was a feint. So, before going on indoors patrol, Tatsuya would stop by the disciplinary committee office and wrap one around each arm. He'd made a habit of it.

As usual, after classes had ended this day, he'd walked to the disciplinary committee HQ—only to find Lina there. Even from a distance, there was no mistaking her beautiful golden locks. The premonition of trouble on the job almost made him do a U-turn, but he suppressed the impulse and made an effort to speak to her like normal.

"Good morning."

He'd gotten used to how the disciplinary committee members greeted everyone with that regardless of the time of day. He slipped through the crowd of people—well, at a glance, there were only five—and quickly ran through his preparations.

"Ah, Shiba, hold on."

Tragically, though, Kanon caught him. He didn't let the despair show on his face; such were the benefits (?) of his daily training here.

"What is it?"

His voice carried an utter lack of both subjective and objective enthusiasm. The fact that Kanon didn't care one bit about that, though, was both one of her charming points and one of her flaws.

"You know Shields here, right?"

A conclusion in the form of a question. Tatsuya had no choice but to nod, of course.

"She wants to observe the disciplinary committee's activity; she says she wants to see the way Japan's magic high school students govern themselves. You're on duty today, right, Shiba? Could you take her along with you?"

If you want to make this harder for me, Tatsuya thought. He didn't know Lina's intent, but he felt there was a high chance of something truly troublesome happening. That was clear, considering all the male students surrounding Lina (who were all upperclassmen) were currently giving him very unamused looks. Being in the disciplinary committee would spare him from any jealous stares for the moment, but if he paraded around the halls side by side with Lina, he couldn't even begin to guess at the beds of nails he'd fall onto afterward. However, there was enough rationale behind Tatsuya being picked for the request itself, so...

"All right."

There was no choice for Tatsuya but to give up and accept it.

She'd only just transferred in, so this wasn't particularly surprising, but it would be his first time alone with Lina. Students roamed the school building, so strictly speaking they wouldn't be completely alone, but the awkwardness would remain, regardless of how popular she was.

In Tatsuya's defense, it wasn't going to be awkward for him because Lina was drop-dead gorgeous. It was because Lina wasn't completely hiding the fact that she'd come to scope him out. She might have been intending to conceal her stolen glances at him, but from his point of view, it was all out in the open.

Still, it wasn't as though Tatsuya could come out and call her a spy, so the murky stress kept on piling up inside him like the ashes from a volcano.

"Did the school you went to not have a system like this?"

But he couldn't retreat into silence forever, either (even though they'd only gone some ten yards away from the disciplinary committee office at this point). Wondering why the quiet felt so heavy, he did something unusual and did her the favor of bringing up the topic himself—though thinking calmly on it, it was a pretty mean-spirited question.

"Huh? Umm…"

He only realized it was mean when he saw Lina clearly at a loss.

He'd heard that the various people who were Sirius were traditionally combat magicians who stuck purely to the front lines; Lina, at the very least, probably hadn't received any espionage training whatsoever. Tatsuya started to feel very *whatever* about the situation.

"…I guess a freshman wouldn't really know about that stuff."

He started to feel sorry watching Lina like that, so he gave her a little help. He didn't need to expose her identity, and he'd rather she not get defiant.

"W-well, no, they wouldn't. I wanted to know more about how this school does things, since they let you be a part of these activities in your first year."

She had a slight susceptibility to letting on too much about herself, but this part of her made Tatsuya think she was smart.

Even though it was after the fact, she connected the pieces.

She might be even more quick-witted than my sister...

As expected, the piercing eyes stung, but nobody actually resorted to force, perhaps realizing they couldn't show any shameful behavior to the transfer student.

With Lina in tow, he patrolled mainly the practice rooms and the science labs. He explained them to her like it was just another tour of the school.

At the edge of the special lab building, where it descended into the back schoolyard, Lina stopped.

"Are you tired? Should we go back?"

Of course, he knew she hadn't stopped for something like that. He just decided to say it as a way into conversation.

"No, I'm fine," came the reply, somewhat stiffly.

"What is it?" he prompted.

Lina pushed her hesitation away. "Tatsuya, you're an alternate—a Course Two, right?"

"Yes, why?"

It had been a long time since someone had said that to his face. Rather than giving him that *not again* feeling, it actually felt new to him, so he asked what she meant by it.

"I was wondering why your uniform is different from everyone in Class A. Miyuki sounded unhappy when she explained it."

As though remembering it, Lina let out a giggle. It was, indeed, a very Miyuki-like episode, and Tatsuya could only smile painfully.

"But when I asked Kanon, she said you were top class in First High when it came to the real thing."

The way she pronounced the name sounded like *cannon* to Tatsuya's ears—instead of *kah-nohn*—but he decided to interpret it not as *cannon* but as *canon*, as in the hymn, which would make more sense given the mystical origins of the name, and ignored it—he would feel bad for Kanon if it was the former.

Because he was thinking about unnecessary things, he was late understanding what Lina was trying to say.

"Tatsuya, why are you pretending to be a poor student—an Irregular? And why do you show your true strength so easily? It's like everything you do is all jumbled up. I just don't get why you act like that."

He listened to the end and finally understood what she meant.

"I don't know what Chiyoda told you, but I'm not pretending. I really am a poor student."

Fortunately, thanks to her explaining her question so well, it wasn't much work to put together an answer, but if she hadn't, it could have been a major hole in his facade. *I should refrain from thinking about unnecessary things*, he thought.

"The practical skill tests evaluate speed, scope, and intensity. The test is based on the international standard. But in real combat, those three things aren't the only things that decide if you win or lose. After all, physical ability is an important factor in battle, too. What I mean is, I might be a poor student when it comes to the practical testing, but I'm good in a fight."

That was the excuse he always used—but it was also the undebatable truth. Tatsuya had no doubt this would wrap everything up nicely for her, or let him off the hook, at least.

"…I agree. I think test-taking skill and real skill are different things."

So Lina saying that was completely unexpected. What was she getting at?

"In the future, I'd like to be a magician who can be useful in real combat, not just a bright student."

An aura of dubiousness began to waver around Lina.

"How disquieting." The warmth—the heat—from Tatsuya's eyes vanished.

"Oh, you understand? That's amazing." Presented with his gaze of ice, or rather steel, Lina gave a brilliant smile.

Not a flowerlike smile, but one with the kind of beauty a sharpened blade might have.

Lina's hand shot upward.

Tatsuya saw the heel of her palm fly at him. With minimal movement, he caught her right hand, thrust sharply out, by its wrist. The palm strike aimed at his jaw was stopped in front of his throat.

Lina made her right hand into a finger gun and shoved her index finger up. A finely shaped nail plunged toward his face.

Tatsuya twisted Lina's right hand to the outside.

Her face clenched, and the psionic light gathering at her outstretched fingertip dispersed before firing.

"That was dangerous."

"I thought I could get away."

"I hope you're ready to explain yourself."

"Could you let go of me first? This kind of hurts. And it's a little embarrassing to stand like this."

Because he'd twisted her hand up and out to the side, the distance between Tatsuya and Lina's bodies had closed a fair bit. Depending on your perspective, their position might make it look like he was assaulting her—like he was forcing a kiss on her.

As soon as she said so, Tatsuya let go of her hand...but not a fragment of embarrassment was on his face.

"That really hurt. It... Well, it didn't bruise. How did you control your power like that?" As she rubbed her right wrist with her left hand, she rolled up her sleeve, then made her surprise evident.

"You tried to bust a hole in my face. I would think a little bit of pain is only natural in return."

"It was just a clump of psionic particles. It wasn't physically lethal. At most, it would just make you feel like you'd been shot."

"And that isn't enough of a reason for me to treat you roughly?"

She'd given him an ingratiating smile, but his expression didn't loosen.

Lina sighed and held up her hands. "All right, I get it. Please, I beg your forgiveness for my rudeness, good sir Tatsuya."

She bowed politely to him, renewing her attitude. When she looked back up, there was an odd twist in Tatsuya's lips, which had been tightly drawn back until now.

"...Something else?"

"...No, don't mind me. And could you speak normally? When you pretend to be elegant like that, you're like a different person."

The twist at the corners of Tatsuya's mouth seemed to be because he didn't think it suited her.

"Are you saying I'm not elegant?!"

"It's out of character."

He was slightly worried that she wouldn't understand his usage of the Japanese loanword *kyara* for *character*, but he decided she was fluent enough with Japanese that it wouldn't be a problem and saved himself the trouble of rephrasing.

And, for better or worse, she understood without an issue: "That isn't true! I was invited to have tea with the president once, you know!" she cried, letting herself get carried away as she emphasized just how "high society" she was.

"Really, now..." smirked Tatsuya upon hearing it. A chilling aura emanated from his grin.

Lina reflexively covered her mouth. The expression Tatsuya had just given her looked like the smile of Mephistopheles.

"The president, hm...?"

Many people in power avoided magicians who could kill without a weapon. In Japan, this barrier around politicians was actually less overbearing than other places; there were some countries where magicians were forbidden to come closer than a set distance to politicians unless they voluntarily imbibed a slow-acting poison that could only be treated with regular periodic administrations of an antidote.

As for magicians who could meet the president of the USNA personally...

"You tricked me, didn't you...?"

Lina glared at him, frustrated. But she'd read too far into it.

"You wound me. The conversation going that way was pure coincidence. In fact, this was more like you self-destructing, wasn't it? You were the one who attacked me, after all."

This is what it meant to be at a loss for words. The only thing Lina could do was continue staring, mortified, at him.

"And? Would you explain why you did something like that?"

"...I wanted to know how skilled you are."

"How skilled I am? For what?" He frowned, dubious.

Lina looked away. "Nothing, really... Just curious."

"Curious... Let's leave it at that, then, shall we?" said Tatsuya, having seen through her clear evasion.

She sniffed, as though sulking. "...If I must say," she began, moving her gaze back to him. "I was wondering if you'd come to the States."

"Me? To America?"

"If you don't get good grades even though you're really good, I just thought maybe you'd want to be somewhere where you could be seen as better for what you do. The international standard is the mainstay in the States for magician ranks, too, but not in certain places. The USNA is a free country, and it's even more diverse. You would be able to get the evaluation you deserve."

"That's a very interesting thought." The unexpected invitation seemed to have softened Tatsuya's attitude slightly.

Lina pressed on, sensing it was working. "Then—"

"If I can take that at face value." But Tatsuya spoiled her enthusiasm with a sardonic tone. "Lina, where exactly do they not use the mainstay for measurement? Are you talking about Arlington?"

Arlington, once a military academy, was now the biggest supply of magicians and magic engineers for the USNA Army.

"...Yes. But that's not the only—"

"Lina, standards of evaluation are for choosing who is right for a specific purpose." But though Tatsuya's tone may have been cold, there was none of the skin-crawling chill in it. "In the sense of choosing suitable magicians for the armed forces, Arlington isn't all that different than Japan's National Defense Academy. Though I suppose they have a wider reach."

If anything, he looked as though he were teasing a friend.

"Well, whatever."

"Huh…?"

And then, suddenly, he muttered, sounding like he really didn't care about any of this.

Lina, who couldn't keep up with the sudden shift, could only express her confusion through her voice and expression.

"Lina, you wanted to test my skills. Is that right?"

"Y-yes…"

"Then this incident is over. Please stop doing things like this from now on."

Shall we be going back now? he asked with a look, his expression now exactly the same as usual.

At least, Lina couldn't tell the difference between it and how he usually seemed.

"You're not going to ask?"

She could understand that Tatsuya was trying to pretend that entire thing never happened. That, of course, would be better for Lina. But she couldn't figure his intentions in doing such a thing.

Tatsuya had said he wouldn't question her, but even knowing she might bring his goodwill to naught, she couldn't help but ask the question.

"Ask what?"

"Ask what…? Like my identity… You don't want to make sure of it?"

"I don't care. There's plenty of things in the world people are better off not knowing."

Lina couldn't tell if that was self-concealment or what he truly felt. This person, Tatsuya Shiba, was too far beyond comprehensible for her.

"...You're a jerk, you know that?"

She glared at him with upturned eyes, muttering. Tatsuya lifted his shoulders in a shrug.

As she followed behind him, she was aware that the word she had used, *jerk*, certainly didn't have a simple meaning.

[4]

January 14, AD 2096, 11:00 PM, Shibuya.

Late on a Saturday night, the roads were filled with young people, and not a car was in sight.

Cars were scarce here because of changes in transportation systems and commute conventions. The automatic cars and one-person transport trains operated all twenty-four hours of the day. And in a big city like Shibuya, you didn't even have to use shared vehicles; the powered walking paths strung about underground would get you to the station quickly.

And now that the infrastructure for working from home had been streamlined, there was almost no reason to cling to an office until the late hours. The business style of the age was that if a job was urgent, a person would simply not go to the office, instead doing the work at home, then providing it to the company through private lines. These days, the office was a place to talk business, not do paperwork. And if you were doing straitlaced business anyway, you now never had to talk business this late at night.

Nighttime Shibuya was a city of young people, with no adults to be found.

Still, in terms of whether you could see the same sight at this time in other cities, that wasn't the case.

Shibuya, Shinjuku, Ikebukuro, Roppongi... Of the cities with downtown areas geared toward young people that had flourished before the war, the only place you could see such groups hovering about and gathering late at night anymore was here in Shibuya.

During the twenty-year period of chaos, at different times, Shinjuku, Ikebukuro, and Roppongi had faced destructive activity from foreigners and angry young people boycotting foreign businesses, and had been devastated in the process, leaving behind moth-eaten ruins in places. During the reconstruction process, the government had opted for aggressive peace-restoring measures, rebuilding these cities with fairly cramped downtown districts.

But Shibuya was the exception.

Before the war, people in Shibuya had already felt incredible devastation as young people's resistance intensified. However, the boycott of foreigners ended more quickly, actually allowing this city to avoid the complete destruction the others had seen. But because of that, the government had left the place in a lawless state at night, so it would be hard to say which was the better deal.

Had it been a lawless zone both day and night, the government—now less tolerant of disorder than before the war—would have proceeded with its "redevelopment." Current administrative authorities had grown quite bold when it came to the limitations of private rights regarding real estate.

But Shibuya had a completely different face during the day.

When the sun was up, it was a city for business, where respectable employees came and went in a hurry.

When the moon was out, it was a nightlife district where young wannabe outlaws roamed.

Unable to sink their hands into it all at once, the related authorities still hadn't gotten anywhere with redevelopment.

And tonight, once again, not long after the New Year, a large number of young people were gathered on the streets, living it up everywhere you looked, laughing with, flirting with, and punching one another.

Among them was a strapping young man with features that cut deeply into his face.

His outfit so light you wouldn't think it was the middle of winter—a sweatshirt with a jumper over it—Leo floated aimlessly through the midnight Shibuya streets. Not floated in a literal sense; his jeans and sneakers were planted firmly on the ground. But you wouldn't get the feeling from his gait that he had a particular destination in mind.

Leo had a certain bad hobby. No, not a hobby—more like a habit.

He was a wanderer.

He didn't walk, run, or shout—he wandered the night.

The closer it got to midnight, the more he wanted to float about with no destination.

Leo considered it an instinct carved into his genes.

Germany had been the first country in the world to realize magician conditioning technology based on genetic engineering, and he was part of the third generation of the original line developed, the Fortress—or *Jousai*—series.

The Burg Folge was a series of engineered magicians developed with an emphasis on physical durability. At the time, close combat was thought to be a weakness of magicians, so they were genetically modified not to increase their magic powers, but to bolster their physical abilities. They weren't so much engineered magicians as super-soldiers who could use magic, or perhaps, an enhanced human who could use both superhuman physical abilities and magic techniques.

Despite the engineering methods not including ways to deal with chimerism, it wasn't difficult to imagine scientists using a far stronger and larger mammal than humans as a reference for the genetic modifications.

They hadn't removed the Burg Folge body limiters from the outside—that type of measure was already known to result in a high chance of loss of magical capability—but instead raised his body's abilities themselves.

Perhaps as a result of such forceful genetic modification, many of that first Burg Folge generation died at very young ages, and even those that did grow up mostly went crazy and died.

One of the few survivors had been Leo's grandfather.

And because of that, Leo held a fear inside him.

You certainly wouldn't think it, looking at him from the outside, but he lived his life with a terror in the furthest reaches of his mind.

Would he, too, go mad one day?

Would his inhuman factor devour his human factor and cause his mind to break?

He was true to his impulses because he thought that by releasing them, he could delay the moment when his mind creaked and broke. Because he knew of a precedent: His grandfather had lived free and died of old age.

That was why he wouldn't go against his impulse to wander at night.

Wherever his heart pleased—under the moon, under the stars, under the jet-black clouds, he would walk aimlessly.

Some nights it would be the heart of the city, other nights the entertainment district, other nights the suburbs, and yet other nights mountains far from human civilization.

He didn't have a set place. He chose his paths on a whim, based on his mood that day.

He'd happened to come to Shibuya today, which made the next thing that happened pure coincidence.

A young man in a dark suit, wearing a gray trench coat, which was new but had wrinkles here and there—

"Huh? Are you Erika's older brother, the police chief?"

The person he passed happened to be someone he knew. That was all, but he spoke to the man anyway—which was another simple whim; he didn't always speak to people he knew whenever he saw them.

A moment later, a wave of murmurs began to press into him.

Leo hadn't been that loud, certainly. Just loud enough to make the person he'd just passed aware that he was there. Nevertheless, glances gathered on him from the sides of the road, none of them particularly favorable.

"Could you come with us?" answered the man walking next to "Erika's brother" as he gave a bitter face. He knew this man's face, too; it would be a little hard for him to call the man young, but he remembered. Not only his face, but his name.

"You were Inagaki, right? What do you need all of a sudden, sir?"

Without answering his question, which could have been dubbed rude, Inagaki grabbed Leo's wrist.

It would have been easy to shake the man off, but Leo obediently followed.

They took him to a small bar down an alley. The sign out front had the word BAR in English on it, but given the place's look, Leo didn't feel they had any need to use English.

"Bartender, we're borrowing the upstairs room."

Without waiting for an answer from the bar's owner, who was polishing glasses on the other side of the counter, they went up the stairs right in front of them. The men brought Leo into a cramped room; it only had a small round table and four chairs inside, but it felt filled to the brim. The door was a thick one with an airtight structure, like an air lock on a spaceship, but it went terribly with the antique furniture inside.

"I'm a minor, you know."

Right before Inagaki could open his mouth after turning the air lock's handle with both hands and making sure the door was firmly locked, Leo took the initiative, voice sounding innocent.

As Inagaki made a sour face, Toshikazu Chiba looked amused— not like he was having fun, but like he found this interesting—and laughed.

"Saijou, right? I'm surprised you recognized us. We were concealing our presence pretty well."

With just that, Leo realized what Toshikazu hadn't said. "...Did I obstruct an investigation?"

His sharpness seemed to catch Toshikazu off guard. "Well, well... You aren't just muscle. Well, I guess Erika wouldn't have helped you if you were just a meathead."

Leo scowled reflexively, but goodwill versus malice aside, he knew she'd helped him a lot by teaching him techniques and lending him a weapon, so he didn't argue anything aloud.

"I think your family might be raising its daughter wrong," he said, his only counterattack being a meaningless jab.

"You're not wrong," said Toshikazu with a dry grin. But behind his levity, the glow in his narrowed eyes made Leo sense something that ran deep.

Sensing it would be dangerous to go any further than that, Leo shut his mouth.

"You don't have to worry about the investigation. We were only concealing ourselves to avoid pointless trouble, not because we were tailing anyone. Officers aren't looked upon kindly around here at night."

"Yeah... You're right about that," said Leo, nodding deeply and a little sympathetically.

The sharp gaze Inagaki was giving Leo changed into a somewhat friendlier one. "Chief, isn't this a good stroke of luck? What do you say we ask him?"

Leo obviously didn't understand what he meant by only that, but he didn't hurry them for an explanation. Toshikazu nodded, then turned back to him; Leo waited calmly.

"Saijou, what might you be in Shibuya for today?"

"Nothing in particular, sir."

"Hmm. Do you come here a lot?"

"Not really a lot, sir, but I come here every once in a while. I think I was wandering around here on New Year's Eve, too."

"Two weeks ago... Then would you know of any strange incidents happening in the city's downtown area?"

Inagaki didn't stop Toshikazu, even though he was about to give details about an incident under media blackout. He knew they'd scoop the story up by tomorrow anyway.

"Strange incidents, sir? They happen basically every day. By the way, weren't you stationed in Yokohama, Chief? How come you're investigating incidents in Tokyo?"

"We belong to the Ministry of Police. We get bumped around Japan. This time, we're investigating a string of freak deaths happening in the city."

The words flowed out, light and smooth. But Leo wasn't disturbed by the tone.

"Freak deaths... A psychotic killer? And serial?" he asked, frowning.

Toshikazu adjusted his opinion of Leo upward without letting it show on his face. "That's right. I mean, you'll know tomorrow anyway, so..." He trailed off, exchanging glances with Inagaki.

Inagaki nodded, then took a cell phone out of his suit's inside pocket. Opening the foldable device, he called up an image file on the screen. When Leo saw the images slide past one by one, he gulped.

"The most recent victim was three days ago, discovered in the park on Dougen Hill. Estimated time of death is somewhere from one AM to two AM."

"Right smack in the heart of the city?"

He thought "right smack in the heart of the city" sounded strange, but Leo couldn't think of any other words to more appropriately express his state of mind.

Weren't freak incidents supposed to happen deep in the mountains, far from civilization?

"This might be the heart of the city during the day, but it's Shibuya—anything can happen here at night."

But after Toshikazu gave a bitter response, all he could do was nod—he was right. Leo knew personally how strangely two-faced Shibuya was these days.

"Getting to the point... Seen any strange people lately? I don't mind if you've only heard rumors."

"Everyone wandering around this city at night is strange. What kind of person exactly are you looking for?"

Leo's remark was valid, and Toshikazu let out a pained grin, even though he knew it wasn't the time. "You're right. But if we knew anything about the criminal, the investigation would be going a lot more smoothly..."

Toshikazu thought to himself about what to explain first; Leo watched him silently.

"Let's see... The victims' corpses we just showed you."

Inagaki didn't try to interject. He didn't move to stop his superior from revealing investigative secrets to a civilian, either.

"They all died from emaciation. All seven had no external wounds whatsoever."

"No external wounds? Poison?" asked Leo, expression changing.

Toshikazu shook his head. "As far as is known, they're all clean for drugs, too. And despite having no external wounds, approximately ten percent of their blood was missing from their bodies."

"All of them?"

"All of them."

"I see... Yeah, definitely freak deaths. This is more like a mystery incident than a psycho killer," sighed Leo, letting neither fear nor unease show.

"It might look like an unnatural phenomenon, but in reality, these were crimes committed." Feeling perplexed at his attitude, Toshikazu went back to his original line of questioning. "Anyway, would you happen to know anyone who seems like they'd pull occult stuff like this? Especially people who have recently come from elsewhere, someone particularly rumored about."

"People who came here recently..." Leo groaned, his arms folded before the question came out, until finally he unfolded them, a look of resignation on his face. "Sorry, can't think of any at the moment."

His tone was rough—no, disorderly, as though saying, *Manners? What are those?* But strangely enough, it didn't feel mean.

"I can go ask some friends, sir."

"Huh? Oh, no, you don't need to do that. That's the police's job, and whoever this is might mark you if you start sniffing around."

"...Well, I suppose, but..."

It went without indication at this point: Toshikazu and Inagaki were really feeling how difficult this investigation would be. If not, they wouldn't have exposed investigative secrets to a young man they just happened to know.

"I'm not gonna ask them anything dangerous. I may not look it, but I've got a good sense of smell."

"Really? Well, all right."

"Chief?!"

Still, letting a high school student aid the investigation was going too far; it was too dangerous. Inagaki thought so, at least, panicking until his boss reached out to stop him. Then he brought a business card out of his pocket.

"If you find anything out, send me a text. You'll only need to put in the key once; after that, it will automatically update."

Toshikazu and Leo both ignored the lieutenant's better sense.

"Pretty strict, eh? If I hear anything, I'll let you know."

Leo stood up, went to the air lock's handle, easily turned it with one hand when it had taken Inagaki two, then went down the stairs.

January 14, AD 2096, 11:30 AM USNA local time, Washington D.C.

Japan time, January 15, 1:30 AM—the middle of the night.

Lina, who had gotten into bed, was roused by her roommate, Sylvia.

"What's going on, Silvie?"

Lina had been an official soldier for three years and had spent half that time as the Stars commander. She was used to being dragged out of bed for emergencies. She instantly woke herself up and asked Sylvia for an explanation, voice clear.

"Emergency message from Major Canopus," answered Silvia.

Lina ran to the phone without a word.

"I apologize for the wait, Ben. And that this is voice only."

"No, I apologize for disrupting you during your rest."

As far as Lina knew, Benjamin Canopus was one of only a few people in the Stars with common sense. Maybe the first-degree members were equipped with most of it. He was aware of the time difference, and that it was the middle of the night, but had called Lina anyway. It had to be something important.

"I don't mind. What on earth happened?"

"We've located where last month's fugitives went."

"What?!"

The deserter incident that occurred last month with Alfred Fomalhaut, a first-degree Star, hadn't been just a scandal; it had imparted a serious shock to the USNA Army leadership.

The incident hadn't ended with Lina personally ending First Lieutenant Fomalhaut's life. Seven other magicians and magic engineers had fled the USNA Army at the same time. Among them was another Stars member, albeit one of their lowest-ranking ones—someone in the satellite-class. The mission Lina had left with Major Canopus was to trace those fugitives and deal with them. And now he had located them.

"Where are they?!"

"Japan. We believe after landing at Yokohama, they went under the radar in Tokyo."

"Why Japan…?" muttered Lina in astonishment. "And right here in Tokyo?!"

But Canopus didn't have an answer to that question, either. It wasn't only Lina who'd asked that question, and it wasn't only Canopus who couldn't answer.

"...The Joint Chiefs of Staff have decided to dispatch an additional pursuit team."

"Does the Japanese government know?"

"No, it's a secret operation."

A pursuit of fugitives that would include espionage and combat activities in a foreign country would give an entirely different impression to that foreign country's government. It was possible it would develop into a breaking of national ties if that government deemed it a grave provocation against its sovereignty. Lina was again made deeply aware of how vital the Pentagon saw this incident as.

"Commander, this is the message from the General Staff Office. Reprioritize the mission currently given to Major Angie Sirius as secondary and pursuit of the fugitives as most important."

Lina took a long, deep breath before answering the transmission. "Ben, tell them I said, 'Understood.'"

"Roger that. Do be careful, Commander."

After a considerate word to her, the call ended.

She probably wouldn't be getting back to sleep tonight.

The classroom that Monday morning was rife with talk of the freak incidents.

On Sunday morning, after the breaking news was broadcast on the country's second-largest news site, media outlets began having a ball with articles about the string of bizarre murders. They were in wild excitement, unrestrained in their enthusiasm, enough so even to daunt their readers.

But that was also how fast news spread in this world.

Of course, most of them emphasized the occult aspect in particular, to fan the flames of a sensation.

"Good morning! Hey, hey, Tatsuya, did you see the news yesterday?"

But perhaps it was a sign of the age of Tatsuya and his friends that they jumped on the bandwagon even though they knew they were being worked up. And, as expected, both the friend who would never dance and then one who probably would right away came to ask him about it first thing in the morning.

"The news—of the vampire?"

He knew exactly what they were talking about, but it was common courtesy to ask and make sure.

And as he'd thought, Erika nodded happily. "It can't possibly be a one-man operation, right? I wonder if it's a professional crime organization. I vote for it being an act of the organ traffickers—no, blood traffickers!"

Before Tatsuya could sit down, she leaned up against him, then twisted to bring her face closer.

At this point, Tatsuya was thinking, *Not that it matters, but your body is pretty soft*, which really didn't matter. But he constructed a more serious face and shook his head.

"That wouldn't explain why only a tenth of their blood was gone."

The authorities had probably wanted to keep that a secret so as not to disturb people, but the fact that the victims had about one-tenth of their blood missing made the term *vampire incident* come automatically with the other sensational words.

"Maybe they didn't plan on killing them? Maybe they thought they could use them for a blood factory if they kept them alive."

"But then they wouldn't have left the bodies on the street. And the fact that there's no markings of blood being taken doesn't make any sense, either."

A few of the articles had settled on the inclusion of a magician who erased the traces after drawing the blood with a needle, but a single healing magic cast wouldn't erase the needle mark permanently.

"Hmm, I see... Yes, no markings is definitely mysterious."

"Could it be an occult murder like they're saying on TV?" said

Mizuki from the seat next to him, entering the conversation, face clouded in a frown—and just a little on edge.

"An occult being... If there really were vampires out there, I feel like we would have known a long time ago."

In the process of modern magic being made into a body of theory, those who had inherited ancient magic began to appear from behind the veil of legends. If there had been some apparition or specter with a physical form, it would have been made known along with the sorcerers. At least, that was what Tatsuya thought.

"Then you think it was all done by a human, and not by anything occult, Tatsuya?"

"What about you, Mikihiko? Do you think this is related to *youkai* and monsters and things?"

He gave an implicit no to Mikihiko's question with the same tone.

Mikihiko groaned. "Hmm..." He shook his head. "...It doesn't seem like a normal person did it, but I can't say for sure..."

Tatsuya gave a mean smirk at the unclear answer.

"Still, magic was considered the number-one occult practice before a hundred years ago," said Erika, leaning in. "Tatsuya, do you think this crime is related to magicians?"

"Not concretely, no. They are saying the street cameras' psion radars weren't picking up anything, after all."

As soon as he finished talking, he shook his head as though changing his mind. "...But more advanced magicians can fool those radars, and someone using outer magic like mental interference spells probably could have committed the crime in the middle of the city with no one the wiser."

"That's unfortunate. I hope humanist trends don't get stronger from this," Mizuki muttered darkly.

Modern humanism was, broadly speaking, a form of discrimination against magicians.

A movement trying to ban magic usage based on the teachings of a minor Christian sect (perhaps *heretical sect* would be a more appropriate term), it stated that magic was not a power humans were allowed to have.

Because of their statement that "Man should live with only the power he is afforded," they were named the humanists and had expanded their influence in recent years in the heart of America's East Coast.

If they simply said "We're not using magic," then there would be no harm done, but radical humanists had engaged in several violent acts against the very existence of magicians; in the USNA, they were under close watch by authorities as a group of potential criminals.

"Oh, yeah, I saw someone on TV getting real excited talking about that!"

"Hey, mornin'. What're we talking about?"

Overlapping Erika's words and interrupting was, as always, the one who sat in front of Tatsuya—there was no homeroom teacher to suggest seat changes, so it was no wonder—Leo.

"You're late today, aren't you?" Tatsuya asked, lifting his hand to respond to his classmate's abbreviated greeting. Though his appearance might have given you other ideas, it was rare for Leo to slide into the room right before classes started.

"Yeah, I was up late doing stupid chores… Anyway, what were you talking about?"

"The vampire incident everyone's talking about," answered Mizuki.

Leo's face scrunched up. Tatsuya thought he heard the word *again* come muttered from his mouth, but just then, the message indicating the start of first period appeared on their terminals, and he had to end the idle gossip without asking.

Miyuki appeared in the cafeteria with no blonde-haired companion next to her.

Lina hadn't promised to be there, so Tatsuya didn't harbor any doubts or dissatisfactions about it. Thus, the remark he made was less because he was curious and more because it simply came to mind first.

"I see Lina's not with you today."

But his little sister's answer was outside Tatsuya's expectations. "She's absent today, Brother. She said an urgent family matter came up."

"Really…?"

Absent so early on in the exchange program? thought Tatsuya, but he didn't know any magician transfer students aside from her, so he couldn't say for sure it was abnormal. Besides, if he was right about her true identity, she would have many things to prioritize over school. And she wouldn't have told Miyuki or Honoka anything other than that it was "a family matter," either. So Tatsuya didn't inquire any further.

Erika and Mizuki acted as though it was on their minds—of course, the difference was that Mizuki was worried and Erika was curious—but they, too, knew there was no reason they'd get an answer if they asked Miyuki. Instead, the same as always, the seven, with one missing (not Lina, but Shizuku), sat down around the table.

"Come to think of it, is Shizuku doing all right?" said Erika, looking at Honoka.

"Yes, she seems to be doing fine. And she said her classes aren't very hard," Honoka replied promptly, not feeling any doubts about it—with modern communication infrastructure, the Pacific Ocean didn't separate them by very much. "She did say she was surprised that they still had discussion-style classes where the teacher participated, though."

Everyone gave surprised and curious reactions to this episode. Studying abroad was practically nonexistent for students of magic, so they got almost no information about what kinds of classes were held in other countries.

"I wonder if Lina is having trouble with things here, then."

"It doesn't seem like it."

Miyuki smiled even as she rebutted her friend's concerns. In reality, Lina didn't seem inconvenienced by the difference between American and Japanese class structures. Miyuki's smile was cold, her tone purposefully crafted to make it sound like Lina had never gone to anything *but* a Japanese magic high school to begin with.

Her coquettish, devilish smile fortunately wasn't spotted by anyone else. Their friends' attentions were soon glued to Honoka's next bombshell remark—or rather, bombshell news.

"We talked about it a little on the phone yesterday, but Shizuku was surprised at the news of the vampire incident, too. She says something similar is happening in America, too."

"What?! Is that true?"

"I asked Shizuku the same thing. Apparently it's happening around Dallas in the mid-South, though, not on the West Coast where she is."

"That's the first I've heard of it…" said Tatsuya in a surprised and impressed tone—he'd been diligently checking on all USNA-related news recently, considering the warning he'd gotten from his aunt.

"They're putting a lot of information control on it over there, too. Shizuku didn't hear about it from the news; she heard it from a well-informed student at the school she's going to," explained Honoka with a bashful smile, as though happy she'd drawn Tatsuya's interest.

As he nodded, there was a light in his eyes, too strong to be standard curiosity.

While Tatsuya and the others were talking up a storm about their friend in America, the blonde-haired, blue-eyed high school student who had come there to study abroad was in the middle of a meeting at the USNA embassy.

"What you mean is, a neural structure never seen in normal

humans had formed in Freddy's—rather, Lieutenant Fomalhaut's cerebral cortex?"

The meeting was eating into her lunchtime, but nobody, including her, insisted on a break.

"The term *normal human* may invite misunderstanding." The one who answered was, despite not wearing the white coat, a man who looked very much like a scientist. "The autopsy turned up a neural structure we've never observed in *any* human's cerebral cortex before, including magicians, in Alfred Fomalhaut's cerebrum. More concretely, a formation similar to a small-scale corpus callosum had formed in his prefrontal cortex."

Seeing that many of those in the meeting were giving him muddled expressions (including Lina), the scientist began to explain again, this time in a more lecturing manner.

"You all know that a human's brain is separated into a right hemisphere and a left hemisphere, correct?"

After seeing everyone in attendance nod, he continued. "The two hemispheres are connected via the corpus callosum near the center of the brain. In different terms, the only place an average person's brain will have a structure connecting the hemispheres is that place near the center."

"The prefrontal cortex is on the surface of the cerebrum... No structures are supposed to connect the left and right brains on the surface, right?"

"Correct. In other words, something a human shouldn't have was in the brain of Lieutenant Fomalhaut."

Lina finally grasped why they'd needed to call her here. This certainly wasn't something they could have told her over normal channels.

"What function could it serve, then? I've heard the prefrontal cortex is closely linked to thinking and judgment... If new brain cells formed there, did they affect his thinking?"

"Among us USNA magic scientists, there is support for a hypothesis that says the brain isn't an independent organ for thought, but rather one for communication, which receives information sent by psycheons. Pushions, as some call them, are the true bodies of thought. In other words, the cerebrum receives information from the *mind*, and can also transmit information about the physical body to the mind."

The scientist gave an insincere smile and shook his head at the question from the high-ranking martial officer sitting across from him.

"According to this hypothesis, the new neural construction that formed in Lieutenant Fomalhaut's cerebrum was a link to an unknown mental function that has never before been downloaded."

Those at the meeting once again gave bewildered looks. Lina, who had been thinking carefully, raised her hand to speak.

"What is it, Major?"

Though prompted by the presenter, she couldn't speak immediately. It was only after three seconds had passed that her question passed from the rosy lips that men couldn't help but be drawn to.

"…Doctor, is it possible that unknown mental function is an unknown magic interfering with the mind from outside?"

The scientist's response was immediate. "I believe you're asking whether Lieutenant Fomalhaut could have been manipulated, but unfortunately, there is no such possibility. This may be a hypothesis, but there is no doubt to the idea that the mind and body react to stimuli individually. You may be able to influence someone else's mind, but it would never result in a structure forming in their brain. Unless the spell recreated the person's mental structure itself."

The idea of recreating someone's very mental structure reminded Lina of the legend of a certain magician. That magician, however, was already dead. She was supposed to have passed away after a twenty-year hospitalization, without ever marrying or producing children.

Lina shook her head a little and reset her thought process.

Afternoon classes were still being held, but seniors were already allowed to skip classes. With an uninterested eye toward the freshmen and juniors confined to their classrooms and practice rooms, two seniors, one male and one female, had met in a club room with nobody else in it.

There was no amorous air about the room, though—even if their parents were considering they marry one day. (Out of several possible choices, that was.)

The lack was only natural; this secret meeting may have been secret, but it was no rendezvous. Katsuto and Mayumi had come to this place representing the Juumonji and Saegusa families.

"I don't know why we had to come all the way here, though."

"Sorry. I decided this way would be least conspicuous. As part of the Juumonji family, I'd like to avoid doing anything that would result in inciting the Yotsuba."

"Well, my family and the Yotsuba are in a state of cold war, present tense, since two months ago. It's all because that tanuki of a father is sticking his nose where he shouldn't."

Mayumi's bitter remark caused Katsuto to crack a smile. "I didn't know you could talk that way, Saegusa."

"Oh my, I'm so very sorry. Was that in bad taste?"

Her overly theatrical flirtatiousness made his smile turn into a pained grin. "When I talk to you, sometimes I think I'm not being treated like a man."

"You misunderstand. Out of everyone I know, you're the ace when it comes to manliness. It's just…"

"It wouldn't develop into a relationship at this point."

"Well, we *have* been rivals for three years—ever since we enrolled."

After a short round of hushed chuckling from both of them, their faces got serious at the same time. There had been a heavy tension drifting between them even while they were laughing, though, so the mood itself didn't exactly change.

"Juumonji, I have a message from my father—rather, from Kouichi Saegusa, current head of the Saegusa. We desire a coalition with the Juumonji family."

"That doesn't sound peaceful. A coalition already, not just cooperation?" Katsuto pressed, his eyes asking for an explanation.

Mayumi, of course, was happy to explain as much as he needed to understand. "How much do you know of the vampire incident?" she asked.

"Only what's been reported. We don't have as many pieces under our control as the Saegusa."

That could be taken as modesty. Mayumi's lips softened a little. "Your family does go for the whole one-man-army thing, after all. We may only have quantity, but as far as we know..." She paused suggestively.

And before Katsuto could prompt her to continue, she added, "There are about three times as many victims in this incident as they're reporting. As of yesterday, we confirmed a twenty-fourth."

Even Katsuto couldn't maintain his stoicism at that surprise. "...Is that just in the Tokyo area?"

"They're all concentrated in the city—in the center of the city, in fact."

Katsuto folded his arms and thought about this. Mayumi waited wordlessly for him to speak.

"The Saegusa have information on victims the police don't," he said eventually. "And the victims are only appearing in a small, limited area... Are the victims related to the Saegusa?"

"You're half-right. All the victims the police don't know about are magicians connected to our family. Even the ones who aren't a part of our family are either magicians or people with aptitude for magic. Students of the Magic University, for example."

"Which means," said Katsuto, expression turning grim, "the criminal is going after magicians."

"...Juumonji, you're scaring me a little."

Apparently, his expression was a little too daunting for the female high school student to look at—leaving aside whether she was acting or telling the truth.

He grunted. "Sorry."

And even if it was an act, it was certainly effective enough to make him yield.

"We don't know if the serial killer is one person or several, but I think we're certain this 'vampire' is after magicians."

As a sadness began to drift from Katsuto for some reason, Mayumi returned to the conversation without trying to help him out—her true character was still that of a devil.

"Chronologically," she continued, "the Magic University students and faculty were the first victims, and then they came after people connected to us when we started investigating. And meanwhile, the victims were increasing regardless."

"You're right. We can't leave this be." Katsuto nodded deeply, the damage he'd received from Mayumi still showing at the edges of his expression. "Do we have any clues? If they're strong enough to harm Saegusa magicians, they must either be enhanced soldiers or magicians themselves. And it's likely they're from outside the country. Any suspicious foreigners who came to Japan around when the incidents started occurring, or at least to Tokyo?"

Mayumi shook her head. The Saegusa had probably already figured the same thing and looked into it. "But in terms of foreigners who came to Japan around the time of the incidents' beginning…"

She shut her mouth then, but as Katsuto urged her on with his eyes, she continued hesitantly. "Quite a few transfer students and magic engineers from the USNA have entered the country. One of them came to our school as an exchange student, but… Juumonji, do you suspect her?"

"She's suspicious, but I don't think she's the criminal." Katsuto's answer was immediate. "I don't think she's completely unrelated, but we should be able to leave her alone for the moment."

"If you say so…" Mayumi didn't seem to be seriously suspecting Lina, either. She lowered her eyes, showing a lack of confidence.

Katsuto asked something that was on his mind: "But if this is the situation, then I'd think we should cooperate with the Yotsuba as well."

The suggestion made sense, but this time it was Mayumi's turn to scowl. "To tell the truth, I think so, too…but we're the ones who broke the rules. Unless my father apologizes, I don't think we're going to repair relations with them."

"And your father has no intention of apologizing to the Yotsuba… I suppose I understand, considering the feud between Sir Kouichi and Lady Maya… Still, it's unusual for the Yotsuba to be this hardened in their attitude."

At best, the Yotsuba were on the road of sovereign independence, and at worst, on one of superior self-righteousness (not necessarily in a bad sense), and they had maintained a stance of not caring what the other families did. They simply strove to improve their own capabilities as though possessed, and their position at the top of the Ten Master Clans with the Saegusa was predicated solely on their magical power. Even among the clans, they were an oddity.

Katsuto got the chills whenever he thought about what they were doing behind the scenes, but nevertheless, as far as he knew, they would never show clear antagonism that would cause a fracture in the Master Clans Council. He wouldn't say it to Mayumi, but the Saegusa were generally the ones who planted those seeds, so to speak.

His thoughts about what could have happened must have been showing on his face.

"I don't know the details, either, but…" Mayumi began reluctantly, "that tanuki of a father of mine secretly got into a certain section of the National Defense Force Army's intelligence division that the Yotsuba have their hooks in. And they found him out…"

"…I see."

In that case, the Yotsuba's firm stance made sense. Mayumi looked about to start gnashing her teeth in frustration; Katsuto could only say those two words. She was probably firing off ninety-nine abusive phrases at her father in her mind.

After a short time passed, Mayumi eventually seemed to calm down, and she turned to face Katsuto directly again. "What do you think?" she asked, tone calmed as well. "Can we expect the Juumonji to fight alongside the Saegusa on this?"

Katsuto immediately nodded. "You can."

"I know you're always quick to decide...but that really was fast," sighed Mayumi. He hadn't shown a bit of hesitation.

"Like I said before, now that I've heard the story, the Juumonji can't leave the situation alone, either."

Of course, her remark wasn't enough to make him waver.

[5]

Nighttime in Shibuya saw no end to people. That, however, did not apply to the city of Shibuya at large.

As midnight approached, for a short time, there were places without any people, like bugs eating away at the town. For example, the tight, narrow blind alleyways between buildings, or the tiny little parks just there to fill space between main roads and back roads. Like this particular tree park, no bigger than a parking space, with but a single bench in it.

Of course, just because people weren't passing by, that didn't mean there were no figures to be seen. Two of them, in fact, were in this park. One wore a long coat, a scarf, and a round, wide-brimmed hat pulled over its eyes. It was the sort of shadowy person you couldn't tell the gender of, much less the features. The other wore a stylish half coat with a knit sweater underneath, plus mini wrapped culottes and thick leggings—a young woman.

Right after the hatted figure rose from its position covering the woman's corpse lying on the bench, a new figure spoke to them from behind.

Incompatible again?

A long coat, a scarf, and a hat. The figure wore the exact same thing as the first and spoke in a voice that didn't vibrate the air.

No good. This time, I tried completely blocking the connection after sending a copy in, but as with previous attempts, it simply absorbed the psions in the sample's blood, then returned without anchoring.

The first answered the second in the same silent voice. The two figures were conversing through thought waves.

Does this mean the copies won't work after all?

That isn't possible. We ourselves are the original duplicates, after all.

Hmm... Perhaps they must have desire in addition to the capacity in order to become like us.

Does anyone have no desire?

You suggest there are other conditions?

We need more samples to be sure.

...That hasn't changed.

I am me. Just like how you are you. Nothing has changed.

Yes, you're right... Hm?

The two figures ended their thought conversation and looked in the same direction.

Someone has broken the psychic barrier. Two...no, three?

I had strengthened the barrier because we were currently conducting trials. They must possess quite high capacity.

We are two. Should we withdraw?

No, this is a rare opportunity. If they are strong enough to cross over the psychic barrier, they may be compatible. Fortunately, the one behind them is trailing the other two by a distance. We could likely disable the first two before the third catches up.

Very well. Everyone else, understand?

Indications of affirmation came back. Leaving the corpse on the bench, the two figures disappeared toward the streetlights.

Leo was walking around the streets of Shibuya again tonight. However, it wasn't his usual aimless wandering—he was going around to acquaintances of his, asking after any rumors of shady people, following eyewitness reports. In other words, traveling with purpose.

Even Leo didn't understand why he was so fervent about playing detective.

For justice? Other unfair crimes occurred.

A sense of territory? It wasn't as though Shibuya were his hometown.

Curiosity? He wasn't actually that interested in who the criminal was.

The closest thing he could come up with was simply that he felt like he couldn't leave this alone.

After searching his own feelings, that was the conclusion he arrived at.

He walked through the night. He plunged through the darkness. For a while now, he'd been hearing an intermittent noise, like the sounds of bug wings flapping. Not in his ears—but crossing the very pit of his consciousness.

He didn't know what it meant. Leo could only recognize it as mere noise. But his gut told him it was voices talking.

Voices trading words at the bottom of his consciousness, close to the region that used magic. He drew ever nearer the transmission source, as though being sucked in.

The Stars were the core magical force of the USNA. But even so, not all American magicians in the army belonged to the Stars. Of the three strategic-class magicians currently recognized by the state, Angie Sirius was the only one assigned to the Stars. The other two were stationed at the Alaska base and the Gibraltar base abroad.

Nevertheless, there was no denying that the Stars magicians were the central axis of magical combat for the USNA Army. In particular, the magicians granted first-magnitude code names made up the strongest magical force in the world. Therefore, the desertion of one of the first-magnitude magicians, Alfred Fomalhaut, was a major shock to the USNA leadership. They couldn't bring the incident to an end with the execution of Fomalhaut alone. They needed to deal with every last one of the other fugitives and make an example of them.

Two people were walking quickly through the streets of Shibuya that night—USNA Army hunters dispatched to deal with the fugitives. They belonged to Stardust, a unit of magicians directly under the USNA Army Joint Chiefs of Staff, the dust that couldn't become stars. Still, they had combat power as magic soldiers, and by abandoning versatility in favor of specific strengths, they strengthened their abilities to levels rivaling those of most Stars personnel. The members selected for hunting down the fugitives were a team that excelled in search and pursuit. They could identify psionic wave patterns and detect their traces, a technology Japan hadn't yet put into practical use—in other words, they were strengthened magicians with a specific ability.

And on this night, the women had already caught the psions of one of the fugitives, a Stars satellite-class soldier, Deimos Second—also known as Charles Sullivan—and had chased him to within walking distance.

"He's in the empty lot up here."

Nodding to her hunter partner's words as she stopped, the woman took a device out of her coat pocket. On it, she called up a map and saw that this alley led straight to the park they'd detected Sullivan at. There was an entrance to the right of their current location, as well as one around a right turn.

"One signal. Let's use a pincer. I'll go right."

A fashionable coat, a short skirt, colorful tights, and short boots. The female American magician, blending in as a young woman out for a night on the town, gave her partner an instruction, her tone of voice the only thing inconspicuous.

"Got it… He's moving. Hurry. But we attack at once."

"Roger that."

The two hunters split—one left, one right.

Between the hat pulled low and the scarf was a gray mask emblazoned with the design of a bat with wings unfurled. Walking, the figure in the long coat, which exposed practically no skin at all, directed its gaze toward the exit of the alley. Hidden behind the mask were lips slightly curled in scorn.

Pursuers from the army. Sending only two Stardust after me—they've gravely underestimated me.

I'm sure it's because they only knew you from before.

As the thought waves reached him from his compatriot, who was no longer visible, *that which was Charles Sullivan's* ridicule changed to a pained grin. Ever since becoming his current self, he couldn't hide anything from his compatriot. He had virtually no privacy. But for the *current* Charles Sullivan, it wasn't uncomfortable. It was only natural for them, and any reason he might have had to be uncomfortable was gone anyway.

When he focused his mind on a spot behind his forehead, he could see the thoughts of all his companions. They shared his consciousness through a new antenna, which had grown between his right and left lobes. He was both the individual known as Charles Sullivan and part of "them."

I see. If they only know me as a satellite-class, then I can predict what measures they'll take. I won't need backup.

After Sullivan sent that thought out, a rustling noise returned to him, like the sounds of wings flapping inside a beehive.

I will make preparations anyway, just to be sure.

The sounds took form as an answer given by his compatriot, hidden nearby.

The encounter happened a moment later.

"Deimos Second, deserter. Put your hands in the air and open them."

A young woman's voice called out to him from in front. At the same time, a silent noise, like nails on a chalkboard, washed over him from behind.

The noise was psionic waves emitted by a Cast Jammer—a form of magical interference using portable anti-magic weapons developed by the USNA Army Magic Research Division. The interfering waves from a Cast Jammer weren't a noise that indiscriminately blocked all magic like Cast Jamming, which used antinite. A Cast Jammer was a device that obstructed a CAD's functions. By duplicating the psi-wave interference caused by using multiple CADs at once, it blocked the reading in of activation sequences. Normally, this interference would only occur because of psi-waves from the same person, but owing to the development of technology to analyze an opponent's psionic patterns, the USNA Army had, though on a limited basis, succeeded in disabling CADs.

Not everyone could use the equipment. Using a Cast Jammer required a high level of skill in typeless, psionic wave–emitting magic. Additionally, its effective firing range was a mere five meters. However, as a means of jamming magic without antinite, Cast Jammers were a revolutionary secret weapon for the USNA Army.

With the muzzle pointed at him, Sullivan raised his hands over his head, opening his fingers, as instructed. The instruction, though it would have been incomprehensible to a normal person, was meant to prevent the use of CADs. According to the data the two women, both pursuers and executioners, had been given, Deimos Second couldn't use magic without a CAD. His physical abilities were at most at the level of a regular soldier. If they simply blocked his magic, then he would be no match for the women, both magicians and biologically enhanced—or rather, that's how it should have been.

"The decision has been made to eliminate you on sight. However, if you'll provide information about the other deserters, our orders are to lower your punishment by one degree," warned the hunter, her finger on the trigger.

Sullivan, hands still up, shrugged.

"Deimos Second, we will give you ten seconds to consider."

"I don't need it."

As though confused by Sullivan's response, which showed no nervousness, much less tension, she didn't fire her bullet.

"Stardust Chasers, Number 17, Number 18—Hunter Q and Hunter R, right?"

With her code name guessed right, Q's relaxed finger tightened again.

"Neither of you can defeat me."

At the same time as Sullivan's light remark came a gunshot. A suppressor silenced the report so much it sounded like a toy air gun. However, the bullet fired was more than capable of taking a person's life.

A muffled scream went up behind Sullivan. The fired bullet, instead of striking Sullivan's chest, which was directly where the muzzle aimed, had instead bored into Hunter R's chest.

"Didn't you hear? You shouldn't have used a gun against me," explained Sullivan in a tone like he was looking down on an inferior.

"A trajectory distortion spell?!" came the astonished voice of Q. They knew he specialized in magic that influenced the trajectory of moving bodies. But they'd also heard he couldn't activate it unless he used a CAD.

"The Cast Jammer didn't work…?" gasped R, clutching at her chest.

"No, no," said Sullivan, not turning around. "Your Cast Jammer is working fine. But…"

Both Q and R sensed him smirk underneath his bat-patterned mask.

"I no longer require a CAD."

Q shoved her gun into the holster hidden under her skirt. Both the hunters drew knives from their coat sleeves, then charged at Sullivan at once, from in front and behind.

Their thrusts were a product of their enhanced physical abilities, too fast for a normal human to avoid. But Sullivan, who they were sure hadn't undergone enhancement, fluttered this way and that, evading their strikes. His dodges weren't solely due to athletic ability. R's blade came at his neck; it curved unnaturally, missing him to the side. As R pulled her knife back, her stance compromised, Q slid in close and made a feint before Sullivan could attack R.

"Changing our knives' trajectories?! How can you use such powerful magic?!"

"Do you not understand? I am not the same person I used to be!"

"Enough nonsense!"

Switching from a thrust to a slash, Q's knife veered from its course for a diagonal swipe. It cut through Sullivan's coat and slid against the surface of the carbon armor he wore underneath. From behind, R charged in, aiming for a gap in the armor, plunging her blade's tip up from underneath.

"Urgh!"

But R's knife only grazed Sullivan's open chest. In fact, as the blade's trajectory twisted, she lost her balance with a grunt.

With the deft motions of a street magician, a knife identical to the ones the hunters held appeared in his hand.

Sullivan's knife then swung down at R's back.

Its tip, however, bounced off a transparent wall built in midair.

"A vector reflection spell?! This strength, it's—"

"Major!" Q shouted over Sullivan's words.

Instantly understanding what she meant, he pounced toward R, who was still regaining her balance.

A blade fell from the sky.

Midjump toward his adversary, he slid to the right, avoiding the short sword falling from above. Barely hitting the ground, he rotated, and the short sword that had been coming at Sullivan knocked away the knife aimed at Q and R.

Using the opening, Sullivan jumped at the wall of a building. Jumping off opposite walls three times, he reached the roof of one of the buildings that formed the alleyway.

Looking up at him was a red-haired, golden-eyed masked magician attempting to chase him by the same route.

But as new psionic waves energized from the other side of the alley, *she* was forced to abandon her pursuit.

No—she knew she had to prevent any more victims, so she began to dash deeper into the alley.

The sudden swelling of Leo's fighting sense didn't hasten him onward but rather stopped him in his tracks. What he'd said to Toshikazu about not doing anything dangerous hadn't been an empty promise. He instinctively knew that what lay ahead was not a place he should tread out of simple curiosity.

He took a transmission unit out of his pocket and sent a short text to the address Toshikazu had given him.

The vampire is here.

Leo sent it with public location information turned on, so if the police chief noticed it right away, he could apprehend the suspect. Deciding to withdraw before getting any more wrapped up in things, Leo turned on his heel—and noticed a figure lying on a park bench.

His goodwill and caution struggled against each other. In the end, his defensive instinct was the one to yield. It was less that he liked people and more that he had little sense of fear. Had he inherited the weakness of his ancestors, being born powerful? Still, without letting go of his caution, he carefully stepped closer to the young woman lying limp on the bench.

"Hey, are you all right?"

He gingerly reached out with a hand and gently shook her shoulder. The woman gave no response, so he put a hand to her throat.

Leo flinched backward. Her skin was cold, and she had no heartbeat—though, no. Actually, his fingers could feel a faint pulse.

Rattled, he took the transmission unit out. He made an emergency call—not to the police, but for an ambulance. As he was saying there was one person, and that she was about to die from bleeding out...

...reflexively, he turned around and brought the device up in front of his face.

The transmission unit shattered.

After he leaped back, his brain realized that the weapon had been an extendable police baton.

And before his eyes, he found an odd opponent.

Underneath a round-brimmed hat was an eerie white mask with only the eyes cut out. A long coat reached down to the person's ankles, perfectly concealing body lines to the point that it blurred even their gender. However, their gender wasn't the half of it—he couldn't even tell if they were *human.*

In the back of his mind, the noise like buzzing bug wings began again. Just like before, he couldn't understand it. But for some reason, this time, he felt as though the "voice" was giving a warning for its comrades to withdraw.

While Leo was preoccupied with the noise, the masked stranger closed the distance in an instant. It was a self-acceleration spell, Leo realized, but he couldn't see any signs of an activation sequence expanding. They came so fast it was like they'd built a magic program directly. Caught off guard and with no time to use a hardening spell, Leo took the sideways baton hit on his left arm.

A dull sound of something being crushed.

At the sight of the *twisted police baton,* a confused grunt made it out from behind the mask.

"Why, you! That hurt!"

Leo's uppercut to the body caught the stranger in the chest. A hard sound rang out.

His opponent staggered heavily backward, and Leo shook his arms out as though they stung. But none of his bones seemed broken.

Even his left arm, which had received the duralumin baton directly, was moving without difficulty.

"Carbon armor under your coat? What do you need all that for?"

Should've brought a weapon, he thought with bitter resentment, keeping his eyes fixed on the masked stranger and taking up a stance. No doubt about it, this had to be one of the vampires.

The stranger tossed their baton aside and stuck both hands forward. They took up a low-profile position with the left side jutting forward, with their left fist at jaw height and right fist in front of their solar plexus. Leo thought it looked like a Chinese *kenpo* stance. And he noticed one other thing, too: The fists were small, almost like a woman's—

With a gust of wind, the stranger attacked—self-acceleration plus assistance from a tailwind, generated out of a fluid-motion spell.

A thin, razor-like blade came flying at him with the wind; it bounced off Leo's already magically hardened jacket.

He intercepted the stranger's downward hand chop with his left arm.

The stranger grabbed it.

In the same instant, a sudden sense of exhaustion washed over Leo. Because of that, his right fist stopped.

The stranger's right hand reached for a spot on his chest above his heart.

Leo gave a burst of spirit and forced his right punch to follow through.

The moment the stranger's right hand reached Leo's chest, Leo's fist plunged into the stranger's *danchu*—a vital spot at the top of the sternum.

The stranger let it carry them into a backward somersault as Leo finally lost to his exhaustion and fell to his knees.

He felt his hit connect. But he also knew it wasn't a decisive blow. Letting go of his consciousness now meant accepting defeat.

With no proof whatsoever that it wouldn't mean an end to his life, too, he drove himself to look up.

The stranger was already standing erect. They were clutching their chest, but as Leo had thought, the injury didn't seem to have taken any of his opponent's combat power away. Still, for some reason, the stranger didn't move to follow up their attack. They weren't even looking at Leo.

He followed the stranger's gaze, hidden by the mask, and saw that there was an *oni* standing there.

Red hair, golden eyes. It looked small, either because of the distance or because his mind was hazy.

Through his murky awareness, he thought he saw the stranger beginning to flee through the now-sideways night streets, and the *oni* chasing after them.

Lina, who had become the masked magician Sirius, locked eyes with Leo, who lay sprawled on the road, for a moment, herself seemingly at a loss. But her hesitation only lasted an instant; Angie Sirius decided to pursue the stranger. Because she'd prioritized saving the hunters earlier, the stranger wearing the bat mask—Deimos Second, aka Charles Sullivan—had already gotten away. She couldn't let this white-masked stranger flee as well.

"Silvie, have you identified their psionic wave pattern?" asked Lina. Silvia was in their mobile base.

But the answer she gave wasn't a favorable one. *"I'm terribly sorry. There's too much noise for me to pinpoint it."*

"What about the cameras?" Hearing their psion radar wouldn't do her any good; maybe she could chase them using low-altitude satellite cameras…?

"I have them for the moment. But this is a city, with plenty of obstacles, so I don't know how long I'll be able to trace them."

"Understood. I'll continue my pursuit."

Realizing she couldn't rely on any technical support, she quickened her pace. Despite how late it was, the roads were filled with young people. The stranger blended in with them, quickly thinning their trail of psions. Lina turned up the gear on her self-acceleration spell so she wouldn't lose sight of the stranger's back as they ran at an inhuman speed.

As though noticing she'd closed the distance, White Mask suddenly changed course.

Out of the busy streets and up a hill toward a residential area. The greenery increased, while human presence decreased.

For Lina, that was advantageous. With fewer people, it would be easier to tell the stranger's psions apart. She chased after White Mask as they veered left and right on their path, using the person's residual psions as a guide. Angie lost sight of their back more frequently now, but her extrasensory perception of psionic patterns was now far stronger. Her experience told her she was almost there. And when she finally caught up, in a park—

She was covered by psionic noise.

Cast Jamming?!

Lina erased the thought from her mind. Her self-acceleration spell effects were still all there. Although it was hard for Cast Jamming to affect a spell a person applied to themselves, it was only relatively hard—not completely impossible. And even given Lina's—or rather, Sirius's—magic abilities, Cast Jamming's effects couldn't completely block her spell. That meant this noise had to be something else.

Shoot!

She immediately knew what it was. Or rather, she was told.

She'd lost track of the residual psions from White Mask, whom she'd been chasing. But they hadn't disappeared—she could no longer tell them apart.

Now she finally understood why this person had led her somewhere with fewer people. If it got easier for her to tell her enemy's psionic wave patterns apart from others', her enemy would also have an easier time telling *her* patterns apart. This noise was a type of long-distance magic; in order to pinpoint Lina and create this noise, this White Mask person had brought her to an empty park in the middle of a residential area where everyone was asleep.

...It pains me to admit it, but I can't do this alone.

"Major, what's happening?!"

Worried about Lina's sudden halt, Silvia, her voice slightly panicked, came over the radio.

"I lost them. I'm returning to our mobile base," she said, frustrated but succinct about her failure.

Erika Chiba's morning started early. Her daily routine was to work up a good sweat from training before the sun rose.

Until the age of ten, she'd done it because her father had told her to.

Until she was fourteen and learned who she really was, she'd done it because she wanted to be a greater swordswoman than the rest of the Chiba.

Until last March, she'd done it out of pure force of habit.

But ever since last April, ever since she'd met *him*, she'd done it because she wanted to, of her own volition. Because she wanted to grow stronger.

She didn't hold a sword for morning training. Her father, who had his eye on Erika's aptitude, had raised her so that she could use the secret sword technique Mountain Tsunami—or rather, he'd raised her solely for that purpose. Her skill was a speed technique, fast as lightning, which changed into a gale that slashed and a thunderbolt that severed. And as part of training for that, she was assigned to strengthen her leg muscles. Because of that, long training runs were treated as especially important.

She'd lost sight of her goal during those days of momentum and had been on the verge of neglecting her footwork on the road. But ever since she'd decided for herself to grow stronger, as long as she was at home, she never missed a single day of it.

This morning was no different as Erika rose from her bed when her alarm clock went off. Constitutionally, Erika wasn't very strong in the morning. Her body would react, but her mind wouldn't wake up. Still, this bodily habit had been engraved into her by thousands of repetitions, and it slowly brought her feet out of bed.

Stifling a yawn, with only her gait unsteady, she headed for the bathroom attached to her room. It was no more than a room with a shower and a vanity unit, but still she had the whole room and its fixtures to herself. Such was the luxury of being the daughter of a wealthy family.

The current Chiba head was, at the very least, not a miser who would discriminate among his children in terms of who got what physical accommodation.

Despite it being the middle of winter, she didn't turn on the hot water; she only fully woke up after washing her face with the freezing cold. Erika had just gone over to her closet to change into her workout clothes when she saw the "incoming text message" light on her phone blinking out of the corner of her eye.

The sun still hadn't risen; in precise time, it was 5:30 AM. She'd gone to sleep at 11:00 PM last night, and she didn't have any unread messages left, so this one must have come in the middle of the night. Then, a growing premonition caused her to go over and look at it rather than leave it for later.

Due to its simplicity, the text message was still used in this day and age. And when Erika saw this one, she scowled. After reading it over, she began to mutter, a creaking, gnashing sound coming from her teeth as she did.

"My brother is such an idiot… What is he making that idiot do…?"

She tore off her pajamas and changed her underwear.

Then, from her closet, rather than her workout gear, she took out a sweater and a skirt.

* * *

The bad news reached Tatsuya just before he left the house to go to school.

It was a plaintext message sent to his portable device, not a call on his house phone. Normally, the text format was only used for disaster forecast delivery, giving this particular one an ominously urgent impression. Of course, such a vaguely urgent message would, once read, be overwritten and then disappear like all the others.

The sender was Erika.

"Brother, is it poor news?"

Miyuki, keenly picking up on the shift in her brother's emotions, looked up at him with worried eyes.

At the moment, the idea of distancing his sister from any sources of unease didn't exist for Tatsuya. "Erika tells me Leo was attacked by the vampire and brought to the hospital."

"…She's…not joking, is she?"

The media had a way of making everything more dramatic than it was. Even something happening in an adjacent town would be extensively reported—you could also call it exaggeration—which made you think it an event from a fictional world with no relation to you. To say nothing of this crazy vampire crime incident. It was, perhaps, no wonder they didn't feel a sense of reality from it. However…

"It's true."

However crazy it might have seemed, averting his eyes from the truth would have brought naught but a disadvantage. Only by confronting a threat head-on could they come up with plans to counteract it.

"He's receiving treatment at the police hospital in Nakano. Thankfully, his life isn't in danger, so we can wait to visit him until after school."

"…Yes, Brother."

For Miyuki, Leonhard Saijou was no more than a friend through her brother. If Tatsuya said it was okay to do it after school, then she had no reason to argue—no matter what she thought deep down.

Erika didn't go to school that day.

She'd contacted Tatsuya, Mizuki, Mikihiko, and the school office about it, so everyone would have known.

However, what nobody would have known was that Leo's hospital room—which Erika was monitoring under the pretense of looking after him (from the perch of a hallway bench)—also had upperclassmen inside, visiting.

Attendance was no longer mandatory for seniors, so the time wasn't an issue. But she couldn't have predicted that students who weren't related to the club committee or the student council would come to visit him. Even the current chairperson of the former or the president of the latter would have been within the realm of possibility.

Giving a glance to Erika where she sat next to the entrance, Katsuto faced the door, his interest in her immediately gone.

Mayumi greeted Erika with a model businesslike smile, then also turned to face the door.

Erika didn't stop her as she knocked on the private room's door. After all, Erika wasn't nursing him; she was just keeping an eye on him—more precisely, she was keeping watch for any uninvited guests who might come to visit. So she had no reason to stop them.

She stood up, and without a word to the two seniors, passed them by and walked away.

Erika was headed for one of the hospital offices. Her brother and his right-hand man were there.

Erika entered without knocking, and Toshikazu awkwardly dropped his gaze.

His cheeks were a little swollen and red, though it was mostly gone at this point. It only made Erika regret not punching him harder. She found herself thinking that she should have gone for the full-frontal, hip-action slap, not just a regular, if vigorous, backhand.

After all, she almost never got the chance to whack this "idiot brother" of hers without resistance.

She should never have let even the tiniest chance of unhindered honesty escape her, if it could lighten the resentment toward him that had been piling up since she was little.

"…Umm, young lady? You wouldn't happen to be thinking anything dangerous, would you?"

Erika, her darkly unhappy thoughts interrupted, turned a stinging glare on Inagaki.

He winced, eyes wandering under her gaze.

Erika's father treated her coldly, but she had many sympathizers among their students. She had a bright personality and a coquettish prettiness, and above all, was the only one who could use the secret sword technique Mountain Tsunami. She had mastered it in real combat; she held what was basically an idol position in the Chiba school, and it wasn't for her bloodline—as she was the daughter of the family head—but instead, for her sword skills and personal charm.

Under her glare, many a student of their dojo would probably have to deal with several uncomfortable feelings.

And besides, Inagaki couldn't oppose Erika with his level of skill. If he was ever assigned to be her practice partner, she would readily push him around. In addition to her original talent, her skills had skyrocketed in the last half year. It was said the only swordsmen in the Chiba dojo who could rival her anymore were the family head and her two older brothers. For all intents and purposes, she had reached full mastery of her art; and the students whispered openly that the only reason she hadn't been certified was out of consideration for her older sister, who only had average skill and talent when it came to swords.

"Toshikazu."

The man reluctantly looked at her. She spoke the word with a masculine brusqueness, which perfectly matched her attitude, not bothering to conceal her irritation.

"The Saegusa's and Juumonji's direct descendants just went to visit him." *You know what they're here for, don't you?* she asked with only her threatening gaze.

Inagaki stiffened further at Erika's relentless stare, but Toshikazu, as expected, didn't seem to want to be apologetic with his sister anymore.

"The girl rescued along with Saijou last night was apparently a member of the Saegusa."

"That's all?"

"And a warning from our superiors not to probe any further."

Toshikazu shrugged, lifting his hands toward the ceiling with an exaggerated gesture.

Erika had half expected that answer. She clicked her tongue. "Kasumigaseki is one thing, but isn't Sakuradamon our turf?"

"Well, we're assigned to Kasumigaseki."

"Useless," muttered Erika bitterly. But she had enough reason left not to vent her frustration any more. "The bugs?"

"All broke when they entered the room. I hadn't expected the Fairy Princess's Multiscope to be so efficient."

Fairy Princess was a derivative of Mayumi's nickname Elfin Sniper, a pseudonym used mainly by magical athletes in ranged sports. *Fairy* implied *small*, which fit Mayumi to a tee, but that meant nobody used it to her face.

"Still useless... What about the one we planted outside the room?"

"That one was disabled by sound-blocking. Juumonji's barrier magic," answered Inagaki in a businesslike tone.

Erika couldn't even muster a *useless* this time. "Then just a guess. I'm sure you have a guess, right?"

Toshikazu shrugged again under Erika's glare. "Really just a guess, though. It seems like the Saegusa are hiding victims."

"...You mean they're hiding corpses?" His "guess" was shadier than she'd expected, and she couldn't conceal her surprise.

Concealment of corpses was a method of destroying evidence. Though it meant something different from directly disposing of a corpse you'd killed yourself, it nonetheless couldn't be called wholly legal. Even though the Ten Master Clans had supralegal rights, they would never get in the police's way with grave criminal acts of mass murder...

That was when Erika realized the underlying meaning. "Which means this vampire incident is related to magicians, right?"

"Probably. We don't know whether they're victims or perpetrators, though."

"Victims? I can understand dealing with things in secret on their own without relying on the police if the crime was done by magicians, but if magicians are the victims, then why would they need to hide it from the police?"

Toshikazu smirked at his sister's truculent remark. "And that's what makes me think this incident isn't going to blow over so easily."

After school.

With the usual members in tow, Tatsuya visited Leo in the Nakano police hospital. After asking for his room at the reception desk, they headed for the elevator. But shortly before they arrived there, his name was called out from the side.

"You all came!"

"You're still here, Erika?"

He knew the basic situation from her text message this morning: Erika's eldest brother was in charge of the vampire incident, and Leo had been cooperating with him when he'd been embroiled in it. Erika, to make him take responsibility, had taken the day off school and gone to the hospital they'd brought Leo to.

But that message had come before they'd gone to school, and now it was evening and the sun was about to set. The expression *still* in regard to her presence was more than appropriate.

"It's not like I was here the whole time. I went back home and got back about an hour ago, since I figured you'd all come," Erika explained as the group filed into the elevator.

He sensed nothing of a lie in her tone or face.

It was just so natural that it came off as suspicious, and Erika was probably the only one who didn't notice that.

"Erika, is Leo okay...?" Mizuki whispered as she stood next to Erika in the elevator. She'd see for herself soon enough, but she was still uneasy. Depending on the person, such emotions easily outstripped logic.

"He's fine, Mizuki. I told you in the text message, remember? His life isn't in danger."

The steadfast attitude was something that didn't suit everyone. As Mizuki breathed a sigh of relief, Erika looked down at her with warm eyes, but if an untidy man had done the same, he doubtless would have been treated coldly.

Mizuki appeared to not be the only one with such concerns, but the rest didn't say it. With the air around them stiffened quite a bit, Erika knocked on the hospital room door.

"Please come in." A young woman's voice came from inside.

"Thanks, Kaya."

Paying no mind to the obvious confusion on her friends' faces, Erika opened the door and shuffled them into the room.

The fastest to collect himself in situations like this was, as always, Tatsuya. Before Erika disappeared behind the curtain hung at the entrance, he proceeded into the hospital room. Miyuki followed him not a hair behind, and Honoka, seeing that, trotted to catch up with them; Mizuki and Mikihiko traded glances before stepping inside and closing the door behind them.

Waiting for them in the rather wide—in other words, quite high-grade—private room was Leo, sitting up in bed with boredom plastered on his face, and a young woman with ash-blonde hair sitting on a folding chair spread out next to him.

She was probably four or five years older than them. Her hair, which resembled the Einebrise proprietor's, gave the same ethnic impression. And her features, if deepened a little and gender-swapped, would be just like Leo's—it made their blood relation easy to imagine.

"This is Kaya Saijou, Leo's older sister."

Before anyone could put the question into words, Erika introduced the woman. Her identity was as Tatsuya and the others had expected.

Kaya rose and bowed politely in their direction. Her bow couldn't be called elegant or polished, but it was still a clear departure in terms of politeness from students.

"She seems like a nice sister," Mizuki murmured to herself after Kaya disappeared behind them out the door, watching her go. It was an honest statement.

Tatsuya felt the same, and no objections rose to the others' faces, either.

Leo, though, winced slightly at this assessment.

"You sure got hit hard." Tatsuya, noticing this, didn't delve any further. Leo's family matters were no business of his to begin with.

"Yeah, this sure doesn't look good for me," said Leo with an embarrassed grin. The pained look from before was gone without a trace.

"You don't appear to be wounded, though."

"As if they'd get me that easy! It wasn't like I was helpless."

"Then where did you get hurt?" Tatsuya asked the natural question of Leo as he grinned fearlessly.

Leo's smile disappeared in an instant. "Not really sure…"

But that didn't mean he was down in the dumps. He was tilting his head, his expression not frustrated at his defeat, but truly baffled by it.

"During the brawl, my body suddenly lost its energy. I used the last of what I had to get in one good hit so I could run away, but then I couldn't stand up anymore, either. While I was lying on the road, Erika's brother, the police chief, found me."

"And it wasn't poison, right?"

"Yeah. They checked everywhere, but there were no cuts or stab wounds, and even a blood test came up clean."

It was indeed a strange story. As Tatsuya mimicked Leo's gesture to tilt his head in wonder, Mikihiko got a word in.

"Did you see who they were?"

"Well, I mean, I *saw* them. Hat pulled low over the eyes, a totally white mask, a long coat with hardened body armor underneath. I couldn't make out any looks or features. But…"

"But?"

"I can't shake the feeling it was a woman."

"…A woman was fighting evenly with you with physical strength?" said Mikihiko, eyes widening.

"It's not like that's impossible or anything," argued Erika. "Give a grade schooler a drug and even she could strangle an adult man to death."

"You're right, but…"

"But?"

"It's possible she was never a normal person to begin with," muttered Mikihiko in a low voice.

Erika's eyes went wide. "Huh?! Miki… You can't possibly believe there's *actually a vampire around*, can you?"

"My name is Mikihiko," he complained sullenly. But nobody could blame her for reacting like that—even among magicians, very few actually believed in the existence of mythical monsters like vampires, even if they did enjoy the gossip.

"Do you have some idea?"

But the response Tatsuya showed didn't belong to either the majority or that rare group. He didn't believe in *youkai*, but he also didn't reject the idea that their spawning point could be *something other than a normal human*.

At his attempt to draw Mikihiko out, the latter answered hesitantly, though with a hint of confidence. "I think what Leo encountered was a parasite."

"A parasite? You don't mean in the traditional sense, right?" asked Erika, tilting her head, this time asking seriously—and with visible curiosity on her face.

That apparently brought his mood back around, because Mikihiko began with a professorial air, "A *paranormal parasite* technically, but just a *parasite* for short. Once the existence and power of magic became clear, international cooperation didn't only happen over modern magic. Old magic wasn't allowed to stay sequestered in its shell; internationalization was unavoidable. International conferences held by those speaking about old magic were held several times, mainly in the United Kingdom, and during those, they designed a common and precise terminology and set of ideas."

"We know that international cooperation served to make old magic flourish. What about it?" Tatsuya interjected, throwing a damper on the geek parade.

Mikihiko cleared his throat and regrouped. "*Parasite* is one of the terms they defined. People from different countries had different names and connotations for them, like *specters, evil spirits, jinn, demons*, but *parasite* is now what they call anything with magical properties that can feed off a human and remake them into something else. Internationalism might have come, but old magic's focus on secrecy didn't change, so I'd think it would be only natural for most modern magicians not to know about it."

"So specters and evil spirits really do exist..." whispered Honoka under her breath.

Tatsuya placed a comforting hand on her shoulder. "Nobody thought magic existed, either. But now we know it does. Just because we don't know what something is doesn't mean we need to be afraid of it."

Tatsuya hadn't acted like this spontaneously—he was aware that his presence held major sway with her. So when he saw her body twitch at the sensation of his hand and her blind unease wiped away, he withdrew—even though he had to pretend he didn't see how reluctant she was for them to part.

"Is that the identity of our vampire?" he asked, turning to Mikihiko. Being scared was a disadvantage, but ignorance was a worse threat.

Without answering his question directly, Mikihiko, seeming to have resolved himself to action, turned back to face Leo. "Leo?"

"Y-yeah?"

Action enough that his glowing enthusiasm overwhelmed his classmate.

"Would you mind it if I took a look at your ethereal body?"

"My ethereal body?"

The term didn't seem to make sense to Leo, and he parroted the syllables right back. To an extent, nobody could blame him. *Spirit form* was one thing, but *ethereal body* wasn't a term very often used in modern magic.

"Your ethereal body is an information body shaped the same as your physical body, created from spirit matter. It connects your mind and body," Mikihiko explained simply. "Your ethereal body is a bundle of spirit energy—in other words, life force. It's thought that monsters that feed on human flesh and blood take in a person's spirit energy through their blood or flesh to fuel themselves."

"In other words, vampires drink blood, but what they're really sucking is the spirit energy they get from it?" asked Erika.

Mikihiko nodded, expression tense. "Vampires suck blood, and man-eaters eat flesh. But since neither of them are physical creatures to begin with, they should only need to absorb spirit energy. If the teachings passed down by us old casters are true."

"Going by that idea, it wouldn't be strange for there to be a vampire who only sucks out spirit energy," said Tatsuya quietly.

Mikihiko nodded again. "If I take a look at Leo's ethereal form,

I think I'll know for sure... To tell the truth, from the start, I never thought this vampire incident was done by just a strange person, or that they were simple bizarre crimes. Not only because there was no sign of blood being drawn—my intuition as an old caster was telling me so, but I didn't have any proof until now. It was just my gut talking, so I didn't tell anyone about parasites. But that means it's my fault Leo was attacked, and—"

"Don't worry about it, Mikihiko."

As Mikihiko started to blame himself, Leo cut him off. It took a moment for the words to sink in. "...Really?"

"Yeah. Actually, I want you to do this. No way to cure me if we don't know the cause, right?"

Leo's words held two layers of *forgiveness*. Mikihiko, meaning to respond to his trust, drew his face back farther, then reached for the bag he'd placed at his feet.

Using an amulet, ink and paper, and other traditional spell tools that even Tatsuya was seeing for the first time, Mikihiko completed his check of Leo's status. And Mikihiko didn't bother trying to hide his surprise. The idea probably didn't even occur to him.

"What to say... I thought Tatsuya was pretty amazing, but Leo, are you really human...?"

"Hey, now. That's not very nice to say."

A joke would have been one thing, but Mikihiko's murmur was serious, and even Leo couldn't seem to laugh it off. He was clearly offended. But Mikihiko was so surprised he didn't care—or, rather, he didn't even notice. "Well, I mean...I can't believe you're up. With this much of your spirit energy eaten, a normal caster would have fallen unconscious and stayed that way."

"Leaving aside what exactly spirit energy is, you can even tell how much he's missing?" asked Tatsuya, evidently impressed.

Mikihiko nodded, not entirely subdued. "Your ethereal body takes the same shape as your physical body. The container can only be so large, so I can make a rough guess as to how much spirit energy there was to begin with, and how much is gone."

He narrowed his eyes and gave Leo another suspicious stare. "Right now, Leo has so little spirit energy left that a normal person wouldn't be able to sit up—in fact, they wouldn't even be conscious. The fact that he's sitting up and talking to us means his body has some high stats on it."

For Mikihiko, those words came casually.

The expression *high stats*, however, bored a hole in Leo's heart; he'd inherited genes that had undergone modification to raise his capabilities. "Well, my body's special order."

Nevertheless, Leo gave a grin. He knew his classmate didn't mean anything by it, and anyway, ugly displays of venting went against his code.

"Anyway, the reason my strength drained was because the masked woman ate my spirit energy or whatever, right?" he asked, quashing his mental tumult.

"I think so. But…"

"But?"

"…If she could absorb your spirit energy just by touching you in the middle of a fight, she shouldn't need to take your blood. I don't know how she takes people's blood without leaving a trace, but…why would this parasite be going through the needless trouble of taking it in the first place?"

Tatsuya didn't possess that answer. The truth was that the blood hadn't been stolen, it had only been *lost*, so at the present time, he had no way of arriving at the correct explanation.

Visiting hours ended, and the visiting five—Tatsuya, Miyuki, Mikihiko, Honoka, and Mizuki—left the hospital room behind them.

Erika had said she had something to talk to her brother Toshikazu about, so she had stayed behind. Nobody took those words at face value, but nobody felt like pointing that out, either.

"Oh, right—Mikihiko."

"Yes?"

His name suddenly called, Mikihiko, who had been chatting with Mizuki, turned to look at Tatsuya dubiously.

Miyuki and Honoka were to either side of Tatsuya.

They didn't have their arms linked, but they weren't much farther away than that.

It wasn't clear whether or not Mikihiko thought, at that moment, that popular guys could all go jump off a cliff.

Whatever he thought, though, Tatsuya probably wouldn't care, either. "There's something I forgot to ask before," said popular young man remarked.

More accurately, he'd purposely not asked it since there could have been listening devices in the room, but it would have been hard for anyone, not just Mikihiko, to glean that dangerous ulterior motive from his tone of voice.

"What is it?"

"All this talk about specters and evil spirits and parasites—do they appear that frequently?"

Though he wasn't eating or drinking anything, Mikihiko almost choked. Tatsuya's tone was a casual one, so he'd listened just as casually, but it ended up being an outrageously profound question.

"…Well, it's not that rare for them to show up. Old stories always write about them hiding somewhere and doing bad things, but most of them are the work of human mages pretending to be devils. We have an accepted opinion that the famous Shuten-douji from Mount Ooe, for example, was actually a shaman who drifted in from the western regions."

It might not have been a conscious act, but Mikihiko put a hand to his chin, striking up an obvious "thinking" pose.

"As for the odds that a mage would meet a real demon… In a single school, we're talking about one person every ten generations. And even then, in most cases, they only find one that wandered into this world by coincidence. A real demon causing harm to people and needing a mage to exterminate it is an emergency that only happens maybe once in a hundred years, through the entire world. The last recorded extermination of a real demon in Japan was nine hundred years ago when Abe-no-Yasunari exterminated a fox spirit."

"But this vampire incident is the work of a real demon?"

"That's what I think."

"Do you think it's a coincidence?"

"I can't say the chances of it being a coincidence are zero, but..." Mikihiko's answer was extremely careful. "There is no doubt that recorded observations of demons decrease the closer you get to modern times. I don't think this incident happened without any cause."

Tatsuya's reply was a simply murmured "I see."

After Tatsuya and the others went home and he saw Kaya return in their place, Leo collapsed onto the bed as though his strength had run out. Erika was still in the room, but he couldn't be stubborn about it anymore.

"...Well, I know the truth," said Erika. "Why try to act tough? You did really well."

"...I'll take...that...as a compliment?"

"That's what it was." Erika gave a gentle smile as Leo closed his eyes painfully.

"Umm, Erika... Will my brother really be all right?"

But Kaya, who was watching their exchange, certainly didn't seem in the mood for smiling. It was natural, since she was a family member.

Erika, though, replied in a truly curt voice. "He'll be fine. We have the finest doctor the Chiba family knows treating him. This may be rather difficult to understand for someone who isn't a magician, but when your energy dries up, it takes more time to recover that than your physical strength. All the treatment he needed is done with. He'll get better given time and a specific medicine."

Erika noticed Kaya shiver a little when she said "someone who isn't a magician," but no comforting words came from her mouth.

"I have to be getting back to my brother. If you need more for something, please don't hesitate to ask anyone—a nurse, my brother's subordinate, or me."

With an insincere bow, Erika left the hospital room.

Leo didn't bother trying to complain about her attitude.

"Maybe you should let up a little, young lady," said Inagaki to Erika as soon as she entered the room they were using to listen in on Leo's. He left out the part about what she was supposed to be letting up, but Erika knew what he meant.

And, knowing what he meant, she snorted, brushing off his sentiments. "I'm not about to tell anyone to start liking magicians. Parent or brother, whatever—what's scary is scary. Which means I'll just keep that in mind when talking to her. Anyway... You've heard this all before, right?"

The last sentence was directed at Toshikazu. Her eldest brother, leaning back heavily on a chair, arms folded behind his neck to hold his head up, tore the headphones from his ears in one rough movement and sat up.

"That was a pretty interesting talk," he said. "If the Yoshida's second son's reasoning is correct, what will you do, Erika?"

"In this case, it doesn't matter if he's right or not," she replied, her eyes scornful, as though he'd asked something stupid. She looked down at her brother, still sitting in the chair. "Even if it was only temporary, he passed through our gates as a Chiba student. I was even the one personally initiating him, so you could call him my first pupil. How could I sit back and watch after something like this happened to my pupil?"

"Such a cold reason."

"It doesn't need to be anything else. That's more than enough for me to grind whoever did this to dust. I don't care if this vampire is a man or a woman—they're the one who came looking for a fight. All I need to do is accept it."

Even Toshikazu, her older brother, couldn't tell whether that was her real reason or if she was hiding embarrassment.

But he did know one thing for sure: She was entirely serious about this.

While Tatsuya and the others were visiting Leo, Lina was visiting Maximillian Devices' Tokyo branch offices. This was where her neighbor Mikaela Hongou, aka Mia Hongou, was working, and one of the secret bases for their fugitive pursuit team.

A magic high school student coming to tour a CAD manufacturer wasn't an unusual thing, though not as common as a university-level student. Passing through reception with a letter of introduction prepared by the embassy and on the strength of her First High uniform, Lina came face-to-face in one of their conference rooms with the Stardust member she'd barely saved last night, as well as a woman in a tight skirt suit.

"Major, thank you for your timely assistance last night."

"Please, be at ease."

Gesturing for the two women who met her with a salute to take a seat, Lina sat down on the sofa herself. When she closed her eyes and let out a big breath, the now *redheaded* girl opened her *golden* eyes.

Different colors, a different face from Angelina Kudou Shields.

But there was no look of surprise on the two Stardust faces. This girl, with the golden eyes and cold features, was Major Sirius to them.

"What did the damage look like from last night?"

"We underwent maintenance, ma'am. It won't affect the mission."

Lina—no, Angie Sirius—frowned at how the hunter spoke of

herself like a tool, but doing that in this form only served to increase her cold impression; it didn't look like she was displeased.

"I see. I'll hear your report, then."

"Yes, ma'am."

Lina felt that her order lacked enough words to mean anything, but the hunter seemed to understand it. "After finding Deimos Second, we used a Cast Jammer in accordance with the data we were given beforehand," the hunter said. "However, the Cast Jammer was ineffectual against him."

"Did he interfere with the Cast Jammer's operation?"

"No, ma'am. The Cast Jammer was functioning properly. According to what Deimos Second said personally, he no longer needs a CAD to cast."

"No need for a CAD... Are you saying Sergeant Sullivan became psychic?"

"Affirmative, ma'am."

Lina's dubious question met with a clear yes.

"Deimos Second did not, in fact, use a CAD, and only used vector reflection magic."

"You mean he didn't use any other spells?"

"Affirmative, ma'am."

"In addition, Deimos Second's physical abilities outstripped our enhanced ones."

The increase in the fugitive's physical abilities was new information. After thinking for a moment, Lina asked the two hunters again, just to make sure.

"Sergeant Sullivan's psionic wave properties hadn't changed, correct?"

"At the very least, we were able to identify it as his, yes, ma'am."

"While pursuing Sergeant Sullivan, I made contact with someone who appeared to be his comrade. Were you able to observe their psi-wave properties?"

"...I'm terribly sorry, ma'am. Apart from the major's and Deimos's psi-waves, we couldn't perceive anything."

"I see..." Lina closed her eyes again and stayed silent for a short time. "...It looks like we can't rely on past data. The next time you find the deserter, hold off on your pursuit and don't engage him directly. I'll deal with him personally."

"Yes, ma'am."

As the two Stardust members stood and saluted, Lina returned it, then left the conference room behind her.

Silvia was waiting for Lina in a hallway in the Maximillian Devices Tokyo branch office.

"This way, Commander."

Lina, with her red hair and golden eyes, nodded and followed after Silvia. She was brought to a women's changing room for employees.

"Please enter, Major. I've confirmed that nobody else is inside."

As Silvia unlocked the door and entered, Lina followed, giving a quick glance around before slipping into the changing room. At the sound of the lock from inside, Lina breathed a sigh of relief.

Her hair and eye color had changed.

Her red hair became golden, and her golden eyes turned a clear sky blue.

"This form is so much easier. It's tough to hide the fact that I'm using magic to change my appearance."

"Major, we don't have much time. Please change clothes before any employees come."

Lina seemed to be too relaxed, so her subordinate immediately scolded her.

Lina winced. As she removed her garments, she said, "It looks like the chasers couldn't identify White Mask's psi-waves, either."

"I see... It looks like the abilities the fugitives gained vary pretty widely."

As though she had been expecting Lina to say something, there was no surprise in Silvia's voice. Only a disappointed air drifted from her shoulders.

"I wonder why they were attacking Japanese people," said Lina, now in her underwear, reaching for her First High uniform.

"Why, ma'am?" repeated Silvia dubiously, not understanding the point of her remark.

"They're on the run. Shouldn't they want to hide what they are from us?"

"Ah, I see."

With that, Silvia figured out what Lina found strange. She was asking why the deserter would brave the risk of being caught in order to attack Japanese people.

"I don't know that, but…"

"But what?" prompted Lina, changing her stockings for leggings and buttoning up the front of her one-piece.

"But I get the feeling the strange ability he gained has something to do with it."

"The strange ability… You mean the vampire one, taking blood without leaving a wound?" Lina asked, putting on her blazer and inner gown and tying her hair back.

"Well, I don't know if we should be calling him a vampire, but… Lina, what are you doing?"

Silvia, who had been looking elsewhere to get her thoughts in order, returned her gaze to her commander and saw the blonde-haired, blue-eyed beauty holding the hem of her fluttering school gown up in front of a full-length mirror, twisting and turning.

"I, uh, this is…"

As her commander shot up straight and looked down red faced, Silvia heaved a deep sigh.

[6]

Two fists thrust out.

A whirl of bodies switching places—a whirl of attacks exchanging with defenses.

Tatsuya was in the middle of his customary morning partner work with Yakumo.

They weren't merely exchanging blows.

Their fists weren't only thrust out straight—they carried out their assaults from above, below, left, and right with fists, chops, and palms. The other would evade, catch, and twist, parrying the tangled hands a hairbreadth away.

Tatsuya and Yakumo—now, at last, their skills contended evenly.

As one, they thrust their right hands out.

The opposing strikes flew past one another, and then they were back-to-back.

Tatsuya switched his weight to his pivoting foot, then took one step away from his position.

The elbow strike he expected did not come.

He turned around.

Yakumo, just like Tatsuya, had distanced himself.

He had predicted the same attack, taken the same evasive action, and in the end created more distance than needed. But he had no time to give a painful grin at the result.

Tatsuya took a step toward Yakumo with his lead foot.

Equal in martial arts.

Tatsuya's advantage was in physical strength.

Tricks hadn't amounted to much.

That meant Tatsuya's only way to beat Yakumo was to stay on the offensive, not giving him time to use his wiles. This state, with more distance between them than necessary, was a disadvantageous situation that Tatsuya would have wanted to avoid. He stepped in and tried to fling out a fist, but a moment later, he detected a distortion in Yakumo's presence.

Curbing his own impatience at his recent string of bitter defeats, Tatsuya cast an anti-magic spell that dismantled information bodies.

Yakumo's body swayed and disappeared. Tatsuya's Program Dispersion had nullified the man's illusion art.

Revving his five senses up to full strength, he searched for his master's real body.

Right or left? Even Yakumo wouldn't have had the time to get fully behind him, so—

Tatsuya's judgment was not mistaken.

His presumption, however, was.

Because Yakumo was *in front* of him.

But he was twelve inches behind where Tatsuya had aimed.

Tatsuya needed an instant to make the decision but swiftly continued with the strike he'd halted a moment earlier.

It wouldn't hit at this range, but with Yakumo starting his attack motion, he'd decided to get in closer and bring this to a double knockout.

However, Yakumo's body didn't follow his own fist.

Tatsuya, lured in by a feint and an afterimage, flew into the air as Yakumo threw him.

"Boy, you sure had me on the ropes," quipped his teacher, finally letting go of Tatsuya's arm as he lay slammed on the ground from

Yakumo's joint-locking technique. His words didn't necessarily sound self-effacing.

Tatsuya, unable to take the fall properly because Yakumo had one of his arms, had neutralized his momentum to barely avoid breaking bones, but couldn't kill the impact completely. It took several coughs before he could go back to breathing normally.

"...Master, what was that?"

As Tatsuya finally managed to stand back up, Yakumo scratched around his temple with a hand to answer—probably a pantomime, pretending to wipe off a cold sweat. "Boy, I really didn't think you would break my Cocoon Water Mirage."

His behavior was ludicrous, but his surprise was the real thing. His feint, which had left an afterimage, had been an unplanned, spur-of-the-moment move. He hadn't predicted that his art from a moment before it would be broken.

"Cocoon Water Mirage... That wasn't one of your usual illusion arts, was it, Master?"

"You could tell that, too, eh?" Yakumo sighed, resigned, but didn't fully hide the amused curling at the edges of his mouth—though he probably never intended to. "That odd ability of yours to read a spell just by looking at it is the definition of a threat to your enemies. But that doesn't mean there are no ways to use it against you."

"And that illusion was one of them?"

"Well, Cocoon was originally for deceiving the eyes of things not of this world. As for how it works... Actually, I'll leave it to you to think about. I'm sure you'll figure it out quickly."

Tatsuya wanted to say, *Stop putting on airs*, but he didn't. He felt, of course, that demanding that someone reveal the trick behind their magic was a breach of etiquette, but Yakumo had said something that piqued his attention more than that.

"Master?"

"Yes? Why do you look so serious...? Well, that's normal. But why the scary voice?"

Whether calling his serious face *normal* was a compliment or an insult wasn't quite clear, and Tatsuya couldn't determine which it was. But he didn't engage the man—he decided not to react.

Yakumo gave him a dissatisfied look for some reason, so he probably understood. And Tatsuya wasn't in the mood to go along with his "jokes."

"You referred to the eyes of 'things not of this world.'"

"Oh, I see."

He didn't need to finish his question. The immediate reply made it seem like Yakumo had predicted what Tatsuya would ask.

"Humans aren't our only opponents. It's not rare to fight things supernatural."

The answer was one Tatsuya had predicted from the context, but it also went against his background knowledge. "A friend of mine, an old-magic user, said that encountering actual demons was an extremely rare thing…"

It wasn't about whom he chose to believe; Tatsuya wanted an answer he could satisfy himself with.

"You must be referring to the second son of the Yoshida. Well, he's not wrong, but…that's a surprising lack of follow-up from you."

Yakumo paused for a moment. Told to think about it harder, Tatsuya sank into the sea of his own thoughts, and before long, arrived at an answer.

"What Mikihiko said isn't wrong. But that doesn't mean it's completely right, either. Is that what you mean? It might be rare to randomly encounter real specters or goblins, but if it's not a coincidence—if someone did it on purpose—it's not rare?"

"You just barely get passing marks for that." As his words suggested, Yakumo's expression was far from satisfied. "Hmm… I guess it's hard even for someone as knowledgeable as you to avoid the traps of symbolism and preconceptions."

His remarks had gotten even worse. Tatsuya thought to himself that calling someone *knowledgeable* to their face was embarrassing (not that it would make him blush), and he wished his teacher would stop. Still, Tatsuya's reaction was quite relaxed, since it wasn't the time for compliments, even by accident.

But Yakumo's next words blew Tatsuya's relaxation out of the water.

"You've had experience yourself contacting things not of this world once or twice. What, exactly, do you think what you modern magicians call 'SB magic' uses as a medium?"

An "Oh" made it out of Tatsuya's mouth.

"You get it now. Modern magicians call them spiritual beings—spirits, in other words—and those certainly aren't of this world."

Tatsuya had indeed overlooked that. He stared at Yakumo as the man continued his explanation.

"Yes, whether something is intelligent or not is secondary. Bacteria might not be intelligent or sapient, but they get into our bodies, interfere with how they work, and make us sick. Even viruses only have imperfect multiplication abilities. And even if, academically, they're not classified as 'creatures,' nobody would argue that they're not living things that damage a person's body."

"You're saying there's no doubt spiritual beings—these 'spirits' that are no more than independent information bodies cut off from phenomena—are things 'not of this world'?"

"To be precise, they might be better called 'things without life or flesh.' Also, has anyone confirmed that spirits don't have a mind?"

It took over a second for Tatsuya to answer this question.

"...Nobody has. And I know someone who would say just the opposite."

And Tatsuya had experience being somewhere with that friend as he remotely controlled spiritual beings. The spirits had shown autonomy in carrying out the commands given to them; rather than believing it was all built into the algorithms in magic programs, it almost seemed more logical to believe the spirits themselves had minds of their own.

"Master, may I ask one more thing?"

"Go ahead."

"According to modern magic, spirits are independent information bodies created when information bodies described by the Idea along with natural phenomena disengage from physicality. And because they record the original phenomenon's information, you can recreate that phenomenon from the information by defining a direction in a magic program. This is what we think of as spirit magic."

"I think that's correct, for the most part. Making such logical connections is something modern magic is one or two levels better at."

"Then if parasites can feed off a person's ethereal body and change the person's properties, what information bodies would they be based on?"

After hearing what Mikihiko had said, Tatsuya had been thinking parasites might be information bodies that interfered with a person's structural information. It seemed like Yakumo was substantiating that by using bacteria and viruses for his examples.

"Parasites, eh...? That's a British expression. Unfortunately, I don't know what information organisms they originate in. They interfere with people's minds, though, so I'd think they're based in spirit phenomena."

"'Information organisms' originating in the mind..."

"I believe that humanoid specters and animal *youkai* might be creatures from this world that have been altered by wraiths, a type of information organism. And just as spirits originating in physical phenomena drift through a shadow world back-to-back with this one, the wraiths originating in mental phenomena might come from the shadow world back-to-back with our mental world. Our lack of encounters with them isn't because they don't exist, but because we don't yet have the proper technology to observe minds. It might be an anomalous idea from the perspective of those in London, but that's my own unadulterated theory."

The title of old-magic authority isn't for nothing, thought Tatsuya, *for the first time in a while.*

◇ ◇ ◇

For the following two days, Leo was bedridden. He was in a severe enough state that a normal person would have been unconscious, so it was only natural he'd need more than three or four days before being discharged. It would have been more worrying if they did discharge him now, whether he forced them to or they gave up on him.

At least, that was how Tatsuya thought of it.

Of course, there was someone who didn't think that way.

"I wonder if Leo is all right..."

Mizuki was the prime example of the type of person who didn't think that way.

"He'll be fine," said Tatsuya. "Aside from the bruises, he wasn't really wounded, and Erika said none of his bones were broken or organs injured, right? You're not thinking she lied, are you?"

Incidentally, Tatsuya did indeed suspect that Erika, who wasn't here at the moment, had lied.

"Well, no, but..."

Still, with Mizuki's personality, no matter what she really thought, she could never call a friend a liar. Even though Erika wasn't here—actually, precisely because she wasn't here—Mizuki doubtless wanted to avoid talking behind her back.

Also, Erika wasn't here—*here* being the classroom before school started—not because she was staying to look after Leo, but simply because she hadn't arrived at school yet. Yesterday, she'd come running in just in time; she'd probably do the same today.

"Come to think of it, Mikihiko isn't here yet this morning, either."

His remark didn't have any particular connotation. He was thinking about Erika not being there yet and then happened to notice Mikihiko wasn't, either.

But that was all it took for Mizuki's face to appear to draw back for a moment.

Tatsuya clamped down on the pleasant smile he felt coming up and wondered what to say to her—or whether to say anything at all. He was certain that whatever Mizuki was worrying about wasn't true, but he couldn't decide whether he should tell her or not.

"Morning!"

"Good morning, Tatsuya, Shibata…"

As Tatsuya sat at a loss, Mikihiko and Erika entered the classroom, the former with exhaustion lingering on his face and the latter with an air of ennui about her.

As soon as they took their seats, the start message screen appeared for the day's first class.

During lunch break that day, Tatsuya's group did something a little different than usual. Erika didn't go to the cafeteria; she was slumped over her desk. When he listened closely, he could hear her snoring softly. It was probably because she couldn't nap during the terminal-based classroom lectures.

Mikihiko complained that his head was pounding and went to the nurse's office as soon as he finished eating lunch. He seemed like the type of person who got a headache rather than a fuzzy mind when he was tired. It was probably just exhaustion, so Tatsuya entrusted Mizuki to go with Mikihiko.

And as for Tatsuya…

"Sorry for calling all of a sudden, Shizuku."

"It's okay. What's up?"

"Umm, Tatsuya says he has something he really needs to ask you."

He had asked Honoka to give Shizuku a call.

"Sorry for calling so late," he said. "I thought about sending you an e-mail, but it probably would have seemed garbled unless I told you in person."

Modern communication systems, even on small, portable information devices, could display such clear video it was like seeing the person in real life. Shizuku, with whom he'd been reunited over the screen of his portable terminal, and who had used her own device's calling function to respond, looked a little more mature than he remembered, despite less than a month having passed.

"It's okay. It's still only eight." The girl on the screen narrowed her eyes slightly into a smile. As always, it was a hard expression to read, but they understood the smile was a pretty happy one.

Honoka and Miyuki stared hotly into their own devices. Unfortunately, Tatsuya had Shizuku displayed in his main window, and vice versa. The subwindows, even smaller on the already-tiny portable device screens, wouldn't easily convey subtle changes in expression, unlike the main window.

"Anyway, what did you need?"

"Right," he said. "I asked Honoka, but it looks like a vampire is making a mess of things over there, too. I wanted you to tell me if you knew any details about it."

On the screen, Shizuku quirked her head to the side.

"...Shizuku?" said Honoka.

"...Oh, that. You mean a real vampire has appeared in Japan?"

"'In Japan'...?"

"Right now, they're still treating it like an urban legend in America. At least, the media isn't reporting on it."

Though they may have been different from the ones in legends and fiction, things called blood-sucking vampires—or spirit-sucking ones—did indeed exist. If people there were talking about the real thing, there must have been an incident occurring. In other words, the USNA still had a media lockdown on the whole thing. It could be a far more deep-rooted issue than Tatsuya gave it credit for.

"I don't mind if they're only rumors—I'd like to know any details you can give me."

"Did something happen?" Shizuku leaned forward on the screen.

Tatsuya wavered over whether to tell the girl alone in another country the truth that her friend had been a victim.

"Leo ran afoul of what seemed like a vampire."

But he immediately decided he should.

Of course, even he couldn't explain why he did so. It was just an instinctive judgment.

…Though maybe it was because of some sort of premonition.

"Thankfully, his life isn't in danger."

"That's awful…"

But he still hadn't wanted to give her needless anxiety. He didn't forget to follow up on what he said so Shizuku wouldn't take too much of a shock, but unfortunately, it didn't seem to have much effect.

"No, he'll be fine. Please, don't make that face. Leo drove off the vampire personally. He just happened to take damage from their strange ability, and they're taking good care of him in the hospital now."

Tatsuya's "consolation" certainly couldn't be said to be skillful. For someone weak willed, saying he was in the hospital would have inflamed their anxiety even more.

"He's really all right? That's good…"

But fortunately, Shizuku wasn't the sort to drown herself in pessimistic ideas. After seeing Tatsuya give a firm nod, she sighed in relief. This sort of communication could, perhaps, be called unique to videophones.

"I get it. That's why you wanted to know what's happening over here," said Shizuku. It was not an interrogative but a declarative remark.

Tatsuya gave his affirmation again. "But it's not absolutely vital." And he didn't forget to remind her of that. "Really, whatever you know is fine."

"But you think America has some clues. Right?"

"Sort of. To be honest, I'm thinking the criminal behind the vampire incident came here from America."

Shizuku wasn't the only one who gasped. He hadn't told this theory to Honoka or Miyuki yet, either.

"So I really want you to stay away from anything dangerous,

Shizuku. Don't cross any bridges you don't need to. It's not like information I can get from you is crucial."

"...*Okay, I won't. So don't get your hopes up waiting for me.*"

"Just to be sure, you're referring to information when you say to wait for you, right? I can believe you when you say you won't do anything dangerous, can't I?"

"*Of course.*"

Shizuku was neither an idiot nor fearless, but even after making sure a second time, he still felt uneasy.

To Erika's knowledge, three factions were making an organized response to the vampire incidents, which were continuing to claim victims in the metropolitan area.

The first was law enforcement, with the Tokyo MPD as its main strength, followed by both the Ministry of Police's Wide-Area Special Investigation Team (also known as the Japanese FBI) and Public Safety (which was also under the Ministry of Police's jurisdiction).

The second was the Ten Master Clans' investigation team, with the Saegusa family taking the lead and the Juumonji family following. With backup from the Cabinet Office Intelligence Agency and cooperating partially with the police, it was a part-officer, part-civilian group. In this case, though, unusually, the civilians were in the position of power.

And the third was a private retaliation unit the Chiba family had organized with cooperation from the Yoshida, an elite old-magic family. In other words, Erika's group.

"Maybe we should have cooperated with our upperclassmen after all...?"

The Chiba's unofficial but proper request to the Yoshida had abruptly made Mikihiko a collaborator, and this was exactly the tenth time since yesterday he'd asked that question.

It went without saying who he was talking about: Erika, his partner on this incident.

"I would think just getting to use the surveillance systems, like the street cameras and such, would give us a big efficiency boost," he said.

"It wouldn't matter," remarked Erika. "The police can use them fully, and they still haven't gotten any leads."

"I still think it would have been better to have help, even if it meant relying on others."

"That's why we're helping each other out, isn't it?"

"I didn't mean just us..." As Erika sped up her walking pace, Mikihiko stopped trying to give her advice. He trotted back up next to her. "I don't think we'll get anywhere just walking around for no reason, though..."

He was complaining to himself now. It was too soft for Erika to hear, and even if she could, she would have ignored it. After all, her stubbornness was the exact reason he was with her at the moment.

Shinto-type old magic was the sort passed down in the Yoshida family. They had a deep knowledge of divination as well, albeit not as deep as onmyoudou families. Religious traditions in Japan didn't provide much of a barrier against other technology creeping in; you could see how unprincipled they were from the fact that they called themselves a Shinto family, yet used onmyoudou's paper talismans as mediums.

After hearing from Toshikazu that their scientific investigation was at a loss, the Chiba family leader (in other words, Toshikazu and Erika's father) had decided to use technology old magicians specialized in, opting to request aid from the head of the Yoshida, the old-style family they had the closest relationship with. The Chiba leader was so tone-deaf when it came to mysticism that he called himself a simple barbarian without magic technology, so maybe he was trying to fight occult with occult.

Which led to Mikihiko going along with Erika, not as a guide but as a "path diviner."

"Which way, Miki?" asked Erika, stopping at a crossroads and turning around.

Sighing and wishing she'd listen a little more diligently, Miki-hiko planted the rod he carried in the path. The rod was a little less than one yard tall—more precisely, it was three *shaku*. Incidentally, he'd given up on seriously arguing about the nickname when it was set as his default name by Lina.

The rod—more a slender wooden stick that happened to be straight—had tiny characters packed together on it, written in ink. Its cross section, though, had been processed to be almost a perfect circle. He held on to its tip, stood it straight up, then gently raised his hand.

Although he'd "planted" it there, the ground was paved. A mere wooden stick would never pierce it. Despite that, without any support from Mikihiko, it stood on the road.

He took three steps backward, then whirled around. As soon as he turned his back, the rod lost its invisible support and fell right over. It hit the ground with a dry noise, pointing right at the intersection.

"Okay, this way..."

Erika walked off in the direction the rod pointed. She didn't wait for her companion; she didn't even turn back to look at him.

Mikihiko gave a pained grin, picked up the rod, and followed her. But right before he got to her, he took his information terminal out of his inside pocket, suddenly remembering something.

Its transmission function was set to signal mode. After verifying that it was broadcasting an identifying signal and notifying the other terminals registered in their group of their position, he returned it to his pocket.

The pained grin had disappeared from his face. He could sense they were getting close to their target.

A step behind Erika, he slowed down, maintaining the distance and taking the terminal out again.

He called up the group list of people he was transmitting to. After adding a new destination, he put it away for real this time and walked up alongside his classmate.

A caped long coat and a hat pulled down over the eyes. Under the hat, a full face mask with a black bat depicted on gray fabric. Charles Sullivan, formerly a Stars satellite-class soldier with the code name Deimos Second, was using all his newly acquired physical abilities to run for his life.

But no matter how much strength he mustered, he couldn't get away. Chasing him was not the hunters from Stardust, but an executioner given the code name of the star that shone the brightest in the night sky.

The red-haired, golden-eyed, masked magician following him. Several times he sprayed Lina, her form changed to that of Angie Sirius, with psionic noise. Her senses lost track of him each time, but...

"Commander, take a right at the next corner."

The psion radar in the mobile base disguised as a television relay vehicle had locked on to where he was and wouldn't let go. USNA was a step ahead of Japan with this technology—once one of these radars, capable of identifying psi-wave characteristics, pinpointed your psi-wave pattern, it was almost impossible to flee from it save by escaping its range. And since Lina was carrying a palm-sized, miniaturized radar relay antenna, getting out of range was impossible, too.

"Claire, Rachel, get in front of Sullivan," called Lina into her radio. Those were pseudonyms: Claire for Hunter Q, or the seventeenth, and Rachel for Hunter R, or the eighteenth. Lina disliked calling people by their code names, and the ones she'd given them were false names for convenience. Claire started with C and not Q, but they were fake anyway, so Lina didn't see it as a problem.

Signs of magical combat appeared twenty or thirty yards ahead. The two of them were slowing Sullivan down. For Lina, he was already in range. She had a perfect lock on his position.

It might have been night, but that didn't mean there were no other eyes around. They didn't worry about that, since they were playing their game of tag at motorcycle speeds. Ignoring the possibility of the police intervening, Lina took out a small knife—a dagger.

She was going too fast; it didn't look like any pedestrians saw the dagger. The matte black blade wouldn't stand out even in the sunlight anyway. Without trying to hide it, she flung her dagger forward.

It soared under the streetlights, then turned as Lina guided it.

This blade was an integrated armament CAD. Simply throwing it activated its movement spell, and it would follow a route set by the caster and pierce the target. The dagger she threw changed direction several times in midair before shooting at Sullivan's back.

Sullivan sensed the blade flying at him right before it hit. Even the physical abilities of a *vampire* didn't give him enough time to dodge it. But *having recovered his psychic abilities*, he judged that his own skill at influencing the trajectory of physical objects would be sufficient.

He concentrated on the weapon. When he turned around, the hunters he was currently fighting charged him. *Friendly fire*, he willed in his mind. The small blade flying at his front *should have* turned and struck a hunter behind him.

But a voiceless cry of pain slipped from Sullivan's mouth.

His vector reflection spell had zero effect on Lina's movement spell.

The difference in their levels of event influence was too great.

Realizing his own strength wasn't enough, Sullivan immediately flung up his right arm. Lina's dagger dug deeply into it.

Sullivan's body froze.

Hunter R's combat knife gouged his back.

If he were a normal human, it would have been fatal.

But Sullivan whipped his arm around in a sideways punch, sending the knife-wielding R reeling.

The masked magician showed herself then. Her golden eyes pierced Sullivan's through his mask.

Lina now stopped, pulled out a pistol.

Suddenly, an electric attack was fired at her from the shadows of the trees on the roadside.

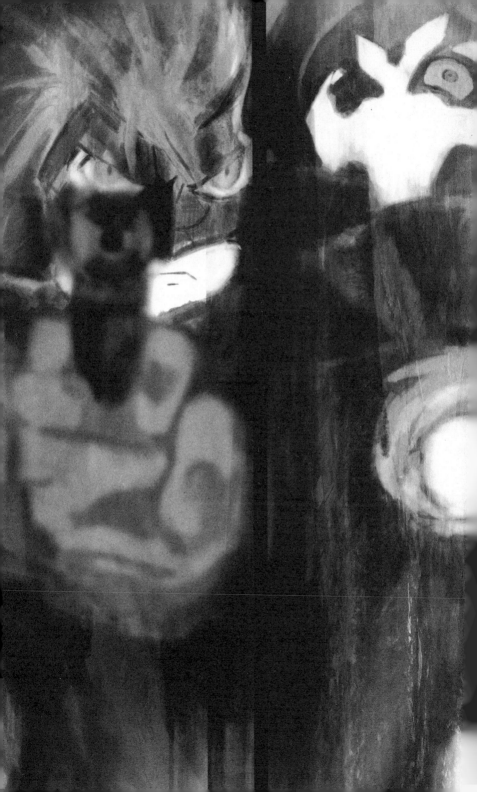

Neither Claire nor Rachel nor Lina had been prepared for it. It was a perfect surprise attack.

But the lightning merely flashed, vanishing before it reached Lina's body.

She had disabled the vampire's spell with a reflexively expanded Area Interference.

Meanwhile, her gun arm was holding steady.

The muzzle was aimed straight at Sullivan's heart.

Lina pulled the trigger.

The *information-strengthened* bullet ignored all his defenses and crushed his heart.

Without basking in victory, Lina got off to another start.

Her eyes were fixed on the lightning-flinging vampire, who was getting farther and farther away.

After walking for about ten minutes and divining their path twice, Erika and Mikihiko heard two soft sets of running footsteps. Rubber soles—probably one making an escape and one pursuing.

They traded glances.

A moment later, without exchanging any signals, they began to run, Erika toward the indications of fighting, and Mikihiko toward the stir among the spirits.

With different senses, but the same hunch: They'd found them.

Erika took a slight lead, and Mikihiko followed behind.

As she ran, Erika took an unsheathed katana from the long, slender case hanging on her shoulder. Though it didn't have a blade, its entire surface was engraved with spell seals—an armament device made by the Isori family. Kei Isori had given it to her as a gift, as a substitute for the Orochi-Maru, since the latter stood out too much in public. It might not have been as strong as the Orochi-Maru, but it had the ability to support momentum-control spells.

Meanwhile, Mikihiko, holding the rod two fist lengths down the shaft in his right hand, swung his left hand diagonally downward. What looked like a folding fan burst from his sleeve; he grabbed it with his left hand.

It was like an iron-ribbed fan, connecting long, slender strips of thin metallic paper to a fan-shaped frame. Each of those strips was a single paper talisman with an incantation or spell circle engraved on it. The ribs, molded to the strips, were lines through which the caster's psions passed. A cord extending from the fan's pivot was hooked up to a psion pattern oscillation unit hidden in his sleeve.

This, too, was a type of CAD. In order to reproduce old magic's two-step activation process of talisman and chanting, Mikihiko had compiled ideas based on advice from Tatsuya and had a regular Yoshida family engineer create this: a new type of old-magic casting assistance tool.

After getting themselves ready for combat, the two of them chased the footsteps. Sometimes their rhythm would fall apart completely, probably because the people running were stopping intermittently to trade blows before running off again.

Even if they hadn't been, Erika's and Mikihiko's feet were faster. They burst through a back road lined with midsize buildings, and in a small disaster-prevention park (more precisely, a damage buffer for natural disasters), they finally spotted their targets.

Two figures mingled. One hid its face and body under a hooded coat, and the other wore a mask that covered its eye area.

Both of them appeared female.

"Miki, you take the one with the coat. I'll stop the one with the mask!"

Checking against Leo's testimony, the suspicious one was the one with the hooded coat. But anyone hiding their face with a mask this late at night would always be suspicious. Above all, the large knife the woman held and the skill with which she swung it were powerful triggers for Erika's sense of caution, even when seen from afar.

Without using self-acceleration—only seal magic to heighten her blade's strength—Erika made a cut at the masked woman. Her slash, even without magical acceleration, was so fast that anyone with normal physical abilities, save for a handful you might call masters, would have difficulty avoiding it.

The woman's knife-play was excellent, but not at a master level. Thus, even if she was able to parry Erika's strike, she wouldn't be able to avoid it—that is, if she'd been a normal person.

Light flashed.

Erika's katana cut through air. Her target had moved three yards ahead.

The flash wasn't physical light, but the psionic radiance that accompanied magic activation. Erika had perceived it just fine, so she wasn't surprised that her slash had missed.

She was, however, surprised at the spell's speed.

Erika was confident she hadn't let the woman know of her attack until a moment before it had landed. It wasn't conceit on her part, either: In the instant between Erika swinging the sword up and bringing it back down, this person had chosen a spell and triggered it.

The masked magician had moved right under a streetlight. Either moving into the light hadn't been intentional, or she didn't care if she was seen. Erika didn't need to confirm which.

Something had been engraved in her eyes, in her mind.

It wasn't the woman's beauty, which she couldn't hide fully behind the mask, and it wasn't her balanced limbs, which could be seen even wrapped in thick clothing.

Under the streetlight, the woman's colors surfaced. Inhuman, ominous colors.

Crimson hair, so deep it almost looked black...

...and golden eyes from behind the mask that drew you in.

"...Here I come!"

Her sword teachings, beaten into her so hard they were nearly reflexive now, severed those eyes' gravity. Pumping herself up, Erika kept her eyes on her opponent and widened her vision, placing the masked magician's entire form in her view. Pruning almost every preparatory motion, she dashed toward the woman.

She didn't use motion support magic. Any magical support would have the opposite effect on this opponent; Erika intuited that it would only let the woman predict her movements.

Without using magic, but with *magic-like* movement and footwork, Erika pressed in toward the woman.

Hesitation leaked from behind her mask.

Regardless, Erika raised her katana.

A magical flash sparked from the masked magician. Not a self-acceleration spell, but a self-movement one.

Erika didn't have the ability to instantly analyze magic programs. But in exchange, she had eyes fully trained as a swordswoman's.

In the instant her adversary started to move, Erika perceived the direction and corrected her sword.

After following through on its reverse shoulder slash, it changed direction, going straight down and grazing the woman's crimson hair.

Triggering a momentum control spell, Erika drew the katana back.

Still in a squatting position, the masked woman jumped horizontally. Erika stepped forward to pursue, but she suddenly forced herself to draw back, because—

A knife stabbed down right in front of her foot.

As Erika stopped, the masked woman stood up from her one-knee-down position.

Her crimson hair blew wildly.

Erika's bladeless katana had cut the string tying her hair back, with the force of her speed alone.

The blustering hair reached down to her chest. Curly locks, fluttering in the wind, made the woman look that much more sinister.

If she had black skin, she'd be just like Kali...

Even as the idea popped into her mind, Erika didn't let up, keeping an eye on her opponent's movements. She looked ridiculous, but her skills were undeniably first-rate. In terms of magical technique, a mere glance let Erika say for sure she was even above that. Erika had had the initiative thus far, but her combat sense told her that if she was forced to go on the defensive, her odds of victory would be hopeless.

Letting a chance escape would be fatal.

Fortunately for her, the masked woman was impatient. Even during her fight with Erika, in the end, her mind was on the coat-wearing vampire.

This woman was acting independently right now, but Erika and Mikihiko were a team.

That would give them an opening to slip into, she calculated.

They stared each other down—the masked woman and the female swordfighter.

Behind Erika there was a thunderclap.

The golden eyes looked away from Erika.

Erika immediately rushed her, sword at the ready.

He heard the sound of slicing air behind him.

Mikihiko knew Erika's skills well. He was never taught the ways of the sword, but old magic and martial arts, while not quite having an inseparable bond, had something close.

It was said Erika's skills were second in the Chiba family only to the current head's and her two older brothers', and it appeared that this wasn't hyperbole. Looking solely at her sword technique, she already rivaled her father's ability and might even be close to her next-oldest brother, oft called a genius.

And her opponent hadn't parried her slash—she'd outright

dodged it. That simple fact meant her adversary was strong; Erika wouldn't have an easy time of it. However—

She's not the only one having trouble.

Backing her up was impossible.

The opponent he was facing looked the same as Leo had described: wearing a hat, a white mask, and a long coat.

The person wasn't brandishing any weapons but might have been hiding some.

Aside from some scrapes and bruises, Leo had no notable wounds. No burns or cut marks. In other words, thought Mikihiko, the one Leo had fought wouldn't use fire, electricity, or blades.

If they used a weapon, it would be a blunt one. If not, then strikes.

Their method of attack, at least for the moment, was just as he'd guessed beforehand.

If he'd miscalculated anything, it had been this enemy's incomparable speed and power.

The female vampire—as Mikihiko dubbed her for convenience's sake in his own mind—flung a fist toward him. The thick-gloved hand wouldn't leave external injuries, but it would probably penetrate to his organs instead.

Mikihiko held down one of the ribs on his already-opened iron-ribbed fan with a finger.

Bridal Veil.

Psions flowing from his fingertip triggered his technique, willed but not spoken, and activated it.

A demon's wind-cutting fist. The strike, holding unimaginable power, had such swiftness it almost reached the speed of sound.

Mikihiko had far higher physical abilities than normal people because of his rigorous ascetic training, but he didn't have the speed to dodge a subsonic strike after his adversary closed in on him.

A compressed mass of wind flew at Mikihiko ahead of the woman's physical fist—

—and Mikihiko's body floated, pushed by that wind.

He went with the current, dodging the fist's trajectory, letting the current pull him behind the fist and close to the arm. In modern magic, this event alteration would be accomplished by a compound spell: gravity blocking and inertial dampening, plus a relative posture stabilization. This old spell combined them all under one idea: riding the wind.

As Mikihiko, now to his opponent's side, set foot back on the ground when the technique's effects cut off, he also drove a blow into a joint in his opponent's fully extended right arm with the rod raised in his own right hand.

He swung down meaning to break the joint, but instead, the rod snapped in two with a dry crack.

Half-conscious of and half ignoring the numbness in his hand, he let go of the broken rod.

A barrier? Or weakening?

Dodging a sideways hand chop by jumping as far back as he could, Mikihiko pulled a throwing knife from a hidden pocket. He hurled the small, slender knife with a nominal grip attached at his opponent's arm as it passed in front of his eyes.

But the knife only tore a hole in her coat, bouncing away before digging any deeper.

A barrier!

There was no sign of any spell activating when he threw the knife. That meant she was covering her body at all times with a force field that would repel matter. Her punches and chops, intense strength ill-matched to her slender arms, had to be an effect of this barrier, he reasoned.

Well, then... Using his fingers, he opened the end of the iron-ribbed fan he'd closed earlier.

The talisman with the highest usage rate, placed in the easiest spot to get to...

As far as Mikihiko knew, you couldn't construct a barrier that stopped both mass and energy simultaneously with magical techniques.

There was a small chance she had expanded a multilayered barrier, but it was still worth a test.

Thunder Child.

Thunder Child was a spell that reproduced a small-scale lightning strike in a tight area. It was a degraded, scaled-down version of Invoke Lightning, a weather-control spell that created a thundercloud to emulate real lightning, but though its amperage was lesser, its voltage compared favorably.

With an explosive roar of electric breakdown, lightning fired from the source to other electrodes he'd set up in the air—at the crown of the vampire's head. At the moment this spell activated, it was already sure to hit. A lightning strike traveling at two hundred thousand kilometers per second bolted toward her head.

A beast-like, piercing cry rang out. But that immediately changed into a shout more suitable for the voice. The flash of light, which should have penetrated his target's body and disappeared, instead moved to the woman's hands as she placed them over her head. Electric sparks crackled from her fingertips. The light had a stronger electric force than the lightning Mikihiko had created.

Emission-type magic!

Spells that extracted electrons from a physical body were basic techniques in one of modern magic's eight types: emission. Because it pinpointed the information directly linked to the phenomenon of electron distribution and overwrote it, emission-type magic could generally output stronger electric attacks than old magic's lightning-type spells.

Mikihiko flung himself to the ground, and an electric light buzzed over, grazing him.

Compared to old lightning magic, modern emission-type spells were superior in power but inferior in control. Because of that, he was able to dodge the first attack. But at zero range, he knew he wouldn't be able to avoid the literally lightning-fast attacks forever.

Cursing his lack of forethought for unconsciously assuming his opponent would only use one type of attack, he hastily built a defensive spell. Then he called forth one that created a layer of air as a barrier, thick enough that no electric breakdown would occur.

However, his opponent was already using her magic. He didn't know how that worked, but the spell activated without an activation sequence, and its effects didn't seem to be waning.

Perhaps she really was a demon.

I won't make it—

Mikihiko prepared himself for the worst, but the worst didn't come to pass.

Like a gust of wind blowing out a candlestick flame, psion information bodies rammed into her, erasing the electric light from the vampire's hands.

Erika's down-swung blade stopped at the masked woman's raised left arm.

With the sound of a dull hit, she didn't feel the woman's bone break, or even that she'd cut flesh.

She had probably stopped it with a protector of lightweight alloy bonded with cushioning material—in other words, with a gauntlet.

No matter that, even though Erika hadn't swung with the intent to kill, she'd still not tried to hold anything back.

Before she knew it, a pistol was in her opponent's right hand. Despite the nonsensical mask, she'd been trained to a high degree not only as a magician but also as a combatant. Warning signals flared in Erika's mind, ordering her to muster even more energy from her body.

Knowing how to handle this position, with her katana sinking into—rather, *digging* into her opponent's gauntlet—she pulled the weapon back.

Faster than she could bring up her gun arm, Erika wheeled around to the woman's left side.

A moment before the muzzle was aimed at her, she slammed the katana into the barrel.

There was a gunshot, muffled by a silencer.

The masked woman's right hand reached for Erika's face. Her thumb and middle finger made a ring.

A small sphere of lightning danced on her opened fingertips.

The body moved, overtaking the mind. Erika retreated to avoid the sphere, and before the muzzle came completely up, she charged straight at the masked magician.

I've got you, Erika thought, just as she stepped into range and began to swing down her katana.

A moment later, a shock wave crashed up into her from below, sending her flying into the air.

She nearly lost consciousness from the shock for an instant.

But Erika immediately got back up.

And yet no follow-up attack came.

The masked magician's left hand was holding her right shoulder. Whether by acceleration magic or movement magic, right before she'd knocked her opponent's spell away, Erika's bladeless katana had landed a firm blow on her enemy's right shoulder. The masked magician, still holding her shoulder, directed her gaze toward where Mikihiko and the vampire were fighting.

More specifically, she looked past them—at a boy on a motorcycle pointing a silver CAD at the vampire.

She couldn't see the boy's face behind his helmet.

Tatsuya…?

Nevertheless, Erika's eyes, through hazy mind and combat stance alike, knew the identity of that boy implicitly.

Erika, Mikihiko, and the vampire.

While keeping the enemy and his allies in sight, Tatsuya's eyes pointed at the masked magician, as though her own golden eyes were drawing him in.

The masked magician leveled her left hand at Tatsuya. Her fingers moved as though typing, and less than a moment later came the sign of magic activating.

But that sign was dispersed before it could overwrite the world.

Confusion ran through those golden eyes.

She formed different magic programs three times, and three times did they disperse.

"Oh," he heard someone say. It was Mikihiko. He didn't need to ask why.

The vampire had started to run away.

Tatsuya's eyes, hidden behind the shield, looked away from the masked magician.

It was only for a moment.

And in that moment, he didn't miss what the masked magician did.

She hadn't used a spell. Even if he'd looked away, his "vision" would never miss the magic.

Perhaps the masked magician had realized that.

The pistol, hanging limp at her side in her right hand, while aimed at the ground, fired a bullet.

Sparks flew at the shooter's feet and instantly changed into a flash of light.

Five muffled gunshots came in succession, and the masked magician concealed herself in the flashes.

Tatsuya aimed his magical sights at the masked woman herself.

Aiming for her legs, he activated a partial dismantling spell—or tried to anyway.

But he couldn't feel it hit her physical information.

The eidos, which should have been reflecting off her real body, were at the surface level only; they were empty.

Only the colors and contours had been recorded; all the information about material, mass, and composition was missing.

Tatsuya stopped his spell and lowered his hand.

When the flashing light disappeared, neither the masked magician nor the vampire remained in the park.

* * *

"Are you two all right?" Tatsuya asked. Pursuit abandoned, he got off his motorcycle and removed his helmet.

Mikihiko didn't seem to have any particular wounds.

As for Erika, though…

"…Stop staring at me like that. You're embarrassing me."

"Right, sorry."

Taking a cue from Mikihiko, whose face was red and gazing somewhere else, Tatsuya looked away.

It wasn't as though he had seen her completely bare. He hadn't spotted any damage to her underclothing, either. However, from the bottom of her outerwear to just below her chest were several cuts, giving him tiny glimpses of her body lines. It was almost like an extreme rock-star look.

Considering it that way, he certainly couldn't say much skin was exposed. Maybe it was like how one would be fine wearing a swimsuit at the beach or the pool but be embarrassed wearing it on the street.

"…Hey, could you lend me something to put over this?" asked Erika, her tone implying she wasn't finding them very considerate.

Mikihiko hastily took off his half coat and threw it to Erika. Tatsuya would have offered, except for the fact that his blouson was hiding a shoulder holster, which would have been problematic to reveal.

"Thanks. I'm fine now."

It wasn't like she'd been naked, or even half-naked. Tatsuya's unadulterated impression was that she was making a big deal out of nothing, but maybe that was a kind of beauty of style. And certainly it was several steps better than having no shame about it.

"Erika, are you hurt?" He'd found out what he could from looking at her, but he decided to ask anyway.

"It was a good thing I wore an acton just in case. If I hadn't, things would've been real bad there."

Acton was another anachronistic term, with a further option being *gambeson*, but Tatsuya knew, by good luck or coincidence, that it was completely unlike what actons originally were. Rather than a thick garment worn underneath armor to soften impacts and keep the skin safe, what Erika referred to as an acton was underwear made of multifunctional synthetic rubber that served as armor against bullets and blades. Unlike thick body armor, it didn't obstruct the wearer's movement, and since you could wear it underneath your clothes, it carried the advantage of not drawing unwanted attention. In exchange, because of its materials, it was designed to cling to your body, so those wanting to hide their shape didn't like them. Normally, since she wore outerwear on top of it, there was no reason to mind it, but this time, it wasn't about the wearer; her companions had found the image of the acton clinging to her body tempting.

"It seems like wind blades were in that blast."

"Looks like it… That masked jerk. Next time I see her, I'm making her pay for these clothes."

"I think you hurt her collarbone pretty good."

"That's a completely separate issue!"

Like Tatsuya said, Erika wasn't beaten one-sidedly—she'd gotten in a little going-away present. The hit had been shallow, but just before the shock wave blew her away, her katana had connected with the masked magician's right shoulder.

Tatsuya hadn't been there to see, but between the masked magician's appearance and the way Erika's clothes were damaged, he'd accurately deduced what had happened.

"By the way, Tatsuya, why are you here?"

He could tell by Erika's face that she hadn't suddenly thought of the question—she'd been itching to ask the whole time. Tatsuya considered several avenues of how to answer, but in the end decided to be honest—because he thought it would be most interesting that way.

"What do you mean? Mikihiko contacted me."

Disturbance shot through Mikihiko's face as he looked at Tatsuya as if he were a traitor.

"Really, now?"

But at the indeed highly unhappy voice, Mikihiko awkwardly shifted his gaze to Erika.

"And our savior came to rescue us just in the nick of time. That was a nice play, Miki."

Her words were complimentary, and given what had led to this state of affairs, one should have judged the action worthy of praise.

Still, Mikihiko could only force out fragmented words like *uh* and *well*.

The volume of her voice entering his ears did not, in any way, strike him as a compliment.

"When did you contact him, by the way? I don't remember asking you."

"..."

Of course she didn't remember asking him—he hadn't told her at all. It was entirely his own decision to send their tracer signal to Tatsuya. And without giving him any other information, either. Even if she pressed him further, not even he would be able to answer what he was trying to do by doing that.

Erika's cold gaze on him, a bead of sweat formed on Mikihiko's temple. He was like a frog under a snake's glare. Mikihiko getting out of this himself seemed difficult, so Tatsuya decided that was enough: "I know you both seem confused, but shouldn't we move?"

Erika blinked twice at the voice addressing them from the side and took out her information terminal, which had just barely stayed safe.

"People are starting to gather, you know."

Mikihiko, flustered at Tatsuya's remarks, too, took out his own terminal.

Erika checked the time. It had been about five minutes since they encountered the vampire and the masked magician. It wouldn't be strange for other teams to start getting here.

Mikihiko brought up his tracer monitor. The lights displaying allied search teams were approaching in random curved paths. It was easy to imagine they did so lest they run across any other search teams.

"You didn't get the Clans' permission, right?"

At the moment, there was no penalty set in stone just because they hadn't participated in the official search team that the Saegusa family had organized.

But diving into combat while ignoring the Saegusa-Juumonji search team was the sort of thing they wanted to pretend hadn't happened... Especially if the former student council president found them. Erika and Mikihiko could sense that would lead to all sorts of problems in the future.

As they worried over this and that, Tatsuya, without thinking about anything unnecessary, prepared for their escape.

"Erika, want a ride?" he asked, getting back on his bike.

"Yeah, please." Erika bounded over, jumped into the tandem seat, and clung to Tatsuya's waist.

"What about me, Tats?" asked Mikihiko, fretting.

"Sorry. That would be too many people," Tatsuya answered, turning on the motor.

Mikihiko sucked in an affronted breath, then shouted: "You'll get fined for not wearing a helmet!"

The protest met only Tatsuya's back as he rode away.

(Additionally, in the late twenty-first century, there was no defined penalty for helmet-wearing delinquency. Instead, if a passenger was fatally wounded in an accident, a dangerous driving fatal wound penalty would be applied to the driver's record.)

Mikihiko, coat taken and left behind, stood there in a daze for quite a while.

Lina—still in her Angie Sirius form—returned to their mobile base, which was disguised as a television relay vehicle, and ordered a withdrawal before she even sat down.

There was no question. That, in itself, was as she'd predicted. As she took her seat in the back, the mobile base began to move without a sound. But the vehicle was filled with a dubious air, a desire to ask the question but a fear of doing so. Her hair was a mess and her boots were dirty with the vestiges of flash bangs, almost as though she'd run away. But for Sirius, commander of the Stars, the term *run away* was an unseemly one.

"Major."

The ceiling in the vehicle was high, but her two team members still had to bend over as they stood in front of Lina.

"We're terribly sorry."

Their apology was for falling behind during their pursuit. Lina had been fighting the vampire alone because her other team members couldn't keep up with her movement speed.

"It doesn't matter. There may have been unexpected third-party interference, but I fled as well."

"…Thank you, ma'am."

"Anyway, we've already dealt with Sergeant Sullivan, so I wouldn't necessarily call this mission a failure. Have you recovered his corpse?"

"Yes, Major."

"I see." Lina nodded, looking relieved at the answer that came from behind where the two of them stood. "Please send the sergeant's corpse for an autopsy right away. And did you figure out what I was chasing?" she asked, her expression immediately tightening up.

"I'm sorry, Major. We successfully extracted the psi-wave pattern this time, but it didn't match any of the data."

"Then either she isn't a fugitive…or her psi-wave patterns have been altered."

"I believe it's likely the latter, Major."

"All right. Trace the pattern we picked up."

"Yes, ma'am."

After hearing the answer and instructing the two in front of her to return to their seats, Lina sat back deeply in her own seat.

She brought her left hand to her right shoulder and applied healing magic to herself. She was able to keep a straight face in front of her subordinates thanks to her magic-based *transformation*, but her collarbone had completely broken after she'd forced herself to use her gun when it was already fractured. It hurt so much she wanted to cry.

Nobody told me Erika would be that strong! And Tatsuya used some crazy skill or magic or something to disable my spells… Are all high schoolers in Japan like that?! complained Lina to herself, leaving her own age aside for the moment.

"I'm sorry? Our aunt…?"

Tatsuya had left the room in haste a moment ago, after taking his terminal out of his breast pocket. Once he returned from that disappearance, Miyuki repeated back what he'd just said: the name of the woman he wanted her to speak to.

And after she said it, she was ashamed of her rudeness.

Tatsuya, of course, couldn't blame her for asking the question like that, but even if he could, it would take more than that to make him displeased with her.

"I have something I'd like to discuss with her," he repeated, asking her again to make the call.

Most of the Yotsuba family servants knew Tatsuya was Maya's nephew. They also knew that, as part of the Yotsuba family, Tatsuya was nothing more than a tool—though few knew he was a weapon. Even if he called Maya, it was entirely possible they'd hang up instead of transferring him over to her.

Nevertheless, neither Tatsuya nor even Miyuki was allowed to know her direct number. Anyone who knew the circumstances would unanimously state that the Yotsuba family's information controls were several levels higher than even the prime minister's official residence, and that was no exaggeration.

"If it's your command, Brother… Might you wait a moment?"

"Yeah… I'll go get changed."

Despite their blood relation, he couldn't take the call in his normal clothes, nor could he cut the video feed—for the siblings, that was the kind of person their aunt (and her household) was.

"I apologize for the lateness of the call."

"It's fine. I'm just surprised you wanted to call me, Miyuki."

As always, she featured age-indeterminate beauty and an indecipherable smile when she appeared on the videophone screen. Next to her was Hayama, wearing a perfectly fitted three-piece suit. Tatsuya thought to himself that having a butler sit in on a call between aunt and niece was a little lacking in common sense, but he was also standing next to Miyuki in a dark suit, so the road went both ways.

After they briefly exchanged regular greetings, tension hidden behind her calm expression, Miyuki explained, in an even more businesslike tone—it was probably hard for her to come out and say it—that Tatsuya had something to discuss with Maya.

"Tatsuya? Well, that's another surprise."

Not bothering to conceal the amusement in her smile, Maya allowed Tatsuya to make a remark.

"Aunt Maya, I actually have one thing I'd like to ask, and one thing I'd like to have your permission on."

"You may ask away," nodded Maya in good temper. On the surface, at least.

"Then, if I may… Aunt Maya, would you please tell me how the Kudou family's Parade spell works?"

Next to Tatsuya, Miyuki gave him a blank, baffled look.

On the other end of the video, Hayama dexterously raised a single eyebrow.

Maya gave a laugh, as though she couldn't help it any longer. *"Oh my… Tatsuya, Parade is the Kudou family's secret technique. Why would you think I'd know its mysteries?"*

Laughing again, Maya gave him a no in the form of a question.

"There was a time when you received instruction from His Excellency. Wouldn't you know the idea, even if not the magic program itself?"

Knowing she meant she couldn't tell him, he used her question against her to stand his ground.

"Is the anti-magic spell Parade for duplicating and processing parts related to your own eidos's outward appearance through the application of Information Boost in order to project a different appearance onto yourself? In other words, through masking or disguising eidos, one temporarily alters their physical appearance, while also substituting any magical interference aims with their own disguised eidos to block the usage of magic on the true body?"

But not only did he stand his ground—he added in his own deductions.

"...*I had thought you, of all people, would be very familiar with the impossibilities of transformation magic.*"

Maya didn't express a direct answer to Tatsuya's theory. That was enough for him to know whether his deduction was correct, but it still didn't satisfy him.

"If all you want to do is alter your appearance, you can do it by interfering with light waves, though it's not true transformation. The issue lies in that light interference can't fool my 'eyes.'"

"Brother, you don't mean..." said Miyuki, surprise evident on her face. "There was someone who could keep their identity secret from you?"

"Not only that. It caused my Mist Dispersion to miss."

Miyuki's face paled, and she lost her voice.

As though her shock had been transmitted through the screen, Maya furrowed her brow into a scowl for a moment. Her smile quickly returned, but she was finished playing games.

"*Even if Mist Dispersion didn't work, Trident wouldn't cause a problem, right?*"

"Can you not deploy a two-layered Parade?"

Maya had given him "advice," but she didn't answer his follow-up question. Instead, she answered a different question, one he hadn't asked aloud.

"I do recall hearing that the Old Master's younger brother was more skilled than he was."

"Thank you. Aunt Maya, this incident seems like too much for me to handle. I would like to request reinforcements."

"Is that the matter you wanted permission for?"

Aunt and nephew exchanged looks over the display.

"...Very well. Things seem to be shifting past the scope of our expectations. I will permit you to contact Major Kazama."

Tatsuya bowed, then withdrew from the screen.

[7]

The usual way to school on a usual morning: He and Miyuki left the station, met up with their friends, and headed for school. One member had been missing since the new year and another since the middle of last week, but aside from that, this morning looked the same as they had since last spring.

This morning, however, a very unusual event was waiting for Tatsuya. Before they met up with their friends, when they were still at the ticket gate, an upperclassman called out to him. Both he and Miyuki had noticed her there before she said anything.

This station was mainly used by First High students or related people at this time of day. Unlike with the high-capacity trains of old, you wouldn't see dense crowds of passengers coming off the platforms very often in stations these days. Nevertheless, the siblings walked over to where Mayumi was standing near the wall so they wouldn't get in the way of the students flooding out as class time approached.

No few students cast glances their way, but none of them seemed to care much. It wasn't strange for the former student council president to be standing and talking to the current vice president, and it was widely assumed at First High that the current vice president's older brother was a favorite of the former student council president—including in a gossipy way.

The reality was, of course, nothing that would meet their expectations. Rather than walking to school with her, the siblings left the ticket gates ahead of her. Mayumi only had one thing to say: to meet her in the crossfield club's second room after school.

The crossfield club (a club dedicated to a survival game using magic tactics) was the club Katsuto belonged to. There was a tacit understanding at First High that the club committee used its second club room as an unofficial meeting place, and many were aware that Katsuto used it for private matters even after retiring from the club. As expected, when Tatsuya arrived, Mayumi and Katsuto were waiting for him.

"Alone?"

Surprise rolled off of not only Katsuto, who asked the question, but Mayumi as well.

"Yes, since I was the only one called here."

In truth, Miyuki had firmly insisted on going with him, but he'd managed to wheedle her out of it—going with her to a cake buffet on his dime would be a small price to pay.

Whatever the reason, Tatsuya had indeed come by himself. Technically, Mayumi had only summoned him, but she hadn't predicted Miyuki wouldn't come, too. But without wasting time on that, she got right to the main topic.

"Tatsuya, did you go out last night?"

She led off with one of the several questions Tatsuya had imagined. "Yes, I did," he politely admitted, instead of the more typical *So what?* of people his age.

"On a motorcycle?"

"Yes."

People got talkative when they wanted to fool someone. Right now, Tatsuya had no motive to deceive with loquaciousness.

"…Will you tell me where you went?"

Mayumi, on the other hand, seemed to be having trouble deciding where to take the conversation. She didn't seem to have enough deviousness or experience in feeling someone out. Katsuto, standing quietly beside her, didn't seem cut out for the job, either.

"Yoshida called me while in combat with the vampire. They were fighting the individual there, as well as an unknown magician who was probably chasing the vampire."

This seems like it'll take a while, thought Tatsuya, deciding to push the conversation forward. Mayumi blinked in surprise as he directed an unreadable gaze at her. Even an adult with a bigger wealth of experience—her father, for example—probably would have had a hard time reading his thoughts.

She didn't know what he was thinking.

And that thought stirred unease within her, shook her psychological defenses.

"Since what time?" inquired Katsuto suddenly, maybe throwing Mayumi a life raft, maybe not.

"I only drove there because they called me yesterday. I wasn't part of the vampire search," answered Tatsuya, supplying even what wasn't asked to the question that cut out all sorts of things, like *who* and *what*. It didn't matter what Katsuto and Mayumi thought—Tatsuya had no intention of playing this game of scoping each other out right now.

"You two know that Saijou in Class 1-E was attacked, right?"

There was no universe in which they wouldn't have known. This wasn't a question, but a verification. The answer he got back was, of course, affirmative.

"I'm not the only one who wants to know what in the world is going on. We can't feel safe at all until we've found the criminal, handed them over, and put an end to it. I'm sure you can't tolerate the curtains closing before even knowing whether there's just one perpetrator, multiple, or whether it's an infectious crime, right?"

He was talking to both of them, but now he turned his gaze to Mayumi in particular. "Unless you tell me how much of the situation you understand and how you plan on solving it, I can't very well cooperate."

Though her initiative had been stolen, she seemed to rally her nerves. After a sigh, her false smile disappeared. "If you promise you'll help us, Tatsuya, I'll tell you what we know so far," she said. "But no telling anyone else. I'm sure you know that."

"Understood. I'll help you." Tatsuya nodded without a moment's delay.

That was the answer she'd hoped for, but since she couldn't figure out his true intentions, her eyes narrowed at him inquisitively. "...Does that mean you'll join our search team?"

"You may take it as such if you wish."

"Why this, all of a sudden? You must have seen the notification from the Clans Council."

Those were Katsuto's words. After the Saegusa and Juumonji had created their joint vampire-hunting team, a notification requesting assistance had gone out from the Clans Council to the leaders of the Ten Master Clans, the Eighteen Support Clans, and the Hundred Families. No high school student would have laid eyes on it if they weren't a direct descendant of one of the Numbers, but Katsuto spoke as though Tatsuya had, in fact, read the Clans Council notification through some means.

"As someone who isn't even part of the Hundred, I didn't think there was any room for me."

And Tatsuya didn't hide the fact that he'd seen the notification. Notifications from the council weren't designated confidential, so they weren't actually that hard to get your hands on.

"If I'd been personally requested, things would have been different, though."

His answer reeked of feigned ignorance. But as a facade, though it wasn't perfect, it left no room for complaints, and nothing in particular stood out as strange. Thus, Mayumi and Katsuto, regardless of whatever they were actually thinking, had no choice but to agree in form.

Because, after all, even before the sums of their experience came into play, Tatsuya already had a meaner personality than either of them.

"...But are you sure? Didn't you say your condition was that I share information before you'd cooperate?"

"One of us has to yield, or the conversation wouldn't get anywhere. What? If I decided you'd tricked me, I'd simply change my attitude."

At the too-honest words—or words that looked too honest, but might have actually had something behind them, then something behind that, and then behind that again—Mayumi let out a dry laugh. She'd been the one to bring up this confidential talk, but she already felt like getting it over with quick.

"Great. I'll explain everything we know at this stage. But before that, can I say something?"

"What is it?"

"You really are an awful person."

"......"

There were three bits in the information Mayumi gave that were altogether new for Tatsuya.

One was the scope of the damage. It greatly exceeded Tatsuya's predictions, but that didn't seem all that vital.

The second was that the crimes didn't seem to be the work of a single criminal. Tatsuya had considered accomplices, too, but the possibility of there being more than one vampire was unexpected.

And third was the presence of a third faction obstructing Mayumi and Katsuto's search. At first, when she said *obstructing faction*, Tatsuya's mind had leaped to Erika and Mikihiko. But after hearing the specifics, he learned it was an entirely separate group.

The second and third pieces of info worried even him. That masked magician probably belonged to the group impeding their search. And he had a pretty certain guess as to her identity.

But he didn't know her motive. He got the feeling that once he knew, it would all be very simple, but that just made it more annoying.

"What do you two plan to do when you capture the vampires?"

Avoiding the foolish act of wandering into a dark alley in his thoughts, Tatsuya pulled his mind back to the topic. He'd said he'd cooperate, and even if it was only a surface-level promise, he couldn't neglect to find out their endgame.

"We'll interrogate them and learn their identities and goals. After that..."

"They'll probably be dealt with," said Katsuto, filling in for what Mayumi was having a hard time saying.

I mean... Tatsuya didn't want to hear a female high school student throwing around terms like *dealing with*, either, so he didn't consider her naive.

And their solution didn't insist on humaneness; it was one Tatsuya could understand, both practically and emotionally.

"...Understood. What should I do?"

"Would you mind coming along with us? Starting tonight, if possible—"

"No, Shiba, you move on your own. I'd like you to report any clues you might come up with."

Mayumi stared at Katsuto as he cut off her instructions. Her gaze held no displeasure, but there was enough suspicion to make up for it.

"I understand."

In all honesty, it would have been easier for Tatsuya to do what Mayumi said. Of course, he had no intention of seriously keeping his promise to cooperate with them, which was why he could agree without hesitation to Katsuto's proposition.

Without revealing the cards in his own hand and having heard everything he wanted to hear for himself, he left them.

Once Tatsuya's footsteps had gone out of earshot (concealed microphones for detecting spies' movements were set up around the room), Mayumi opened her mouth.

"Juumonji, why did you tell Tatsuya to act separately?" Her tone wasn't criticizing, but she was unconvinced.

"I thought it would be more efficient," answered Katsuto.

She couldn't feel a lack of confidence from him. "But that could mean giving him to the Chiba."

Mayumi also knew that Erika's group had disobeyed the notification and was acting on its own. The Saegusa might have been a leader in the Ten Master Clans, but they weren't rulers, so they couldn't easily force the Chiba to stop, nor could they levy any penalties on them. But in a situation where a foreign faction was peeking through the shadows, letting them run about on their own was an inconvenient bother. Her true position was that even if they couldn't do anything about the combination of Erika Chiba and Mikihiko Yoshida, she at least wanted to get the Shiba siblings on their side.

"If we hadn't told him the truth, it's possible that could have happened," Katsuto muttered. He shook his head, implying that it wasn't a current concern. "But now that we've shown him our sincerity, he won't betray us. That's the kind of man he is."

"…A thoroughly give-and-take relationship, huh? That's a weird form of trust."

"Even the loyalty of a samurai, at its roots, was about goodwill and service—give and take. I personally think we can trust him much more than someone who was blindly obedient."

"…At the root of absolute loyalty lies dependence, after all. We can't expect that from Tatsuya. And it wouldn't make sense for him anyway."

Katsuto nodded. Mayumi nodded back, convinced.

At this stage, he'd have to be satisfied with putting pieces of the puzzle together even if he knew he was missing a crucial piece. While once again mentally searching through the information he'd acquired thus far, Tatsuya hurried to the student council room, where Miyuki was waiting for him.

It was still light out. But of course it was—today was Saturday. School had ended, but noon had only just passed. He was hurrying not because they were going to be late getting home, but because they were going to be late for lunch.

Miyuki would never eat without waiting for him. Maybe she would if he had carefully instructed (ordered?) her to, but he didn't think he'd be that late today, so he hadn't. He hadn't actually made her wait very long, but knowing he was making his little sister wait was enough to put pressure on even Tatsuya.

——Birds of a feather, one might call the two of them.

Putting his physical abilities to use, he dashed up the stairs two at a time and went to the student council room. When he got there, the door was open, as though it were waiting for him.

The first thing that came into view was a golden radiance.

At almost the same time, Tatsuya stepped to the side and Lina hid behind the door. They both waited, the door between them for the other to walk past. Tatsuya's lips pulled up a little at how ridiculous he must have looked, and then he went through the doorway, the one barring (?) the way gone.

He was purposely ignoring the concept of "ladies first" while making sure not to ignore the lady herself.

"Hey, Lina. How are you doing?" he asked, turning to her as he passed, lightly tapping her right shoulder.

"Hi, Tatsuya. I'm great. Thanks."

Despite the sudden physical contact, she didn't complain of sexual harassment. Her answer was given without a single wrinkle in her brow but with a smile, and as if in exchange, she patted Tatsuya's shoulder twice and left.

Tatsuya waved down Miyuki and Honoka—they'd stood up happily upon seeing him—and took a seat at the table (on a chair at the table, actually) which he couldn't quite decide whether to call a conference table or not. He obviously didn't want to give much thought to its having been purchased so student council members could use it to dine and take tea breaks.

Azusa and Isori were nowhere to be found. He couldn't have criticized them even if they were here, but he was still more comfortable without them. Not because upperclassmen being in the same room made him nervous, but because he'd have to take them into consideration. Azusa, especially, would look frightened as soon as the slightest thing happened (or so Tatsuya figured).

Mayumi's summons had been completely unexpected, so they hadn't prepared their own lunches. Of course, if someone suddenly said "I thought this might happen," he'd doubtless be less impressed and more scared. Knowing a lot would be sold out already, there would be no lack of fuss going to the cafeteria now, so they decided to make use of the dining server in the student council room for the first time in a while.

Honoka used the cooking panel to prepare a drink for Miyuki. Tatsuya's job was to stay put and let himself be waited on... Looking at him objectively would have made him an object of envy, but he cut off that unproductive idea before it made it to his conscious mind.

"What was Lina here for, by the way?" he asked, instead going with the thought that *did* come to mind.

"The school suggested that Lina could possibly be a temporary student council member for the length of her study-abroad program," answered Miyuki as she placed a coffee cup in front of him and leaned over to the side to look at him.

Her straight black hair flowed down like a waterfall before his eyes. His eyes stolen by how she combed it back behind her, he put together the information that had come in via his ears.

"Oh... Come to think of it, you mentioned she hadn't decided on a club yet, and you smelled trouble."

"Yes. It looks like the recruitment wars are growing quite severe below the surface... Apparently, Chairman Hattori was the one to propose Lina's position on the council."

That answer came from Honoka as she brought over a tray with steaming plates on it. She made a U-turn, then they both went around the table, took their own trays, and started eating.

"Her program ends after one school term, so she obviously couldn't join an athletic club," agreed Tatsuya.

"People seem to have a different ulterior motive," offered Miyuki, giving a slightly mean smile. "Apparently some people had the ridiculous plan of making a photo collection of her and selling it."

Honoka frowned and sighed. "Do we even have a photography club?"

It wouldn't be strange to have a club like that, but Tatsuya couldn't remember one existing.

"It was the photography team of the art club. Their idea, dull as it is, is to have her join the light gymnastics club and take pictures of her doing that."

Light gymnastics was a magicians-only gymnastics event performed with lowered gravity and inertia. In floor programs, you'd end up doing a trampoline-like performance without using a trampoline. Mirage Bat, which Miyuki and Honoka had competed in, was one of its extensions.

"I see..." Tatsuya murmured. "That would probably paint a nice picture."

"Um, Brother?"

"Though I'm not sure about them selling it."

"......"

Miyuki looked at him dubiously. Tatsuya looked in the other direction.

He got the same stare in that direction, too.

"...Sorry. I didn't say that properly," he said, looking back at his sister and holding aloft the white flag. If it came to a staring contest with his enthusiastic gaze, the two girls would more than likely be the first to break, but he'd figured using their feelings for something so petty would be incredibly uncool.

Meanwhile, Miyuki knew Tatsuya had no rude intentions, which meant that when humbled like this, she couldn't refrain from feeling awkward and casting her eyes down.

"A-anyway, I've heard similar things here and there, and it's not only Lina—the fires might start spreading to people who have nothing to do with recruitment, too, and, um..."

Honoka showed panic at the strange mood. Despite having an opinionated side to her, she was basically a person with delicate sensibilities (also called *timid*).

"And they thought the student council would be a good fit," remarked Tatsuya, immediately understanding her consideration.

"Yes," followed Miyuki without a moment's delay. "All the other clubs should give up if she refuses even student council work."

Seeing the strange air drifting between the siblings swept away, Honoka breathed a sigh of relief. Unfortunately (?) for her, she was far from the type of girl devious enough to take advantage of them fighting.

"What did Lina think about it?"

"She didn't seem very happy with the idea," answered Miyuki.

"I don't think she wanted to give up her time after school," said Honoka. "I thought maybe that was why she hasn't decided on a club yet, despite all the eager invitations."

Tatsuya nodded, looking convinced.

After their weekend dinner, Tatsuya sat on the living room sofa watching the large screen on the wall.

Next to him, Miyuki sat so close she was almost snuggling up with him.

The screen was divided in three. The main section showed a real-time video feed of the Tokyo metropolitan area from the stratospheric security cameras, with three different points of light moving atop it. The upper subsection had a road map corresponding to the main section and lights moving on it, while the lower subsection displayed text data that scrolled by every thirty seconds.

It was thanks to Captain Sanada that he could use the surveillance cameras on the stratospheric platform. And it was because of the once-in-a-generation hacker Kyouko Fujibayashi's job that he could monitor the tracer signals from the Saegusa-Juumonji family federation, not because he'd squeezed the authentication codes out of Mayumi. Fujibayashi was also the one who had picked out the Chiba search team's signal.

The luminous point thought to be the interfering faction was generated with constant analysis by the Independent Magic Battalion's supercomputer of the electric waves being detected by the interception and monitoring radios aboard the stratospheric platform.

From his long relationship with the Independent Magic Battalion, Tatsuya had had a vague understanding that the experimental magic force was also an experimental cutting-edge tech force (if not, they couldn't have built the MOVAL suits), but once again, he felt like he'd been blindsided by their exceptional capabilities.

And in terms of technology…

"The Stars seem to have better tech than us searching for the parasite," muttered Tatsuya, impressed, deciding the interfering faction was the Stars and watching them move.

They couldn't directly pinpoint the parasite's movements, but they could approximate them by analyzing the routes of the three factions looking for the vampire. And the moving light designated as the Stars, despite not being able to use the roadside cameras and their sensors or the measurement devices on the stratospheric platform, seemed to be tracing the parasite's motions the quickest. Tatsuya couldn't tell if it was a spell they didn't know of or more advanced technology. He also had no way of knowing whether the parasite was the only thing the Stars could trace or whether it could isolate other magical signals as well. The one thing he could say for sure was that the USNA was ahead of Japan in this field.

He'd never believed Japan's magic technology was on the forefront of the world to begin with. He also wasn't conceited enough to think they possessed every kind of tech. Still, he found it hard to suppress his chagrin and his earnest desire to seek answers.

"But now isn't the time for that," he said, cutting off those unneeded thoughts and rising from the sofa's backrest.

"Are you going, Brother?" asked Miyuki, watching the now-standing Tatsuya from the sofa with a pained look.

"Be good and wait here for me." Tatsuya's palm stroked Miyuki's cheek.

She put her own hand over his and pressed his palm to her cheek, almost as if making sure he was still alive. "I will await your return tonight."

"Yeah. Before long, I'll definitely need your strength. When the time comes—"

"Yes. When the time comes, we'll do it together. That's a promise, Brother."

"...Well, I don't think it'll be as dangerous as Yokohama was anyway," he said a little jokingly. Miyuki released his hand with a smile.

Tatsuya had more than just his favorite CAD. As he headed for the conflict with various other pieces of equipment, his sister saw him off at the front door.

She stared at the closed door until she could no longer feel her brother's presence.

And as that presence grew more distant, once her senses could no longer get a clear read on his location, she turned around sharply.

Not a vestige of loneliness was left on her face. In her tightly drawn expression were large eyes giving off strong light.

She returned to the living room and turned on the switch for the large, darkened screen. She wasn't wholly incompetent when it came to machines, but if one were to categorize her as either skilled or unskilled, she would definitely fall into the latter category.

But she was gifted with a good memory. Not as good as Tatsuya's, who could freely control his memory functions as a side effect of his mind being altered, but reproducing the procedure she'd watched him use presented her with no difficulty.

She called up the screens she'd just been watching with her brother. The scroll speed for the text data was a little too fast for her, but she wasn't skilled enough to change the settings, so she would put up with it.

As she watched the points of light move around, she desperately tried to deduce her brother's whereabouts. He'd told her to wait patiently, but just for today, she didn't intend to simply wait. Even if the result was that she went against his order, even if it earned her a scolding later, it was better than doing nothing but watch him get hurt.

And there wasn't a large-scale armed clash happening today. In that sense, one could say it was less dangerous than Yokohama had been.

But even if the scale was small…

Even if any armed action would meet with heavy restrictions…

His enemy would probably be *that* Stars member.

——Even still, there wasn't much Miyuki could do.

On a personal level, she already possessed one of the highest magical power levels in Japan, even at only fifteen. In fact, perhaps her power level was one of the highest in the world.

But her strengths didn't include precognition or clairvoyance.

She didn't yet have the right to move the Yotsuba's forces.

She didn't have a personally built network like Tatsuya.

She didn't have hacking skills like Fujibayashi.

Miyuki had none of the special magic, organizational capacity, or expertise needed to search out her brother. With her eyes still on the screen, she put a hand to her chest.

It was an unconscious act.

At her chest's center, above her heart. She couldn't feel her pulse with her clothing in the way, but in exchange, she could feel something else.

Deep in her chest, near her heart...

...she felt her connection to Tatsuya.

The detestable shackles bound to her brother.

The reset limiter.

The chains and the lock were both with her.

As was the key.

A curse-like secret art that constrained her even as it constrained her brother.

But it was a definite link tying her to him.

——If only I could see, too——

Such were her thoughts.

No matter how far away Tatsuya was, he could always see her, understand her. Tatsuya's "vision" could analyze everything about an existence, and she'd heard he could perceive her location and situation.

That meant she had no privacy whatsoever, but Miyuki didn't find that disagreeable in the slightest.

After all, there wasn't a single thing she had to keep a secret from him.

In fact, she wanted him to use his power to read even her innermost feelings, the ones she couldn't say herself. Even knowing his sight didn't work up to the dimension of the mind, she still wanted it.

On the other hand, Miyuki didn't have the power to "see" someone far away.

Instead, equipped with her inborn mental interference-type magic, she possessed a special haptic perception—a sense of "touch"—that could detect the whereabouts of a mind. If she released the limiters on Tatsuya and thus released her own unusual ability, she could "touch" another person's mind. She might even be able to touch individual souls drifting through the world if she felt like it.

But she couldn't feel a faraway person's "presence." She couldn't penetrate physical distance—which didn't exist in the information dimension—as something nonexistent like her brother could.

That was, indeed, the difference between visual and haptic perception. With a sense of touch, she could feel things that she was told were there, but she couldn't find things she didn't know the location of.

Feeling her brother in her chest, which only tantalized her more, she tried hard to infer the answer.

Struck by an ominous, inexplicable premonition, and wishing she could run to her brother.

How long did she stare at the screen like that?

Suddenly, the doorbell rang to announce a visitor.

She came to and looked at the clock.

Good, I'll send them away, she thought. In other words, if she pretended not to be home, nobody could blame her. It was too late for people to be visiting others' houses.

She looked at the door phone's monitor. When she saw the visitor, she immediately changed her plan. Choosing a change of clothes in her mind, she calculated how long she'd need.

"Would you mind waiting a few moments, please, Sensei?"

The visitor was Yakumo.

Tatsuya watched the battle between the parasite and the masked magician from the trees.

He'd arrived at this park three minutes before the fighting started. When he confirmed that his estimate of where the altercation would occur was right on the money, he smiled without thinking, but right now he was holding his breath, watching for the right moment to jump in.

According to Mayumi, there were multiple vampires, and multiple hunters chasing them. Now, though, the ones fighting were the same two from yesterday. All he'd done was look at how the groups were moving and predicted where the initial fight would break out; he hadn't figured out where, exactly, the specimen would show up.

...This is a coincidence, right?

A shiver squirmed up his spine, threatening to give him away. He managed to stamp it out right before that happened, however. *If you're telling me this is fate, then she's got terrible taste.*

He checked on the battle again. The masked magician was clearly the one on the offensive. The white-masked one thought to be the vampire was looking for an opportunity to flee. And the encirclement to block her escape route was still incomplete.

Four people. Just as predicted. Still, not much.

As the three factions—four, if you counted the police units who weren't cooperating with the Saegusa—played a complex game of checks and feints with one another, four magicians were closing in on this location from four different directions. Given that they were the away team without access to the roadside surveillance devices, he was surprised they could get four people here without the other factions noticing. Still, surveillance wasn't enough to quash all the escape routes in the city, which stretched upward, too.

Probably why this was a game of tag rather than hide-and-seek, but...

The enemy of my enemy is, in the end, a complete stranger. Guess it doesn't always mean they're my friend.

If all the factions chasing the parasite joined forces, with so many people from each team, it would be a simple matter to chase her down. Their different views wouldn't let that happen, though. Personally speaking, his own goals weren't perfectly aligned with Mayumi's or Erika's, either.

But for now, the vampire was the enemy here.

Anyway, how should I do this?

While predicting several responses from the masked magician, Tatsuya drew not his CAD but his gun from behind his waist. It was an illegal carry, of course, but he certainly wasn't about to worry about that now. As the vampire evaded a knife strike and made a big leap, he, in perfectly natural fashion, aimed roughly for her stomach and offhandedly pulled the trigger.

His handgun's average effective firing range was fifty yards, with its effective range in actual combat being twenty yards and closer. These details hadn't changed since the previous century. The weapons were made to fulfill a specific need, after all.

The distance between the trees Tatsuya was hiding under and the mystery woman in the long coat was about ten yards. Though he'd put in more than the bare minimum training time with handguns, he didn't exactly practice daily, so it was hard to get the exact right aim at this distance.

The gun in his hand was a break-action single loader due to a peculiarity of the bullet—which meant this was a one-shot showdown with no do-overs. He would have preferred to aim for a spot where the skin was exposed, but he couldn't, so he had to give up on that.

His opponent was wearing a hat pulled low over her face and a long coat that went down to her ankles, and her face was covered with an entirely white mask, an outfit that left virtually no exposed skin to begin with. Still, he needn't have worried about it.

The suppressor absorbed almost all of the heavy, low-speed bullet's discharge sound. The bullet caught the middle of the coat, just where he'd aimed. With twice the weight of a 9mm bullet making up for its lack of speed, it toppled the vampire over backward.

The masked magician looked in Tatsuya's direction. Her golden eyes held a fierce, penetrating light.

The light of unmistakable hostility.

She tossed aside her knife, and Tatsuya let go of his gun at the same time.

Her hand reached behind her, and his reached into his clothes.

Tatsuya was the first to finish drawing.

But when his finger was about to pull the CAD's trigger, it stopped halfway.

His opponent gripped a midsize automatic pistol. His vision told him a magic program was formed on its barrel.

Its activation speed rivaled that of Tatsuya's dismantling magic. Just holding the single-use armament device would expand an activation sequence, and because she didn't need to press a button, she'd gotten ahead of him.

The spell that was triggered was Information Boost, which strengthened a bullet's attributes as it traveled through the barrel.

Tatsuya used his CAD's selector to switch activation sequences from an eidos-dismantling spell to a body-dismantling one.

He aimed for the chamber of the gun the masked magician gripped. The bullet fired from it.

Their temporal perceptions quickened, a side effect of the high-density information processing from using magic. As he watched the masked magician squeeze her trigger, Tatsuya pulled his CAD's.

About fifteen yards separated them. She, too, was using a suppressor, giving her subsonic bullet a low-noise effect, but even so, it would take less than 0.05 seconds to hit its target.

It was synonymous with *instant*.

But the time it took for the Information Boost to affect the bullet was even shorter.

The bullet's attribute information had been strengthened, including its velocity, in the blink of an eye, but in the middle of its flight, it broke into small pieces.

A sense of shock leaked from behind the mask.

Her confidence is well placed, thought Tatsuya. Normally, he couldn't have blocked that bullet by stopping it or altering its vector. Maybe he could have if he'd had Katsuto's level of skill, but normal magicians would find it impossible. Even active combat units in the Ten Master Clans would have had trouble with it.

In fact, Tatsuya had only been able to deal with it because dismantling spells were effective against Information Boost. If they weren't, he wouldn't have had a solution for it, and would have had a *very* difficult time blocking Information Boost on sight.

But that was a hypothetical situation. In reality, the masked magician was exposing a clear opportunity to Tatsuya.

He shot a spell at the same exact time that his mind acknowledged an opening.

The spell he'd tried to fire initially would pick off the masked magician this time.

Eidos describing color, shape, sound, heat, and position were reflected in his vision. Rather than his opponent's actual body, his anti-magic spell Program Dispersion targeted the camouflage spell itself.

When his spell dismantled the very magic program, the empty, costume-like outer coating tore off in every direction.

—A moment later...

...the demon was reborn as an angel.

The night scene turned into stars and flowed past. Inside a motor sedan driving, almost sliding, over a metropolitan highway, they could see the outside scenery as a 3-D image, but no sounds or vibrations made it in.

From the quiet cabin's back seat, Miyuki hesitantly spoke. "...Sensei?"

The question was for the *ninjutsu* user sitting next to her: Yakumo Kokonoe.

"Hm? What is it?" he said, opening his eyes and turning to her.

"Why...might you be helping me right now? I recall that any contact with the outside world is admonished."

Self-discipline, or strict adherence. They meant different things, but the effects were the same. And the restrictions Yakumo had imposed on himself were both.

"There are actually a couple little reasons." His tone was as detached as it always was, so Miyuki had a hard time seeing through to his thoughts. "I became a priest and renounced the world, but I didn't renounce the *shinobi* arts. This problem goes beyond me."

Not that he couldn't renounce them—but that he *hadn't*. Miyuki couldn't sense any strain or despair in that; it was a completely regular part of Yakumo... At least, that's how it looked to her.

"There are also the duties, the responsibilities of those who inherit those skills... This might also be an extremely worldly affair, but even the priesthood can't stay detached from authority and tradition. I think this is allowed, don't you?"

Miyuki had no way to answer that. No matter who she was, it wasn't something you asked a fifteen-year-old girl.

"Mm..." she said. It was the most she could do, and appropriate. She thought she felt Yakumo's disciple scowl in the driver's seat, but it might have been her imagination.

"I actually heard from Kazama that Tatsuya's enemy might be using the Kudou's Parade spell. If that's true, I need to give a stern warning to the caster—in the place of my own predecessor, who taught them Cocoon, the spell that forms the basis for Parade.

"It's such a pain," he grumbled. But those imprudent words didn't make it to Miyuki's ears.

"Sensei, your master taught the Kudou family the original version of their secret spell, Parade?"

If it had been Tatsuya, he might have thought, *I see, I suppose that kind of thing can happen* and swallowed the whole thing up, but it was a fact that Miyuki couldn't help but repeat aloud.

"Wait, you didn't know that? Lab Nine's mission statement is to develop magicians with rationalized, resystematized old magic packaged as modern magic. They gathered a lot of old-magic casters together for it. My predecessor was one of them."

Miyuki hadn't known that, of course.

In fact, thinking a high school student would know about the magic technician development laboratories, half of which were sealed up as part of the dark side of modern magic, was incorrect. Even if she had been in a position to inherit the products of the most infamous one, Lab Four, she wouldn't have known what was going on in the other ones.

Suddenly, she gasped and gazed at him in pale wonderment. "Then, Sensei, your last name…"

"No, you're thinking too hard," he said, waving a hand and grinning drily. He must have known exactly what her question was. "The surname Kokonoe, 'of the imperial court' and more literally 'ninefold,' is something I inherited from my predecessor."

The air in the vehicle softened a bit. But the temperature soon plummeted again:

"Anyway, that was how my predecessor taught Cocoon to the Kudou, and they improved it into Parade. There are mysteries in it that we normally never should have let outside our gates. If the magician involved with Tatsuya is using it, I need to warn them not to spread it any further. If they don't listen, then, unfortunately…"

Yakumo's tone and expression were still just as detached as always, but Miyuki felt a chill run up her spine. It wasn't just her, either—his disciple's shoulders stiffened as he gripped the steering wheel.

A demon into an angel. A trite notion, but the change was vivid enough to call it to Tatsuya's mind.

Her crimson hair, reminiscent of a dark abyss—into a gold that glittered under even the weakest of streetlights.

Her ominous golden eyes—the color changed to a clear, azure blue.

Her jawline softened, and her features grew more delicate.

Even her height seemed to slightly decrease. Or had she simply appeared taller until now?

This beauty was nothing a tiny little mask could conceal.

I see, thought Tatsuya. If she could even make her body type different, it made sense that she'd been able to blind eyes around the world. If not for the piles of data he'd accumulated, even he probably wouldn't have known.

Without his realizing it, his hands and mind were moving. Five bullets were fired in succession from the brilliantly blonde-haired, blue-eyed girl's hand. All of them were reduced to dust before reaching him.

Right before the seventh shot was fired, the slide flew off the handgun and the barrel broke away.

The masked girl halted. Her gun's attack had been stopped. More importantly, the device she was using had been destroyed *by magic*. It was impossible.

"Lina, stop! I don't want to be your enemy!"

Taking advantage of her shock, Tatsuya attempted to change the situation. His goal today was to apprehend the parasite—the woman—and then find out her identity. That was why he'd gone through all the trouble of procuring an anesthetic bullet with a complicated gimmick—launching a needle when it hit the target—and this break-action, single-loader gun to fire it.

Fighting the masked magician—Lina—wasn't necessary. In fact, it was pointless. He'd hoped his words would end it, but…

It was a bad move—it had the opposite effect. The blue eyes behind the mask shone with a piercing light.

After returning the integrated handgun CAD without a slide or barrel to her waist holster, her right hand came out with, instead of a gun, a small throwing dagger.

The accepted notion was that USNA magicians favored integrated armament CADs. This dagger was doubtless no mere blade—it might even be some kind of armament device.

Her short boots kicked off the soft ground. The speed with which she did this wasn't possibly hers naturally, but at the end of the day, it wasn't extraordinary, either.

Tatsuya removed a lead ball from his pocket and flicked it.

It cut through the wind, soaring toward Lina's right hand—and penetrated it.

No blood spattered.

He hadn't shot through flesh. The ball had passed through an illusion.

Lina continued, waving her arm. The dagger launched from a point about a yard away from its location as seen by Tatsuya's eyes.

Jumping to the side to dodge, his eyes followed its trajectory. Beyond where he watched, the illusion readied a second throwing dagger.

His physical eyes perceived where the girl in the small mask was, and his mind's eye knew it was an empty projection.

What a pain! he cursed to himself. Knowing the theory and experiencing it for real were different; he was out of his element.

The factors described by the information bodies making up the Parade spell were color, shape, sound, heat, and position. Same as Yakumo's illusion art, Cocoon.

Whereas Cocoon projected color, shape, sound, and heat that were exactly the same as those of the real thing but in a different location, Lina's Parade spell placed more emphasis on projecting a different color and a different shape. That didn't mean it had cut out the part about camouflaging location, though. This magic program, which Kudou had come up with and Lina had inherited, was equipped with the same position-blurring function.

Right now, Lina was diverting the calculation power from camouflaging her color and shape into camouflaging her position, trying not to let Tatsuya grasp her real body's coordinates. And if he couldn't identify those, he couldn't use magic on her. It would essentially disable magic that specified coordinates based on visual data. The difference between Parade and illusion arts lay in how the first could falsify one's coordinates even in the information dimension.

In order to apply magic to something, you had to project a magic program onto the target object's eidos. For example, in order to use a file on a computer, you had to specify a path for the directory it was stored in, then use an execute command. But checking the path all the time was a pain, so shortcuts were widely used. If you switched a shortcut with a fake one whose path linked to a dummy file with no contents, you would get an error when you tried to change the file, even though you went through the same process.

Applying this concept to the magical activation process, in most cases, one's visual information was the shortcut icon, and auditory and heat-sensing information would fit into that. Fooling the visual information with an illusion would cause magic not to activate, but if the main body and illusion overlapped, you could usually still arrive at the main body's eidos using the coordinate information. In this case, despite the lag in his activation time, his spells were still working fine.

Even if you projected an illusion somewhere other than the main body, you could also still search for the main body's eidos using the relationship between the illusion and body as a key. But with the coordinates camouflaged and a dummy of the main body prepared in the information dimension, any magic program he fired using his sensory information as a shortcut would end up not doing anything.

That was the system behind the anti-magic spell Parade.

Which meant that in order to break it, he had to either:

—destroy the illusion, and then find and attack the main body before a new illusion was formed…

—or locate the main body's coordinates without relying on his senses, instead going through the Idea, to attack.

The former option wasn't going very well at the moment. Lina was already quick at triggering magic. Her activation speed was enough to rival Miyuki's. She'd probably practiced this spell in particular. Her reactivation time was monstrous.

Tatsuya was able to use the latter method, too. But it was a kind of gamble, shifting most of his awareness from the physical dimensions to the information one while under physical attack.

...No other choice.

As he dodged the fifth dagger, he made up his mind. He wouldn't try to find the main body and attack before a new illusion formed, nor would he directly search for her eidos in the Idea. There was a third option.

He took out of his pocket a cylindrical can small enough to fit in his hand.

And then he tossed it *up.*

For a moment, Lina gave him a dubious expression. But when she realized what the "can" was, it opened her eyes.

——A small shrapnel grenade.

"Je—"

Maybe she wanted to say *Jesus,* but she couldn't finish. Not wasting the time to finish even her short word, she expanded a physical barrier.

Constant deceleration.

Meanwhile, with flash casting, Tatsuya triggered an area-of-effect spell that decelerated object movement speeds at a fixed rate. It was impossible for a weak barrier created by a virtual magic region to completely stop the shrapnel grenade he'd thrown. A halting spell that brought speeds to zero might buckle under the shrapnel's kinetic energy, its event alteration failing.

That was why he used constant deceleration. Even so, decelerating an object to a small fraction of its original speed, like a hundredth or a thousandth, was too much for him.

Weighing the specs of the weapon he'd prepared for himself against the interfering power of his virtual magic region, he cast the spell at a level where it would just barely work.

However, constant deceleration wouldn't completely halt the shrapnel; the spell wasn't for that purpose in the first place. He turned half to the side, then knelt on one knee, moving his arm to protect his shoulder, flank, thighs, and head. The minute fragments tore into it.

Few of them penetrated the artificial leather fabric with simple

bulletproofing on it, but more than ten still dug lightly into his leg and arm.

Self-repair spell: auto-starting.

Kill self-repair process.

Willing the automatically activated self-repairing to stop, he immediately lunged for Lina, who had blocked the shrapnel grenade completely with her own barrier. When she tried to form another physical barrier, he nullified it with a dismantling spell. Caught completely off guard, even she couldn't resist any longer.

"...Tatsuya, you're crazy."

Lina was on the ground facing up, and Tatsuya was on top of her, holding her down. Pinned down, she sounded appalled. But a smile appeared on her lips, which weren't hidden by the mask. It was a relaxed gesture, but it wasn't hard to realize it was feigned.

"I didn't know where you were. Standard tactics say to smoke you out with a nondirectional attack, right?"

"Most would call that an indiscriminate attack."

"Interpret it that way if you wish. Unfortunately, I have no skill with manipulating area-of-effect magic. Anyway, I knew for certain you'd be able to defend against it, so give me a break."

"You got hurt, though. Doesn't seem worth it."

"I had to in order to capture you."

"You wanted to capture me? If you wanted to whisper sweet nothings into my ear, I would have preferred a more romantic approach."

Tatsuya looked into the blue eyes behind the mask and smirked. After bringing her hands over her head, one on top of the other, he used one of his own to suppress her opened palm.

When he brought his empty hand toward her mask, her shoulders gave a jerk. A finger on her thickly gloved left hand tried to move, but Tatsuya pushed it open by force.

"...Tatsuya, that hurts."

"Unfortunately for you, I know how that CAD works. Anyway..."

Tatsuya's hand went for the mask.

Lina closed her eyes and turned away. Her cover was long ago blown—did she still not want to expose her face? He couldn't understand the mentality, but it wasn't like he was tearing off her clothes or anything, so he had no reason to stop.

"Activate, Dancing Blaze!"

As his hand touched her mask, Lina shouted, her face still turned.

The five daggers she'd already thrown returned at her voice and attacked him.

A voice-activated armament device... It keeps a delayed-activation spell at the ready, not an activation sequence? Interesting, he thought to himself, sensing the daggers quickly converging on him.

Two went for his right arm, reaching for the mask, one for his right shoulder, one for his left arm, and one for his legs.

None of them would hit a vital spot.

Come to think of it, Lina's attacks were all to disable me, not kill me... As he considered this, the daggers had already reached his body.

And the instant they made contact, they all turned into fine sand and scattered.

"Corrosion... No, dismantling...?" muttered Lina, overcome with surprise, turning her averted eyes back to him.

Ignoring her, Tatsuya got back to peeling the mask off.

She shook her head fiercely to resist him, but she couldn't shake off his hand.

"You'll regret this, Tatsuya!"

"I've let the target I nearly captured escape. I already regret this plenty."

As he and Lina were struggling about, the parasite had made a clean getaway. Though he had insurance for it, he couldn't deny a feeling of vain effort. Lina was chasing the vampire, too, which made Tatsuya wonder what she stood to gain by helping her escape.

Neither her teary-eyed glare nor her desperate warnings were reason for Tatsuya to hesitate. He unlatched the receivers on her ears, left and then right. As he'd thought, the mask doubled as an information terminal.

He gently removed the surprisingly hard mask. Even Tatsuya, who was used to pretty girls, nearly breathed a sigh at her exposed beauty.

Lina bit her lip and glared sharply at him.

A moment later, a scream that could tear silk exited her lips.

It was too sudden. Tatsuya's eyes turned into dots.

He didn't loosen his grip on her hands despite his shock, thanks to the extremely thorough training he'd received from Kazuma, a man of poor character.

"Somebody! Somebody help me!"

It was exactly the shout of a girl seeking rescue from a rapist.

And the perpetrator—well, Tatsuya—stared at her realistic performance with a dreary look.

Then, as though others had been waiting for Lina's scream signal, he heard footsteps running toward them. Figures wearing navy-blue bulletproof vests with white lines made of reflective material on them over equally navy-blue uniforms, one from each of the four compass directions, were approaching. The insignia shining on the fronts of their caps was an informal crest of a cherry blossom.

As Tatsuya grabbed Lina's left arm and dragged her up, he tore the glove off her left hand. With the sensation of cords splitting and cracking, Lina's white hand became visible.

"Raise your hands and turn around!" shouted the police officer—no, the man dressed as a police officer—who ran to them from the front, pointing a gun at him.

Tatsuya went around behind Lina and shoved her toward the man.

Lina yelped and flew into his chest.

Just as the uniformed man put his arms up to stop her...

...Tatsuya jumped over Lina's head and landed on the man's shoulder.

Like kicking a soccer ball, he rammed his foot into his face.

As he fell down without a peep, Tatsuya launched off his shoulder and broke out of the fake police encirclement.

"...What if that had been a real police officer?" asked Lina in disbelief.

However:

"I'd prefer it if you dropped the charade, Angie Sirius," he answered.

The air audibly froze.

"If they're cooperating with you, it makes no difference whether they're the real thing or not. A hundred years ago, maybe, but current Japanese criminal law applies to foreign aggression crimes even if no martial force was used. If you thought people disguised as the cops would intimidate me, you couldn't be more wrong. I'd like it if you stopped underestimating the resolve of Japanese magicians."

The three remaining fakes looked at the expression of Lina for instructions—their commander, Angie Sirius.

After sighing, she turned to Tatsuya and gave a light, polite bow. "I apologize for my rudeness. I did indeed underestimate you. Hearing and seeing are entirely different. As another magician, I am sorry."

Then, she put her feet together, straightened her spine, and brought her right hand up horizontally to her forehead. Even without a military cap, it was an unmistakable soldier salute.

Before, she had acted as a single magician—from now on, it would be as the commander of the USNA Army's magician forces.

That was how Tatsuya understood her display of intent.

"I am Major Angelina Sirius, commander of the Stars magician unit, under the direct command of the USNA Army's Joint Chiefs of Staff. Angie Sirius is the name I use when transformed like I was before, so please continue to call me Lina. Now, then—"

Her bloodlust, previously tucked away inside the sugar coating called courtesy, was now on full display, and it washed over Tatsuya.

"Now that you know my face and name, Tatsuya, the Stars must get rid of you. It is unfortunate—there were plenty of ways to play around the facts if I still had my mask."

"So that's what you meant by regretting this." With the murderous intent blowing on him like a wind, Tatsuya let a fearless smile show.

"If you had at least allowed yourself to be deceived and captured, we could have finished without needing to kill you."

"Well, excuse me. I seem to have wasted the consideration you were kind enough to show me."

"No, you needn't apologize. We need to kill you because of our own selfish reasons. You may feel free to resist."

One of the fake police officers handed her a combat knife for her right hand and a midsize pistol for her left.

A sword-shaped armament device and a handgun-shaped specialized CAD.

Tatsuya drew his own from inside his clothes.

"This really is a shame, Tatsuya. I'd started to like you quite a bit, you know."

Lina raised her left hand and pointed her CAD at Tatsuya.

Tatsuya raised his right hand and pointed his CAD at Lina.

Lina's subordinates surrounded Tatsuya to the back and either side.

"…Good-bye, Tatsuya."

"I won't let you do that, Lina!"

Suddenly, an imperious voice rattled the freezing midwinter air.

Shock appeared in Lina's azure eyes as she turned to look toward where it had come from.

As if trying to cover their commander's exposed opening, her three subordinates jumped Tatsuya at once.

They swung big combat knives. Extending from their blades in a straight line were virtual regions—Atomic Dividers.

Tatsuya pulled his CAD's trigger. Their virtual regions to reverse intermolecular binding force vanished against the casters' wills.

Slipping past the combat knives, now mere blades, Tatsuya escaped their encirclement. The subordinate he passed on the way fell down, clutching his stomach. Blood started to gush between his fingers.

With a single swing of Tatsuya's blood-soaked left hand, a spatter of blood flew toward Lina's goons.

One of them stopped moving, and one of them charged him.

Tatsuya pointed his right hand at Lina.

Her left hand was aimed at the person who had announced her intervention—Miyuki.

The activation sequence Lina expanded shattered under Tatsuya's Program Dispersion.

A wall of cold that would freeze anyone who stepped into it appeared in front of Tatsuya to block the man rushing him.

His feet came to an abrupt stop.

A figure crept up behind him.

The last officer was already on the ground.

"Gee, Tatsuya, that was quite the pickle."

Yakumo, who had instantly disabled two Stars members, brought his face, looking as detached as ever, close to Tatsuya's.

I can't stay the same as ever, thought Tatsuya, reflecting on his own inexperience. "Such an innocent lie, Master," he said. The constant admiration was getting on his nerves, so he replied sarcastically. "I know you were hiding until your chance came."

Lina's eyes widened.

Miyuki took a position in front of her, CAD at the ready. Tatsuya's right hand was pointed straight at Lina, too. And even though Yakumo's gaze was on Tatsuya, his still had Lina completely in his view.

Lina was now the one surrounded.

"Well, what's the fuss? It looks like you had some things to ask, too," she said.

"Huh? Is that true, Brother?"

Miyuki turned around, expression dismayed. It meant taking her eyes off Lina, but with Tatsuya and Yakumo ramping up the pressure on her, she couldn't make a move.

Miyuki noticed her own failure right away, though, and hurriedly returned her gaze to Lina.

"You had us surround her on purpose so that we could get information from her... I was utterly ignorant of your idea, and I made an assertive move. Forgive me, Brother."

With her eyes on Lina, Miyuki asked Tatsuya's forgiveness in a voice full of sorrow.

"No, I was definitely in danger, so you made the right decision. You don't have to apologize. In fact, I should be grateful. Thank you, Miyuki."

"Brother...I'm not worthy of such words..." his sister muttered, her expression intoxicated. Still, whenever Miyuki apologized to Tatsuya, this was the predictable development. Or maybe it was a kind of ritual, or beauty of form. Considering her eyes still hadn't left Lina, though, she seemed to have a bare minimum of reason left.

"And we can just ask anything we want now anyway," he said, both to Miyuki and to let Lina hear it. He pronounced every sound, every syllable distinctly, making Lina sure that he was talking to her, too.

"...You plan to use force to interrogate me?" asked Lina, the sound of grating teeth accompanying her voice.

"Aren't interrogations usually done with force?" he replied—an indirect yes.

"But it's one against three! That's unfair!" she cried, a full-on frustrated criticism.

"Unfair?" cut in Miyuki, astonished. "How many people did you get just to surround my brother?"

"Now, don't say that," said Tatsuya, trying to soothe her before her astonishment changed to anger. "*Fair* is a superficial term, used to maintain your advantage when you're already in an advantageous position, and *unfair* is a convenient word to bring an opponent to the negotiating table when you're in a disadvantageous one. Tactically speaking, trying to skirt around having to fight when you know your strength isn't enough is correct. It's all over if you take her seriously, Miyuki."

"I see. I understand how it is."

What Tatsuya had said was altogether too blunt, but it seemed to calm Miyuki down, at least.

"Superficial? Convenient?"

At the same time, though, it seemed to rile Lina up.

Incidentally, Yakumo was busy trying to muffle laughter.

"Japanese people are the last people I want to hear that from! You feel no shame taking advantage of insincere words!"

"Aren't you a quarter Japanese, too?"

"...!"

"The Parade you were using was developed in Japan, and you can use it because you have Kudou blood—the blood of a Japanese person, right? Besides, double standards are a specialty of the white establishment. I've never heard of people who *don't* take advantage of insincerity."

Lina glared at him without a word, her white skin flushing red. But since she was both glaring and not speaking, it probably meant she didn't know what to say to that.

As he took her stare with a (mean) grin, he realized the blood-thirsty mood in the air had thinned and let out a dry laugh.

"...What's so funny?" demanded Lina.

"Nothing. Just thinking that if we interrogated you like this, you'd get all stiff-necked and wouldn't tell us anything."

"You could at least call it *stubborn*!"

She really is fluent in Japanese if she knew what that metaphor meant, thought Tatsuya, impressed—even though it really didn't matter.

"The other groups will probably get here soon, too..."

"Hey! Are you listening to me?"

It was best to ignore what didn't matter.

"Lina, let's make a *fair* trade. If one against three is cheating, then why not have a one-on-one contest? If you win, I'll let you go for today. In exchange, if I win, you'll give me honest answers to my questions. How does that sound?"

Even if Lina won, they knew her identity. If Tatsuya won, she'd have to tell him everything. The match itself was one-on-one, but it was certainly not an equitable deal.

"...Fine."

"Wait!"

After Lina racked her brains over it, she accepted the conditions, and at the same time, Miyuki interrupted with an objection.

Tatsuya's and Lina's eyes went to Miyuki.

"Brother, would you approve of leaving the duel with Lina to me?"

"Miyuki, why would you—"

"Remember this, Lina. I will not forgive anyone who tries to hurt my brother. I consider you a rival and a friend, but I can never forgive you for attempting to take his life, even if it wasn't sincere. I will personally teach you your sin."

Miyuki's eyes glowed with a light that was 100 percent serious. Lina tried to laugh off her deep attachment, but it only ended up being a grimace.

"Be assured, I will not kill you."

Miyuki's words declared she was certain of her victory.

"Hmm... Miyuki, you think you can beat me? The one granted the name of Sirius?!"

Upon hearing her challenger's words, Lina's chest began to blaze with her competitive spirit.

The two knockout beauties stared each other down.

"All right. Miyuki, I'll leave it to you. Is that all right with you, Lina?"

"Thank you very much, Brother."

"Fine by me. If I lose, I'll tell you everything. Not that it's possible, of course!"

Consent was present. The curtain was about to slide open on the splendid match between two unparalleled beauties.

Miyuki and the others knew her specialties were cooling magic and freezing magic.

But their true identities were vibration canceling and movement canceling; she wasn't making use of any snow fairies or ice magic. And, of course, unlike in clichéd young adult fantasy novels, she wasn't impervious to the cold through the protection of any spirits.

What needs to be said, regardless, is this:

What's cold is cold.

There was no way the motorcycle's tandem seat wouldn't be cold when she sat down on it in this midwinter's night.

So...

It would make sense for me to cling to him...since it's so cold.

Tightly gripping Tatsuya's waist, pressing her cheek to his back, bringing her chest all the way up, she repeated her excuse like a mantra.

—And there would be nobody butting in and asking if she needed such excuses at this point.

Yakumo spared a glance behind him to the headlights of the motorbike following just behind them and gave a smile that anyone would describe as bad-natured.

From his position, he couldn't completely see Miyuki in the tandem seat, as she was behind Tatsuya, but he could see quite clearly her posture, state, and expression. The emotions the siblings had for each other were supremely interesting to Yakumo.

A moment after his lips curled up, and he felt a heightening of tension from next to him. Someone seemed to have misinterpreted his grin as something stranger.

"You don't need to be defensive. If you keep your promise, we won't harm you in any way."

"...You expect me to believe you in my current position?" replied Lina in a hard voice, eyes fixed straight ahead. No, perhaps it was less *hard* and more *drawn back*.

"Well, I can't blame you for feeling that way."

She was sitting deeply back in the rear seat, with Yakumo on one side and his disciple on the other in such a way that anyone who knew her position would think of them as an escort. She'd just learned the true power of the men sitting to either side, which made her resentment even stronger.

Yakumo had knocked out two of the Stars' elite members in an instant.

The other had suddenly been standing behind her without any of them realizing it, wearing black clothes—a ninja.

The man holding the steering wheel had no apparent openings for her to exploit, either.

She didn't think they could beat her, even three on one, but she wasn't confident she'd emerge unscathed, either.

"But it's all right. You can trust us."

Whether he'd simply sensed her nervousness or also guessed that it was rooted in hostility and caution, Yakumo's tone was exceedingly laid-back.

For Lina, that made him even creepier.

"I'm not interested in the conflict between you and Tatsuya. What I am interested in is the proper handing down of secrets. Like I said earlier, all I want from you is not to reveal the art given to you by Kudou. Handing it down to someone who has no right to it is not handing it down properly."

"...You don't have national interests in mind, either?"

"Nope."

"The peace of the world? The future of human civilization?"

"Not interested. I'm a recluse."

"But you're a magician, too!"

Yakumo was suggesting something that Lina's perspective on the world considered impossible—something that couldn't be allowed to happen. That made it all the more unbelievable.

"I'm a *shinobi*. Not a magician," replied Yakumo, voice gentle—a firm negative.

"...*Ninjutsu* users are a kind of magician, aren't they?"

"Just because you can use magic doesn't mean you have to become a magician."

She knew the meaning of the words he used.

She understood them.

But none of what Yakumo was saying made sense to her.

"It's like how just because you're a magician, you don't automatically have the duty to serve your country."

It didn't make sense, but for some reason, she couldn't argue, either.

Their sedan parked on a dry riverbed in the middle of nowhere.

Lina wasn't acquainted with the place, so she didn't know where it was. Considering how long they'd been driving, they would be in the next prefecture over, but she was surprised there was a place like this in the suburbs of the Tokyo megalopolis.

She couldn't see any light at all.

The sedan's headlights went out, and when the motorcycle's behind them did as well, it made their stage virtually pitch-black.

There was no moon; only the stars guided their way through the dark as Tatsuya and Miyuki walked over.

Suddenly, Lina was struck by an indescribable unease.

They hadn't confiscated her CAD, but she didn't have her transmitter or comm unit on her. They hadn't even done a body check; they'd made good guesses as to all her possessions. All she could do was obediently hand them over.

They said they'd return them later, but she didn't have any way to inform her allies back home of the situation. The observation satellite would be following her location, but it was *ninjutsu* users recognized for their illusion magic who had brought her here. They might even be able to fool the military-grade observation satellite's high-resolution cameras.

This means they're releasing me somewhere I don't even know, doesn't it? At worst, I could be assassinated. Her fingers closed tightly around her clothes where her CAD was stored. *If it comes to that, I'll have to use my trump card.*

"I can imagine what you're thinking, but we'll keep our promise, so don't worry."

It was all Lina could manage not to yelp. She couldn't help but give a jolt at the sudden address. When she turned around, she saw Tatsuya. The starlight was enough for her to make out his expression as he came closer. He was smiling.

"We're just going to ask some questions. Once we've heard what we want to know, we'll drive you to the station."

From her point of view, it was an extremely exasperating grin.

"I'll only tell you if you beat me." Lina's voice was naturally sharp.

"Of course. We'll keep that promise, too."

His iron mask didn't shake even a little, which got on her nerves even more, but she knew blowing her stack now would only make her position worse.

She clenched her teeth, then aimed her sharp stare behind Tatsuya—at Miyuki.

Eyes swelling with fight looked back at her. She was already raring to go.

"Now, then… It may not please you, Lina, but Master will be

the referee. I say referee, but he'll just determine who won or lost. He won't break up the match or interfere in the middle."

"I knew from the start everyone here is an enemy. It's fine by me."

"How sportsmanlike of you."

Tatsuya let her remark slide off him.

Her frustration had gotten worse, but she suddenly felt like she'd calmed down.

"Unworthy though I may be, I, Yakumo Kokonoe, will preside over this duel. Victory will be when one person surrenders or is incapacitated. No killing. It'll leave a grudge."

"I understand. That will be enough."

"I'll end it before that happens."

Miyuki nodded quietly, while Lina gave a spirited acknowledgment.

Their attitudes contrasted, but each had the same unwavering confidence in her own victory.

The situation was fit to explode at a moment's notice.

"All right. Let's get started."

"Master, please wait a moment."

But there was one man here who couldn't read the mood, who would purposely throw a wet blanket over them. Ignoring the strained looks from Yakumo and Lina, Tatsuya walked over to his sister.

He came within two steps of her, but he didn't stop walking.

"Umm, Brother?"

She was confused and unable to read his intent, but he didn't answer.

He took one more step up to her.

As though it were natural, he still didn't stop.

Then, when he was at zero distance from her, close enough to reach out and embrace her, he came to a stop...

...and did just that.

"I-I-I, umm—"

He wrapped a hand all the way around her waist as she passed the blushing stage and fell into a panic. Even though she was just embracing him until a few moments ago—but that would have been a third party's impression. For her, hugging someone and suddenly being hugged were two completely different things.

Tatsuya's other hand slid in behind her head.

At this point, Miyuki couldn't even make a sound.

His fingers combed through his sister's hair,

he brought her face, which had forgotten to resist, to his mouth,

and gave her a kiss on the forehead.

When he released her from the embrace, he saw that Miyuki's eyes were wide.

Not in an embarrassed way—she was simply surprised.

"This... Why...?"

"I had it shown to me before. It might not be perfect, but I remember how. It'll only have a temporary effect, but I'll return your control. Fight to your heart's content."

"...I will!"

Miyuki nodded to her brother's words and gave a strong smile that was no longer intoxicated.

"I'm sorry for the wait, Master," said Tatsuya. Next to Yakumo, Lina was making a face like she'd eaten too much and had heartburn. "I made you wait, too, Lina... If you're not feeling well, I'll give you a moment."

"It's your fault... As such, I'll be quite fine," she replied as meanly as she could while Tatsuya feigned ignorance (at least, Lina thought it was feigned), then turned back to Miyuki.

Miyuki hadn't followed on Tatsuya's heels. She didn't seem to be planning on close combat.

Based on her observations thus far, Lina judged that she was a typical magician who wasn't strong at martial arts. The easiest type for Sirius, executor of treacherous magicians, to deal with.

I'll end it in one attack!

They still hadn't given the signal to start, but she had no intention of waiting for something so trivial. They hadn't agreed to start on a signal.

She would close the distance with self-acceleration, disable Miyuki's magic with Information Boost, and disable the girl herself with physical combat.

Then, while Tatsuya and the others were preoccupied with Miyuki's defeat, she would use a high-speed movement spell to escape.

That was Lina's plan.

But it would end with Lina giving a mute yelp.

An instant before she could use her magic, a gust laced with hail attacked her.

She immediately made a long jump horizontally, dodging the cold torrent of tightly packed hail. When she looked up, a blizzard blew at her, aiming for her side. By manipulating the air's density and creating a wall of vacuum to shield herself, she managed to endure the attack.

"I suppose it'll take more than that."

Someone's muttering floated to her on the night wind.

Lina clenched her back teeth hard.

In terms of magic activation speed, Lina had Miyuki beat.

But if Miyuki had taken the lead, she must have started hers before Lina did.

And those two consecutive attacks had emphasized speed by lowering their power.

In two senses, Lina felt disgraced.

Her plan to take advantage of Miyuki's naïveté had instead made her slip up.

Miyuki had thought she could defeat Lina even with low-power attacks—and as a matter of fact, her first nearly got her.

But now it's my turn!

There was an empty moment, probably so Miyuki could take her down for certain with a stronger attack. But Lina considered that a fatal mistake as she executed two spells in parallel: Information Boost and a self-accelerating spell.

Her self-acceleration spell decreased both gravity and inertia simultaneously, and with it, Lina charged toward Miyuki's side. Her right hand was closed around a decorative button she'd ripped off her jacket.

They'd confiscated her gun, but this would be enough to disable a high school girl.

When she made it within five yards, a sudden flash of instinct stopped her in her tracks.

A strong wind suddenly whipped up and pulled on her. She dug her feet into the ground to resist it.

She fought against the sucking force by using a stasis spell. From that position, she simultaneously activated a movement spell on her button. Bypassing physics' normal rate of acceleration, it was given a speed of three hundred kilometers per hour. But it lost speed not even a meter out and fell to the ground.

Miyuki's senses had a lock on Lina as she charged forward with blinding speed.

She couldn't extract data directly from the Idea like Tatsuya, but she could perceive the traces of magic-induced event alterations. Any magician, albeit at different levels, could do it; and if it was something a magician could do, Miyuki could do it at a world-class level.

Self-acceleration magic applied an event alteration to oneself. Therefore, by following the traces of that alteration in real time, she could locate the caster's position. The skill took advantage of self-acceleration magic's flaw; Tatsuya had taught it to her.

So far, it was going according to plan. Her attempt to provoke Lina by purposely muttering a significant phrase—"I suppose it'll take more than that"—had gotten results.

Her real attack was this next spell.

Deceleration Zone.

The spell itself was relatively commonplace. Used widely both in Japan and abroad, it decelerated object movement within a target area.

But when Miyuki used the spell, the deceleration affected gaseous molecules, too.

The movement velocity of gas particles was directly correlated with the gas's pressure. To be more precise (but still approximately), the pressure of a gaseous body in an enclosed space was proportional to the square of the gas particles' movement speed. If the particle movement was forcibly decelerated, the pressure in the zone would drop, and it would draw in air from the surroundings according to the pressure gradient.

Suddenly and strongly.

Not only the air, but people and objects, too.

If someone who was sucked in didn't have the resistance to defeat this spell, it would deplete their movement speed and they'd be trapped inside the zone.

If someone who was sucked in did have enough resistance to nullify the Deceleration Zone spell, the decelerated gas particles would regain their movement speed, and the gas would expand with pressure in accordance with the amount of molecules—in other words, explode.

Normally, if one didn't have enough magic power to stop a bullet, this spell, which could only decrease the power of projectile weapons, was the next best thing. But in the hands of someone with as much magic power as Miyuki, it was an antipersonnel anti-magic spell with a contingency plan.

Lina, however, fought the current's force of suction and dug in her heels.

She fired something with a movement spell—a button?

A bit of resin only given an initial velocity would never penetrate Miyuki's Deceleration Zone, but by her shooting down such a slipshod projectile weapon, Lina doubtless knew what kind of spell she was using now.

In that case!

Tatsuya told her almost daily that the attacker always needed to think two or three steps ahead. If her plan to finish Lina by drawing her into the Deceleration Zone failed, she simply had to finish her outside that zone.

Maintaining the two-layered wall she'd made on the inside, Miyuki canceled the zone on the outside.

The gas particles, forced into a false deceleration, regained their original movement speed.

The air that had been compressed into a small area had its pressure released, became an explosive blast, and assaulted Lina.

The large-scale event alteration she'd sensed suddenly vanished.

Obeying her training and instincts, Lina flung herself to the ground and covered herself with a barrier against physical objects.

A blast stormed atop the shield. When the lift from the high-speed current threatened to pick both her shield and her up off the ground, she managed to endure with a multiactivation of an inertial increasing spell. As she lay on her belly, she peeled her eyes for a chance—no, an opening—to counterattack.

She wasn't about to casually (?) wait for an opportunity.

Until now, all the initiative had been in Miyuki's hands.

She was just a high school student, and Lina was commander of the world's strongest force.

She felt pride at that fact, of course, but above that, she felt a mental pressure—things were only getting worse.

In any case, unless she could get in even a small counterattack, she'd be overcome.

Excluding very tough defensive magic, even magical combat favored the attacker over the defender. That was the theory.

Lina felt the wind pressure weakening. The blast of wind had come from the cancellation of magic, so it made sense that the wind would stop once all the pressurized air was released.

Lina's right hand gripped her combat knife.

They'd taken her handgun but not this knife, which was for activating Atomic Divider.

The previous Sirius had developed this magical armament device, now a trump card for the Stars.

The spell extended a virtual region, and it needed enough influence to overcome the enemy magician's.

And it couldn't be just barely more—it had to be an entire rank higher.

But at the very least...

I should be able to distract her with it!

Still on the ground, she scattered daggers around so that Miyuki couldn't see.

She canceled her inertial amplification, then got up as fast as she could.

Atomic Divider.

Up on one knee, she swung her right hand's knife across.

The virtual region extended almost at the same time. She felt a strong force of influence unleashed between them that was unlike anything she'd ever experienced.

While the virtual region was still forming, the all-encompassing influence stamped it out.

She knew Miyuki would block it. Just as calculated, you might say.

"Dancing Blaze!"

Before seeing her Atomic Divider get nullified, she fired her next spell.

The daggers she'd secretly spread about floated up and flew off at a blinding speed.

Traveling in an arc a hairbreadth away from the ground, they evaded the space Miyuki controlled.

Four blades attacking you from the sides and behind in the darkness. Block that if you can!

Feeling magic-tinged objects racing her way, Miyuki canceled her currently activated attack spell and switched to perimeter defense magic.

Daggers, flying around the space to attack her, lost their flight energy and fell to the ground.

Significantly more difficult than perceiving each individual object to defend, and even more difficult than barrier magic that specified a direction—omnidirectional, indiscriminate defensive magic. But right now, Miyuki could use it without a problem.

She could stop even attacks saturated with Lina's—Sirius's—magic power.

If she were in her usual state, with some of her control diverted to Tatsuya's seal, she would have a hard time defending against this attack.

She might not have even been able to control such an elaborate spell in the first place.

If she'd challenged Lina to a duel alone, she would have lost... Miyuki mentally offered a prayer of thanks.

It's because you're watching, Brother... I won't lose. I cannot lose!

Seeing her technical, complicated surprise attack beaten by sheer force made both a fear and a fighting spirit bubble up in Lina's heart at once.

And that heartburn-inducingly sweet scene from before suddenly flashed through her mind.

She could only see it as them making light of this battle.

But at the time, Tatsuya had whispered something to her.

Come to think of it, he'd already broken her Dancing Blaze spell. He'd simultaneously dismantled all five daggers simultaneously striking at him.

It wasn't any molecular force neutralization spell she knew about, but the result was that he, by some method, had broken their molecular bonds.

But that wasn't the crucial issue.

It was that he'd dealt with several flying objects coming from different directions all at once.

She thought to herself that it wasn't only Miyuki's power that blocked her attack.

Yes... He wouldn't interfere, but he would have a word. Suits me fine!

*   *   *

Miyuki thought:
I absolutely cannot lose.

Lina thought:
I'll crush her with everything I have.

And both of them called out at once.

"Miyuki!" "Lina!"

"This is it!"

Space froze.

Space boiled.

Their magic power painted over the world, and the two worlds clashed.

A world of ice and snow, glittering like a crystal.

A world of fire and lightning, sparkling with electricity.

The air-freezing arctic hell, Niflheim.

The air-burning incandescent hell, Muspelheim.

One area-of-effect spell decelerated the vibration of gas particles, not only freezing water vapor and carbon dioxide, but also liquefying nitrogen.

One area-of-effect spell dismantled the gas particles into plasma, then further separated positive ions and electrons to create a high-energy electromagnetic field.

The cold reverted the heated plasma to gas, and the heated plasma returned the frozen air to normal.

The two clashing forces shed a curtain of aurora on the ground.

A flickering, overlapping dance of polar lights.

It was truly a wondrous spectacle.

Enough to make one forget that death waited just on the other side.

Tatsuya, his finger riding his CAD's trigger, observed the scene carefully. If one of them lost control of her spell, he would immediately erase the spell itself.

He expected that disabling their two spells at once would be tough, but he was a magician specializing in dismantling and regeneration. He was determined to see this recklessness through to the end.

Amid the dancing aurora, the clash of ice and snow with fire and lightning seemed like it would last forever. But before even a minute had passed, the trend became clear.

The cold expanded, and the plasma diminished.

Miyuki was, originally, a magician specializing in magic that brought about large-scale event alterations over a wide area.

On the other hand, Lina was a magician who focused her power on individual objects and phenomena, causing acute event alterations.

This clash had begun with Miyuki in the advantageous position.

Adding to that, this was Lina's third battle in a row, after the vampire and Tatsuya.

She may not have been aware of her symptoms, but the exhaustion had accumulated.

And now this duel format had put her opponent at an advantage over her.

Miyuki and Lina's match wouldn't be decided by a difference in magic power, but by who could retain her calm rationality for longer.

"Ugh…!"

Lina must have known that herself; a frustrated grunt escaped her lips.

And she reached behind her, pulling out her armament device again. But a multicast in this situation was, no matter how talented a magician she was, tantamount to suicide.

"That's enough, both of you!" shouted Tatsuya, pulling his CAD's trigger.

His Program Dispersion wiped out both Miyuki's Niflheim and Lina's Muspelheim at the same time.

* * *

The cold air mixing drastically with the flames and lightning, a wind that would cause burns and frostbite at once blew around violently. Tatsuya had prepared himself for the inevitable searing pain, but the storm, its fang's fiery blaze and extreme cold, hit an invisible wall right in front of him.

"Brother! What have you done?!"

Her face pale, Miyuki ran over to him.

Lina watched him, dumbstruck.

Protecting themselves from the mere aftereffects, the heat and cold waves, would have been a piece of cake no matter how tired they were. But it wasn't something Tatsuya could manage. He knew his own talents well. At times like these, he envied the ability to use *normal* magic.

"Dear me... Tatsuya, what will we do about this?"

And he didn't know how the man had protected himself, but in any case, the unharmed Yakumo spoke to him with affected shock in his voice— Well, the disciples he'd brought who were behind him were covered in dirt and mud. They must have dived into the earth to escape. The *doton* art, most likely.

"Master...what do you mean?"

Tatsuya knew now how he'd escaped the chill and the high heat, but he didn't understand the question, so he asked honestly, or rather out of reflex.

This time, Yakumo gave him an astonished look that seemed more sincere. "Well, I mean...didn't you decide that whoever surrendered or was incapacitated first would lose? You were the one who suggested this duel in the first place. Why did you go and break it up like that?"

He literally had no words.

If he hadn't done what he had, it would have broken the "no killing" rule, so he didn't regret the act of intervening itself.

But this match was just an excuse to settle the situation to begin with.

In actuality, the question of how to deal with Lina was extremely troublesome.

As an official soldier, her rights as a captive were guaranteed. He wouldn't have needed to care had her identity still been under wraps, but Lina had already told him she was the Stars commander and a major in the USNA Army. And he'd known that previously anyway, so he couldn't ignore her rights as a captive.

Even if she didn't have any during a legal engagement, if she was conducting actual military affairs, she had rights as a prisoner.

And before that, Tatsuya and the others were civilians. They couldn't take Lina, a soldier, prisoner.

He could if he displayed his connection with the Independent Magic Battalion, but unfortunately, he couldn't reveal something that confidential.

If they interrogated or confined her without proper authority, it would only give the USNA a political excuse. And execution was out of the question.

Of course, Lina's side would face criticism for attacking civilians as well, but unfortunately, the rights guaranteed to a magician as a civilian were severely limited. In terms of justice in public international law, Tatsuya and the others had grim prospects.

But that didn't mean they could set her free without doing anything, especially considering the future. How would he resolve the situation…? Tatsuya felt as though it was giving him a headache.

"We'll say it's my loss."

But he didn't have to worry for long. Rescue found him from an unexpected place.

"At that rate, I would have been defeated. If I'd diverted my capacity to other magic, Miyuki's spell would have swallowed me whole and I might have lost my life. I would have needed a few months in the hospital at the very least."

Lina looked at Tatsuya and Miyuki and admitted her own defeat in a sportsmanlike manner.

"Miyuki, I lost. Tatsuya, I don't intend to bother you with disgraceful struggling."

But it was too soon to breathe a sigh of relief at the situation resolving itself.

"I promise I'll answer anything you ask me. However…"

"However what?"

"But my answers will be yes or no. If I can't answer a question like that, then I won't. You changed the conditions Miyuki and I agreed on by spoiling our match, so I hope you don't mind me changing a small condition as well, Tatsuya."

Lina had been beaten more soundly than he'd expected.

She gave a wonderful smile that you wouldn't think a loser would give, and Tatsuya had no choice but to agree to the new terms.

(To be continued)

AFTERWORD

Thank you for purchasing another volume of *The Irregular at Magic High School*. For those new, allow me to take the opportunity to say that it's a pleasure to meet you, and I look forward to your continued support.

The book's subtitle is *Visitor Arc, Part I*. All sorts of visitors keep pulling the protagonists into the middle of the incident. Big-shot guest characters appear as well. There are victims on the protagonist side, too. The incident evolves into a complex three-sided fight, plus a little more. It is just a tad romantic (and I will accept any objections to that). As you can see, this story of the magic high school students is a bit different from the first eight volumes, but I think you'll enjoy it.

Now, there is something I need to excuse myself to everyone for. I'm sorry, but this arc will be a three-parter. Maybe it's the recoil from the Reminiscence Arc being one volume. We couldn't fit the whole Visitor Arc into two parts. Actually, Dengeki Bunko has no word limit (unless it gets way out of hand), so we could have if we'd wanted to…but circumstances dictated we take this approach. It will mean a slightly longer wait for this episode's climax, but my opinion is that I'll create something everyone can enjoy all the more for it.

* * *

The schedule was tighter than usual for this one. I predict that parts two and three will end up creating a busy schedule, too. To everyone involved, allow me to apologize again. And thank you very much. I hope for your support for the next book, too, so that we can deliver the continuation to those who are fond of this story not a day later than we need to.

In closing, I'd like to give another thanks to all the readers who purchased this book. I pray that we'll see each other again in the next volume, *Visitor Arc, Part II*.

Tsutomu Sato

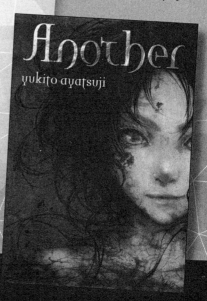

THE
AsteriskWar